to Monique

Chapter One

Having spent the morning rummaging in her boxes freshly arrived from England, Maggie Flanagan felt the urge to fill her lungs with fresh air. She stumbled over piles of books and half-unpacked cases to reach for the bow window facing the lake. As she slid the window up, a gust of air blew her red locks into her eyes. A quacking coming from her pocket interrupted her contemplation.

"Hey, Maggie! I can't wait to see you. About this weekend, does it still work for you?"

"Amy, of course, I've already unpacked your bed! Why are you speaking so softly?"

"I don't want my colleague from the morgue to hear I'm off this weekend, otherwise I'll have a case to investigate urgently. Thankfully, up where you live no one dies suspiciously, but—"

"Come on, you're not going to chicken out so quickly!" interrupted Maggie, hearing hesitation in her friend's voice. "Clearly you need a break, and you've still not learned to delegate, I see. It's about time you do. No excuses, I've already booked dinner for Friday at the Horizon Cafe."

Amy sighed. "You're right, as always... I'll have to tell my hubby to deal with the kids."

"A bit more enthusiasm, dear... It'll be great fun, and the kids will love to have time alone with their dad."

"I'm sorry. I'm truly happy to see you, I just worry about everyone."

"Okay then, get on with your work so that you can come early on Friday!" replied Maggie.

Amy laughed. "Even you're whispering now! I'll be there. And don't drown in your boxes."

"Can't wait to see you again!"

Maggie slipped her phone back into her pocket and looked down toward the shoreline. She saw herself forty years ago, running from the terrace down to the dock and plunging into the lake, her parents keeping a watchful eye on her while cheering her acrobatics from the same position behind the window.

At the thought of seeing her friend Amy, she felt time had collapsed. It had been decades since they'd spent a weekend together at the lake. During her time abroad, Maggie had only returned for short holidays to Canada to see her parents, and she had lost touch with most of her university friends, aside from Amy. Distance and busy lives had put a strain on their relationship, and now it was time to rekindle it. What better way than at the cottage, chatting in front of the fireplace, sipping hot chocolate.

A fluffy white tail caught the corner of her eye, propelled by its owner along the house into the woods. Her curiosity piqued, she slipped on her Wellington boots and jacket and laughed. *I should call them rubber boots now that I'm back in Canada.* She tucked her curly hair under her favourite green Tilley hat and set off to track the snowshoe hare.

She loved early spring, with the birds arriving back from their migration, the chipmunks and groundhogs coming out of their deep sleep, and the sun's intensity growing by the day. This was her first Canadian spring in twenty years.

Losing the hare to the deep blackberry bushes, Maggie decided to check out the trails on the property leading to the beaver dam alongside the border of her land. There she hoped to capture a shot of a beaver with her camera. The sun, unhindered by a canopy of leaves, warmed her back as she walked through the woods. The large pond was still partially frozen with a few open channels leading to the beaver lodge.

She climbed onto Lake View Road, which bordered her land, to catch a better view of a brown mass she could see moving along the ridge of the dam. Sure enough, a large beaver, oblivious to her presence, was busy plugging the breach with mud and branches in the deep end of the water. She managed to freeze its startled look with one click before it dove back under the thin ice out of sight.

Her prize captured, Maggie hastened back to her home, looking forward to her ten o'clock ritual of a warm cup of tea. She had picked up the habit in London. She found it helped her relax and think. She intended to savour every moment of her new life, embracing her choice of moving out of the city back to the Canadian countryside she liked so much.

Maggie loaded the images from her walk onto her computer. She loved blowing up images on the computer to study the details that her eyes missed. The beaver appeared to stare back at her from under his bushy eyebrows, his overbite highlighted by two elongated yellow teeth.

Moving her mouse around the picture, she sat back, surprised by what seemed to be a black handle sticking out from the thin layer of ice next to the breach in the water where the animal had disappeared. Maybe a motorcycle handle...strange. Could a beaver have carried something like this into the pond...from where? How on earth did it end up there?

She suppressed the urge to go straight out again and investigate it, since her boxes were waiting to be emptied, her photo business to be implemented, and the refurbishing of the cottage had to be planned quickly. The roof was leaking and the kitchen needed replacement. Her parents had lived in the log home since she was born and had maintained it well but had postponed the replacement of the roof, having disagreed about an extension to the living room, which in the end never happened.

Energized by her walk and with a log added to the stove, Maggie sat behind her computer. She brushed aside the anxious thought of whether her dream to become a photographer was a smart career change. Instead, she pondered ways to set up her photo studio. She had given herself a year to make it happen. She had heard from the vegetable vendor that the Millers, the owners of Moose Lodge, a restaurant and summer camp for kids, were looking for a photographer for their daughter's wedding. She hoped they would remember her and be open to using an unproven photographer, despite the importance of wedding pictures. It would be the ideal launch for her studio and a way to see old acquaintances.

Maggie hesitated, rubbing her arms uneasily at the thought of calling the Millers out of the blue. If she were in their shoes, there would be no reason to work with her—after all, she didn't have any credentials as a photographer. She put the kettle on and only once her warm cup of tea was nestled in her hands and she was curled up in her tweed armchair did she feel she had nothing to lose by approaching them. She reached into her pocket and pulled out her phone. Sitting in her favourite position, her legs tucked under her, with a flick of a thumb she searched for the Millers' number. As the phone rang, Maggie straightened in anticipation.

"Hello, is this Ms. Sue Miller?"

"Yes?"

"This is Maggie Flanagan. How're you doing?" The silence on the other side urged her to speak. "I'm a photographer and setting up my business in the region." Maggie waited a little for an acknowledgement. "I was in the vegetable store when I overheard a conversation about the upcoming wedding of your daughter."

Ms. Sue Miller was still silent on the other side, increasing Maggie's uneasiness.

"We're neighbours. I'm the daughter of the Flanagans, at the end of Lake View Road. They often visited your restaurant."

"Neighbours you say, the Flanagans, eh? The name rings a bell. I'm better with faces than names. My daughter's already found a photographer, but I'm not sure about him, all the way from Toronto."

Maggie sensed an opening and rushed to say, "I'd be happy to show you my work and meet up with you and your daughter at your convenience. It's always good to compare options."

Another silence. Maggie was at a loss how to convince her until her mother's little voice in her head reminded her that Ms. Miller liked bargains. She had haggled for the price of her parents' boat down thirty percent, to the dismay of her father.

"What about if you've no obligation to buy my pictures, I take them at my own cost, and only if you like them, you can buy the prints you want afterward?"

Maggie heard a shuffle, and finally out came a sound from the phone.

"That seems reasonable and a better deal than the other one, but I need to check with my daughter. She's very picky, and she'd want to see your work first."

"Of course, I understand. I'm happy to show you my portfolio."

As the words came out of her mouth, Maggie worried that she didn't have wedding photos, only a wildlife portfolio, and a few printed portraits from the film era that had gone missing in the removal. Feeling she could no longer backtrack, she added, "I'm available this afternoon."

"Let me check with my daughter. I was planning on visiting her at three o'clock. So four o'clock at her place could work."

As Maggie hung up, she looked at the clock and realized she would never have the time to take new photographs and somehow would have to convince them that her squirrel portraits would translate into beautiful headshots of the bride. She cursed herself for being unprepared but argued that it was an opportunity she had to grasp. How many weddings will there be in Foxton per year? One, maybe two if she was lucky.

For a few minutes she hoped the call would be fruitless, with Catherine, Ms. Miller's daughter, rejecting her upfront. She then would have time to build a website, have a portrait photo book, and be ready to approach clients. As she settled with a rejection, the phone rang and Ms. Miller confirmed the afternoon appointment.

During the following hour it seemed that an upheaval had taken place in the living room as Maggie emptied box after box still hoping to find the portrait prints. Nothing. She pulled out her wildlife portfolio and flicked through it, trying to place herself in a future bride's mind and snapped it closed with anger. I'll just have to be lucky. Maybe she likes animals, but even then...

Maggie printed out a few more pictures and got ready for her visit. She tried to brush aside her apprehension. She climbed into her old blue pickup truck, her father's cherished vehicle. She liked feeling tall and safe peering over the steering wheel at the cars and animals below. Big Jay, as she fondly called it, had a mismatched red door and was rusting around the wheels, but she loved it. At just above five feet, she had to add a cushion to her seat to see the end of the hood. She often joked about it and said it was the driverless car.

She wasn't sure what to expect as she turned onto Graham's Lane, peering over her steering wheel at the white cottage at the far end. As she parked in front of the house, a Great Dane dashed out of nowhere, it seemed, prancing around the car. She had noted the veterinary clinic sign at the entrance and expected to encounter animals, but this dog was a pony's size. Carefully, she rolled down her window and calmly spoke to the dog that was now fully stretched, paws on the door. Reassured by his wagging tail and attitude, Maggie climbed out of the truck, the dog at her waist, sniffing her.

To Maggie's surprise, four people stood at the door, observing her. Maggie recognized Ms. Miller, a little more dried-up with age, like a prune but still with her prominent hawk nose taking central position between ice-blue eyes. Frozen on the spot by the intensity of Ms. Miller's gaze, Maggie quickly glanced at the others, hoping to see the friendly familiar face of the Richard Miller she remembered. She was rescued by a warm smile from a bearded man in beige overalls she didn't know, and as he moved sideways she saw Richard Miller. He hadn't changed a bit. He didn't seem to recognize her, although she noted a surprised look in his eyes, followed by a smile. He still had his full head of hair, which used to puzzle her as a child. Seeing it now, she had to conclude it was real, having turned to a mix of pepper and salt.

This was going to be a little different than Maggie had hoped for. She had imagined that they would remember her parents, or perhaps Ms. Miller hadn't shared it with the group and still couldn't place her. Ms. Miller finally came forward.

"Maggie, welcome, I'm Sue Miller, but call me Sue." Ms. Miller glanced quickly back over her shoulder at the group still standing on the porch and whispered in Maggie's ear. "I'm afraid my daughter is really set on her photographer. Although I'm paying, it's her day…"

As the group approached the pair, Ms. Miller raised her voice. "This is Catherine, my daughter and bride, my husband Richard, and Matt, the groom."

As Ms. Miller turned toward her future son-in-law, Maggie looked up to the bearded man, tilting her head back farther and farther until she could see his eyes. Maggie smiled at the trio. Catherine's sharp blue eyes travelled around her face and body in appraisal.

"Hi, it's really exciting you're getting married so soon."

As Maggie spoke, Matt placed his arm around Catherine's shoulder, looking down at her with love.

Inspired, Maggie said, "I love weddings and capturing the joyful moment to extend it in time. I'm—"

Ms. Miller interrupted, "Shall we go inside, it's a little chilly. We can hear all about it then."

Ms. Miller waved her hands to herd the group toward the door. The family moved in unison, as if following a rehearsed drill. Richard held the door open for Maggie.

Matt, at six foot four with his burly frame, shrank the house to a doll's size as he walked, bending under the doorways. Like a line of ants, they marched behind him via the mudroom into the kitchen. Careful not to step on one of the cats winding its tail around any leg it could find, Maggie quickly moved to a side of the wooden table, away from Ms. Miller. She could see in their smiling eyes yet arched brows that they hadn't expected a pint-sized, red-haired woman.

Looking at each in turn, feeling her cheeks warm, Maggie rubbed her hands together and straightened her back.

"As Sue might have mentioned to you, I've approached her, having heard on the grapevine of the village"—Maggie chuckled to ease the atmosphere—"that you were looking for a photographer."

With a stern face, Catherine replied, "Mom's the one really looking for one. I've already got one from Toronto. Frankly, you're wasting your time."

Unease fell upon the group as Ms. Miller looked reproachfully at her daughter.

"I'm sorry, Maggie, as you can see, my daughter is stubborn, and I'd hoped she would at least look at what you had to offer, given your good deal."

Maggie replied, smiling, "I understand, Catherine, it is your special day, and if you've found—"

Richard Miller interrupted Maggie. "I remember you! You are the wee girl who came and play at the lodge when we had the kids for summer camp, always canoeing to our dock at the time of the bonfire for the scary stories. Like a mouse, we would suddenly see you sitting among the kids without having seen you arrive. You did worry your parents."

Ms. Miller turned toward her husband, hitting her thigh with her hand. "Of course, that's it, yes, the Flanagans, how could I forget? My memory's failing me at times. So sad for your parents, my dear."

Catherine appeared impatient, shifting on her chair, darting glances at the trio, in reaction to which Matt placed his large hand in the back of her neck, as if he were trying to appease a wild animal.

Ms. Miller looked at her daughter. "Catherine, you were just a baby when Maggie wandered up to the lodge in summer. Her parents have the log home all the way at the end of Lake View Road. It takes more time to drive there than to canoe between the lodge and their home. You know which home, you canoed there and back often enough."

Catherine appeared to search her mind but remained silent.

Maggie replied, "I'm so glad you remember. I've such fond memories of those times. And you always had extra marshmallows for me to roast."

Richard Miller replied with a sigh, "Yes, and you gobbled them too! All those years... We heard about your life in England, what an achievement! Your dad was so proud of you, wasn't he?"

Richard nudged Ms. Miller with his elbow. She nodded and sat there, still staring at Maggie.

Richard asked, "Are you back for good?"

"Yes, I am, I love it here. It's so nice to be back..."

Sue Miller interrupted. "I didn't remember you were a photographer. Were you not working in a health company?"

Catherine pulled the front flaps of her cardigan over each other, crossing her arms, and looked at Maggie with a challenging, icy stare. Maggie had first thought that the table had turned once they recognized her, and she could have talked herself into the job. Now, looking at Catherine, her confidence vanished. She felt twenty-four again, faced with bluffing her way to prove she could do the job, even without the years of experience.

"You're right. I'm a biologist, but I've always been a keen amateur photographer, and it's always been my dream to become a professional photographer here in the highlands."

Maggie felt a sense of relief at having told them the truth; she couldn't pretend to the Millers. Before she could carry on talking, Catherine straightened and looked across the table at her mother.

"Well, that settles it, I want a professional photographer."

Matt put his arm around his wife-to-be, seeming already attuned to her ways, and laughed. "Honey, you don't mean that exactly. You've always told me that even though I'm a vet, I could've been a professional craftsman. Give Maggie a chance. At least look at her photo-book."

Catherine appeared to melt under his embrace and deep voice as she huddled up closer to him.

Ms. Miller added, "Matt, you're right, and Maggie didn't tell you yet, but we only pay for the prints if we like them, nothing to lose."

Catherine looked at Maggie, cradling her mug with both hands. "I'm sorry, I shouldn't judge without seeing your work, but you see, I really want the best I can get for the big day."

Maggie replied, "Of course, Catherine, and right you are. It is your special day."

Maggie opened the folder on the table and slid it toward Catherine and Matt. Matt smiled at a close-up of a red squirrel.

"This one is not from here, the ears are different."

"Yes, a European one."

"I like it, very sharp. Not easy to capture."

"I had to climb the tree!" Maggie smiled remembering the moment.

Catherine flicked through the photos of animals, stopping to observe a picture of a horse.

"Oh, that's a friend's horse, a friendly animal."

Catherine replied, "A beautiful animal, a Friesian horse. I like horses. Your animal pictures are very good. But where're your wedding pics?"

Maggie cleared her throat. "I did take some, but it's been a while, those are recent pictures. I love photographing wildlife. It is a way to relax for me."

"I find it hard to judge on this basis. I'd really need to see other pictures. And I've already got someone."

"You see, Maggie, I told you, when she's made up her mind..." added Ms. Miller.

"Yes, indeed, just like her mother. But don't despair, if you do have more pics, send them along to me, and we'll see what we can do," said Richard.

Maggie recognized in those words the kind-hearted man always looking to make everyone happy. She now felt it would be harder than she had hoped to establish herself as a photographer. The conversation moved onto reminiscences of the past and the joyful summer camps held at the lodge. Now and then the discussion was interrupted by a profound sigh coming from the Great Dane lying across all the feet under the table.

Leaving their home, Maggie thought of Richard, and a glimmer of hope for the wedding assignment lingered on. Catherine had shown affection toward her father, holding on to his arm as they escorted Maggie out of the house. Perhaps he could convince her. Or perhaps Matt would. He seemed to like her photographs. Maybe he needed pictures for his veterinary practice.

Maggie sighed as she sat in her truck, ready to go. She thought, *Amy is coming on Friday. Another reason why it's better that this doesn't work out. I can't cancel the weekend now after all those years... Maybe she'll have ideas.*

Chapter Two

Maggie held the Horizon Cafe door open for Amy. She looked at her friend with appreciation, her impeccable straight mane of hair framing her slim face. Amy's large tortoiseshell-style glasses gave her a serious appearance, her forensic expert look. Her large hazel eyes sparkled as the light of the candles reflected in them as they entered. A mix of coffee and baking smells hit their senses, together with country music coming from the back of the restaurant.

Maggie smiled at Amy. "I told you it'd be lively up here. And this smell of apple pie, what about that?"

"Mmm, it does smell nice. I can't believe it, there's even a band playing. Of course it has to be country music...not your favourite, I believe?" Amy slipped off her jacket, looking toward the four musicians drumming the rhythm with their boots.

Maggie scanned the room for a good table, far enough from the sound that they could talk but with a view on the lake that glimmered in the moonlight. She grabbed her friend by the arm, gently guiding her to the last table next to the window. She sat down opposite Amy, pulling herself closer to the wooden table, all the while checking the place for familiar faces.

"Are you expecting anyone?" asked Amy.

"No, not particularly, but I thought an old acquaintance from school might be here. You know. Denis. He's now the local dentist."

"I see, *the* Denis? The one I had to fend off for you with all sorts of excuses... You still owe me for that, by the way. He was keen, that's for sure, poor guy."

"Yes, that one. We were very young, my first boyfriend at high school. He still wanted the relationship at university—he didn't get that it was over. Not my fault, I was clear."

"It didn't work, though, did it, your communication. It was only after I spoke to him at length that he stopped calling you. A sweet guy."

"Yes, just as a friend, but you even agreed with me he was boring."

"Only from the call, though. I've never met him in person. I'd be curious to see him. It'll be a shock for him to see you here, and I won't be here to protect you from him now." Amy laughed.

"I shouldn't have told you. You'll never stop teasing me now. I don't want to hurt him. I did like him a lot at the time. So please be nice if we see him. Anyway, the coast is clear for now." Maggie peered into the orange candleholder. She checked her pockets for her father's old lighter and lit the candle.

"Very romantic, my dear. Denis would love it, you in the candlelight..."

"I love candles. When I went to Amsterdam, they had them all over in restaurants, bars, but also at home. It makes the atmosphere really cozy with dimmed lights. I always have some on at home in the evening," replied Maggie, deliberately ignoring her sarcasm.

Maggie felt slightly annoyed by her friend's teasing but couldn't pinpoint the reason. They had always poked fun at each other, and Maggie rarely took offence.

"You look a bit upset. I didn't mean to hurt you. That's not a good start for our first get-together in years." Amy leaned toward her, looking at her with her large puppy-brown eyes.

"Of course you didn't and I'm not upset. I'm actually looking forward to seeing him and having you meet him..."

A larger-than-life figure dressed in a red knitted cardigan adorned with a flurry of white edelweiss flowers interrupted the pair. A plump, rosy-cheeked face beamed down on them.

"Good evening, girls. How're you doing, Maggie?"

Rubbing her reddened hands against a frilly apron, Heidi smiled at Maggie then at Amy.

"Great, Heidi. What about you?" Seeing Heidi smile in response, Maggie gestured at the room filled with diners and added, "Good to see you're as busy as ever. I tried your pretzels the other day. Amy, you have to take some back home for your boys, they are delicious."

Heidi's cheeks turned pink as she flapped her hand out toward Maggie.

"She's such a sweetie pie. I'll bake them again for you then. Our menu is on the chalkboard over there. Do you want me to bring it to you?"

"Yes please, any specials tonight? Amy can't wait to taste your stew, isn't that true? What's the name again, the beef in broth one..."

Maggie winked at Amy, who smiled broadly, showing a perfect line of large teeth to Heidi and nodding.

"Tonight, I have a wiener schnitzel with a potato salad. Not the *tafelspitz*, I'm afraid. I only do that on Sundays."

"I warned you, Amy, you have to keep room for dessert. Her *apfelstrudel*, a cinnamon apple dessert, is really nice. Do you have any tonight?"

"Yes. So what can I get you to drink?"

Maggie felt so excited and happy to see her friend that she grabbed her hand. "Shall we celebrate—bubbles? Any recommendation, Heidi?"

Heidi flickered her pencil on her pad, looking at the ceiling for a moment, and then with a wiggle of her large hips said, "I still have a bottle of Sekt left, a nice sparkling Austrian wine. But if you prefer, I also have Prosecco."

"Sekt, I like the sound of it," said Maggie.

"Okay, let's do it. But you're driving. You know I get tipsy after a glass," replied Amy.

As Heidi walked away to get the drinks, Amy looked around and said, "It's very cozy here, with all the paintings and photos on the walls. I like the colourful cushions on the chairs. They're so comfy. Does Heidi have any kids?"

"Yes, I think so. I never asked. She'd be a nice mum, but not good for the waistline." Maggie laughed.

"That's for sure. So tell me more about your plans. A photographer, hey, I'm happy you're finally taking it up seriously. You know I got your eagle and fox pictures enlarged for Mike for his bedroom."

"Really, that's so sweet of him."

"By the way, my department at the forensics lab is looking for a photographer in Toronto, but not really your type of pictures, I think... It's not always pics of dead bodies in reality."

"I'd hope so, but you're right. I was thinking more of happy pictures of animals or people...alive. Like the one I took of a beaver this week. Oh, I've got to show you that, there was something strange about it. Anyway, I already blew my first wedding assignment. I only had pictures of animals to show a bride-to-be..."

Maggie watched Amy's lips curl up at one corner, exactly as she remembered when Amy was about to lecture her. As Amy opened her mouth, a frog call from under the table stopped her short.

Feeling the stare on her back, Maggie swivelled around. A woman probably intent on having a totally speechless dinner with her husband appeared offended by the sound. Maggie cast her an apologetic smile, then glanced down at her phone and noticed the Millers' number.

"I must have forgotten something at their place. Nothing important."

"At whose place?" asked Amy.

"The Millers. It's their daughter who is getting married tomorrow."

"Well, pick it up then, come on!"

"No point, the daughter already has a photographer. Anyway, here comes Heidi with the drinks."

Maggie shook her head as she put her phone on the table. "I'd rather celebrate with you our long-lasting friendship than attend a wedding." Maggie turned toward Heidi, who was standing next to the table, busy opening the bottle. "Do you know, Heidi, Amy and I have known each other for...what is it now...twenty-five years?"

"That's very special. To celebrate, the drinks are on the house."

"No, no, I didn't say this for you to invite us..."

"I insist..."

"Only if you join us for a drink then."

"After your dinner, when it's a little quieter; for now you must have lots of catching up to do," replied Heidi as she swiftly moved away to attend another guest signalling her.

Amy glanced sideways at Maggie's phone, as if it were alive. As soon as Maggie picked it up to put it away, Amy held her hand out, nearly capsizing her glass.

"Don't, I feel there's a message, check it."

"Come on, don't be ridiculous. I thought you'd stopped with your premonitions when you were wrong about your son winning his hockey game. He was so upset afterward when he lost."

"I can't help it. And he's over it now. If there is a message, I'm only asking you to listen to it. What's the harm in that?"

"Okay, fine."

Maggie felt a twinge of exasperation. She didn't like letting herself be influenced by irrational impulses, and yet deep down she believed that her friend had a gift. Amy had, after all, saved her life when she told her not go to university one day, following a dream. A fire broke out in the lab Maggie would have been working in. Fortunately, no one was in the room when it happened.

After listening to the message, her heart beating faster, she announced, "This is crazy...how did you know?"

Amy looked at her, her left eyebrow reaching new heights on her forehead.

"Their photographer is sick. They want me to do the job!"

"That's great. I told ya I had a hunch. Better call back then, eh..."

"Oh, but that's not right, you've come all the way to see me, and we'd planned to have a great walk in the park tomorrow. Unless..."

Maggie felt torn, because she valued friendship over any work. Before she could carry on, Amy finished her sentence.

"Unless I join you as your assistant. Someone needs to carry your bag and help you with the lenses. It'll be a lot of fun. I love weddings."

Maggie clapped her hands with pleasure and excitement at the idea. Standing up suddenly, toppling her chair backward nearly falling on the table behind her. With a flick of her hand, Amy sent Maggie off to make her call before it was too late.

Maggie returned after a short while, weaving along the tables, eager to share the news with her friend. Amy craned above the other heads, trying to read her features, as she always used to. For a moment Maggie thought of pretending it hadn't worked out but was too happy to do so.

"It worked! And you're hired."

The pair chatted and giggled through the night, sharing anecdotes and plotting the day ahead over a delicious dinner, culminating with Heidi's *apfelstrudel*. With the effect of the sparkling wine dwindling, Amy's look darkened as she said, "It's all well and good, but I've got nothing to wear for the wedding. I can't come in jeans. You better go on your own."

Maggie's chest tightened; she wanted her friend to be there by her side. And yet how could clothing be an issue? If only Amy could be like her, not too bothered with fashion, and be a similar size. She looked at her friend, tall and slim, always looking perfect. It would not be a simple task to convince her that her jeans would be fine; she would have to think of something else over what was left of the night. The wedding was only a few hours away now.

Chapter Three

Today was the big day, not only for the bride and groom but also for Maggie to prove her photographer's skills. She packed her Billingham bag with all her photo equipment, checking several times she hadn't forgotten anything. It was still dark, but she could already hear the robin singing in the tree.

A tomboy, Maggie chose her outfits so that she could move without concern of revealing too much. She slipped on her blue tailored trousers together with a white blouse, colourful flowers flowing down the side of each arm and around the collar. She laughed as she imagined Amy questioning her choices. Her wardrobe had always been a source of contention.

This thought reminded her of finding something to wear for Amy. Opening the bedroom closet, she flicked through her mother's outfits, and under a plastic wrapping a yellow dress stood out. Maggie would have loved to fit in it, but she had always been plumper than her mother. Hearing movement in the guest room, Maggie grabbed the dress, nearly tripping on it, and ran out to greet Amy.

They bumped into each other in the corridor.

"Ow, is that how you wake up your guests in the morning?"

Maggie reached out with her hand to rub her friend's arm, oblivious to her own pain, adrenaline rushing in her veins from the excitement. "Sorry, are you okay? It's just that I've found it."

"What?" Amy looked at her, perplexed, rubbing her eyes and

scratching her head.

Maggie shoved the dress into her arms, ignoring her friend's sleepy look. "You're coming with me today." Not getting a satisfactory reaction, Maggie insisted, "The dress, it will fit you, I'm sure. For the wedding."

"But, yellow. Not my colour...and it's cold outside, it's an evening dress, not for the day."

"Don't worry, jeans are fine for the day, you won't be on the pictures. And it'll be warm in the evening with the huge fire at the lodge. Come on...please..." It dawned on Maggie that she had forgotten how to approach Amy in the morning: never before a coffee. "I've got some coffee ready, then I'll tell you about my plan."

Amy, dragging her feet, followed Maggie to the kitchen. Two warmed up pretzels and a cup of coffee lay on the table.

Maggie laughed. "Heidi baked them for us. She's so nice. I think I've found a new mum!"

Maggie could see Amy warming up to her proposal as she tore a bit of pretzel and tasted it. Amy's sleepy features were progressively replaced by a side smile as she sipped the coffee, staring at the dress Maggie had carefully placed on the chair next to her.

Maggie waited a little longer for the coffee to take effect, then, picking up her own mug, sat opposite Amy at the kitchen wooden table. "Look, I know it isn't ideal. But there'll be no one you know up here, and the dress will fit you. Pleaaaaseeee! I can't do this job without you. It was your fault I listened to the voice mail and called them back."

Maggie looked away, feigning a sulk, hoping her special pout would have the effect it used to, providing the little nudge Amy required when she was about to agree with her but hesitated.

Amy put her mug down and picked the dress from the back of the chair, holding it up to take a close look at it. She then looked at Maggie's blouse, smiling. "I see you still like your flowers... All right then. Stop sulking! Because it's—"

Before she could finish, Maggie jumped to her feet, looking at the clock on the wall. "Hurry, we have to go. We'll be late otherwise!"

After what seemed like fifteen minutes of chaos, with pieces of clothing being tossed in the air as Maggie searched for her favourite blue fedora and shouts coming from the bathroom from Amy, complaining that she couldn't get her hair under control, the pair stood in front of the entrance door. With one glance at each other, in unison they rushed out of the house to the car. They drove in silence to the Millers' house, Moose Lodge, where the bride, Catherine, would be getting ready.

The Millers lived at the end of Lake View Road in one of the cabins only slightly bigger than the guest cabins scattered around the property. A few metres away from their home, on a little peninsula, stood the octagonal old log building built in the forties. Its popularity had never decreased since the 1900s, when it was a stopover for the wooden steamboat that travelled along the chain of lakes bringing the first cottage tourists to the region. The Millers kept up the tradition and not only ran a restaurant, together with the children's camp, but in summer they also operated a boat service picking up guests at Foxton harbour on Perch Lake, sailing up via King Fisher Narrows to Deep Lake and Otter Lake, with a stopover at the lodge for lunch or dinner then back to Foxton. In winter, the locals regularly gathered around the central large stone fireplace of the hexagonal building for dinner, having reached the lodge via snowmobile over the frozen lakes.

Maggie and Amy walked around the premises, looking for a sign of life. The hexagonal log building had been decorated with white ribbons, blowing in the wind. Peering inside, they could see the tables all decked out with red rose petals and the chairs clad with white covers and large red bows. The tables appeared to revolve around the prominent central stone fireplace that rose up to the ceiling, each with a view of Otter Lake or Deep Lake. Maggie turned to Amy.

"We're in the right place. You see the fireplace in the middle? You won't be cold tonight."

"Yes, it looks cozy."

Finding the door of the lodge locked, fear that she was supposed to meet the bride at her home gripped Maggie. She scanned the cabin for a sign of life. A silhouette in white moved in front of the window.

"That must be Catherine. Let's go, quick, the sun is rising and I want to get a picture of her in the nice light."

"Yes, boss…" replied Amy with a grin while struggling with a reflective umbrella.

Maggie knocked on the door. No answer. She knocked again and opened it.

"Hello! It's Maggie the photographer. Can I come in?"

Ms. Miller sprang out from behind the door and ushered them into the cabin, directing them to the bedroom. Laden with her bag, her large camera already out and ready to shoot, Maggie walked into a wooden room. There in the middle stood Catherine in a 1930s-style white dress, fiddling with a headband of white beads. The bride's hand trembled as she fitted her headdress.

Maggie glanced toward Amy and with a nod told her to help the bride with it. Her friend would know how to handle a stressed bride and provide the perfect finishing touches to the hairstyle, while she could start taking pictures so Catherine would get used to the camera.

"You look beautiful, Catherine! My assistant, Amy, is very good with hair. She can help you with your headdress if you like."

Catherine dropped her arms, letting the band slip to her feet, loose white beads bouncing on the floor around her. At the sight, Ms. Miller swung her arms up in the air then clasped her hands together in a prayer position.

"If you can help her, my dear, that would be so nice… I can't seem to do anything right this morning." Ms. Miller faced Maggie and Amy with a look of desperation in her eyes, soon replaced by a little twinkle. "I'm so glad you could make it. Maggie and…?"

"Amy. She'll help me with the lighting and set up for the

pictures." Turning to the bride, Maggie said, "I really like your dress. I love the thirties."

"Thanks," muttered Catherine sulkily.

"Do you have a preference for the type of pictures you want?"

"I had, but what's the point now? I guess I've got no choice now but to work with you. I want portraits and action pictures and…"

Catherine let herself drop down into a chair in front of a dressing table, looking at Maggie via the mirror. In a defeated tone, she added, "Whatever… My headband is broken, my photographer fell ill, they're forecasting rain for today… Nothing can get worse, I guess."

"Honey, don't worry, it'll be a beautiful day!" exclaimed Ms. Miller.

Amy had meanwhile picked up the band and already mended it. She walked behind the bride, carefully adjusting it to fit on Catherine's forehead.

"Look, you see, Amy fixed it. You look so pretty that it'll be easy for me to make great portraits. It's a happy day. Just relax. Look over there…the sun is rising," Maggie said with enthusiasm.

Catherine's face glowed under a sunray gently hitting her cheek, a small smile curling the corners of her lips.

"Yes, that's it, stay there, look at it, beautiful profile!" Maggie snapped a few pictures and quickly showed them on the camera viewer to Catherine to check if it was the type she liked. The bride's shoulders slid down, releasing the tension as she studied of her newly styled hair in the mirror. She smiled, and touched a perfectly formed curl sculpted against her temple.

"This looks great, thanks so much. How did you do those curls on the side? Wow! I feel better now."

"It's easy to do, just a bit of gel, and with your hair it's really nothing. If I may, I'd add a little blush there and some eyeliner…" replied Amy.

Amy's magic seemed to work. She could soothe any anxious mind when it came to styling.

Suddenly Catherine turned to face Maggie. "Thank you for bringing Amy." She swivelled back and gently applied blush on her cheeks as she went on, "I like the pics you just took. I'm ready for the others you have in mind. Let's go out and do it!"

All four started laughing as Catherine stood up energetically, and pirouetted around the room grabbing her mother by the waist. The tension finally released. The atmosphere was further improved when Matt arrived for the pictures, leading to a series of shots in front of the lake with a laughing bride and groom dancing the Charleston. The morning went by in a wink of an eye with a brief civil ceremony with only family members, then on to the afternoon church ceremony.

In the spur of the action and highly focused on her photography, Maggie had obliterated her own excitement and apprehension at meeting old friends until she was standing in the corner up in the pulpit of the Foxton church, looking down at the rows of pews filled with colourful hats. The reverend had let her climb into his pulpit to get a special shot of the assembly.

Maggie blushed when she saw the crowd, feeling a little shy. As she positioned herself for a better view, her hat popped off her head and fell down straight into the arms of Reverend John Smithers. All eyes were suddenly on her, causing her to check her unruly curls with one hand.

Fortunately, Reverend John Smithers was a jolly fellow and a good improviser.

"How exciting, a special blessing from God for our wedding today. We never know how He might express himself next."

A roar of laughter shook the hats like a wave as he threw the blue fedora back up to Maggie. She was just on time to snap a picture of all heads looking up at her with broad smiles.

Only the close family and friends had been invited to the church ceremony; the rest of the village was expected to join for the buffet reception at the Moose Lodge in the evening. The church ceremony ended with a group picture on its steps. Maggie popped her head to the side of the camera and grinned, opening her eyes wide, to the surprise of the crowd, who instantaneously smiled, and there it was: the photo she was after.

Maggie rushed toward the group, her hands out, shouting, "Stop, stay there!"

Wondering what was happening, they froze on the spot as loud clippety-clops grew in intensity until a carriage drawn by two elegant draft horses, their blond manes neatly braided with white ribbons, appeared at the corner of the road. This was Matt's surprise for his bride. Maggie had known Catherine liked horses from her comment on her portrait of a Friesian horse. The impression was confirmed when Catherine leaped into Matt's arms with a squeal as Matt announced with a smile from ear to ear, "Meet Pea and Pod, your new friends, my love."

Matt lifted his bride into the carriage as Maggie ran around it to capture the moment. Maggie called out, "Look over here, a picture of you both framed by the horses' heads, yes, that's it, great!"

Meanwhile, Amy spent her time trying to keep up with Maggie as if she were her shadow, ready to hand her a lens and at all times trying to keep out of the photographs. As soon as the carriage set off, the guests, eager to take part in the traditional procession, raced to their cars.

Maggie rearranged her curls under her fedora. "I think I've nailed it. And I've got to say, you're a great assistant."

"Phew, I need a rest now. Don't tell me you'll be running around like that at the party. Look, he seems angry," whispered Amy into her ear.

The man marched toward them, his fists clenched by his sides as if he were preparing for a fight. Amy and Maggie took a step back as he approached.

"Hi, my car won't start, the wife is ticked off—late, we'll be late, she says. I need help...yous have a car?"

Maggie looked toward where he was waving his hand at a white van with a sign on the side: *Joe Johnson Septic & Plumbing, always there when you need.*

Maggie replied, "Hi, Joe Johnson, is that correct?"

The man nodded. "Call me Joe."

"I'm Maggie, and this is Amy. Your wife's in the car over there? Well, the blue truck is mine. Why don't you come with us, and you can deal with your car later. We're going to the lodge now."

Joe gestured to his wife to come along. "You've saved my day! She may look nice, but when she gets started."

Maggie nudged her head towards the pair to signal to Amy. She lifted the corner of her mouth and raised an eyebrow as she climbed into her truck. Amy twisted her neck to get a better view of them. "Going to the party?"

Maggie nodded. A pretty brunette with narrow, rectangular glasses sitting on a small nose perfectly positioned between smooth cheeks stood next to the driver's side. *What a symmetrical face—a doll face,* thought Maggie.

"Thank you so much. I'm the bride's cousin and promised to help her with her evening gown, so you see I can't be late. You're the photographer?" As she spoke she climbed into the back seat with her husband.

Maggie replied, "Yes, I'm Maggie and she's Amy. And you...?"

"Oh, Heather, sorry."

"I haven't seen you around, Maggie. Or Amy for that matter."

"I've just moved back from London, UK, but I was born here in Foxton. And Amy is from Toronto, just up for a visit."

Heather's tense features loosened as Maggie mentioned Amy lived in Toronto; perhaps she had considered Amy a threat. She was taken aback a little by Heather's next comment. "So you're back for your kids? Much better here than in a city to bring them up."

"No, no kids."

"Oh," replied Heather. After an awkward silence, she added, "You must need to learn how to relax, then, after living in the city. I teach a yoga class and—"

"Heather, no yoga talk, please... She can go on for hours about it," interrupted Joe, rolling his eyes.

"Come on, Joe, maybe she wants to join," insisted Heather nodding toward Maggie in the rear-view mirror.

Although Maggie didn't see herself performing any yoga moves, hating all forms of stretching, she didn't want to put her off. "I might."

Before Maggie could ask Heather where she was from, Heather said, "It won't be easy to make a living as a photographer here, not like in London...there was one that closed a year ago."

Amy's right eyebrow lifted, together with the right corner of her mouth. Maggie certainly didn't want Amy to get irritated as well; she would have to hide her own feelings. She wanted to be accepted in the village and was likely to meet Heather again. Perhaps Heather was just one of those people who spoke their minds without consideration of how the message might be received. And Heather made a valid point. She had to speak quickly before Amy launched a counterattack.

Joe came to the rescue. "Heather! Ignore her. He was no good, and no one liked his blurry pictures."

"It's all right, I know it won't be easy, but that's fine, and in London I was a biologist."

"Oh...what does that mean?" asked Heather.

Before Maggie could reply, Amy shifted her shoulders toward Heather to face her. "She discovered a new antibiotic and had her own company. But I can tell you she's also a brilliant photographer."

"Come on, Amy, don't exaggerate. I just worked at a biotech company. And I was lucky with my research, that's all." Maggie felt annoyed with Amy. Although she knew her friend meant well, Maggie wasn't the boasting type. She wanted a new deal, and her past seemed irrelevant for her current life.

"Wow, that's amazing...but then what made you come back?" said Heather.

"After the death of my parents, I questioned my life and how I was living. It made me realize that I wanted to try out my dream of becoming a photographer. I was homesick, and I missed all this beautiful nature."

"I wouldn't mind a change of life," sighed Joe. "I'd go live on an island in the sun far away from the winter..."

"Nonsense, you'd get sunburned in no time with your pale skin," snapped Heather.

Joe grumbled a reply that didn't reach Maggie's ears. Heather was silent for a moment as if she were thinking, then asked, "You're right about one thing, Foxton is the best place to be."

Suddenly aware of the silence in the car, Maggie said, "I noticed from your sticker on your van that you're a plumber. I have to do some renovations to winterize the house and also update the kitchen."

Heather smiled broadly, grabbing Joe by the arm as she spoke. "You have your man, but he's not only a plumber—he knows everyone around. Tell her, Joe."

Joe seemed to take up more space in the back as he poured onto Maggie a sea of names, all close friends in the building trade he would gladly arrange for her. He jumped on her interest in solar-powered water heating systems she had mentioned only out of curiosity, seeing he had a sticker advertising it on his car. Joe claimed he could get his friend and reputed installer Leon LeBreton to give her a good deal. He told her how things had gone horribly wrong with another plumber from the nearby village of Greentown and how not to do the installation, thereby attempting to shine in contrast.

As they drove along Deep Lake, one of the series of the chain of lakes toward Otter Lake and Moose Lodge, they caught a glimpse of the tail end of the wedding procession. Maggie attempted to accelerate to catch up with them, thinking Heather would appreciate it, when she was stopped short by a loud shout from Joe.

"Stop!"

The car ground to a halt. Maggie looked for a deer or other animal that must have triggered Joe's reaction. Her heart was still beating, no animal to be seen; only a large hand, index finger pointing to her side window appeared in front of her face.

"Look! I did the solar installation, well, Leon helped. Behind the pine tree, see that humongous cottage..."

Big, yes, but for a family and many friends, thought Maggie, looking at the cottage, *really only a normal two-storey home... with a roof covered in solar panels.*

Heather added, "You know, it's the electric utility director's cottage. Lots of money, our money...with these crazy electricity bills, that's where it all goes."

"Heather, don't start."

"He's really not handy; he can't even use a chainsaw to cut his tree, and he asked my Joe to do it for him. You should show it to her so that she sees your work."

Keen to avoid any delay and not feeling in the mood of more building work conversations, Maggie changed the topic, having accepted their offer of a visit.

"Do you know if Denis Partridge, the dentist, will be attending?"

Amy sat up in her chair as if she had been asleep the rest of the time but was now all ears.

"Do you mean Tina's hubby? I should think so; she'll be there, so he should be there too," replied Heather.

The name "Tina" rang a bell, but Maggie couldn't place it. For some reason it made her uncomfortable. "Tina?"

"Yes, the journalist. She takes my yoga classes. I think you should too..."

Maggie's uneasiness grew. Could it be the dreaded Tina from her school days, jealous of her relationship with Denis? Could he have married her? That seemed impossible.

As they pulled up at the lodge, all cars from the church gathering were parked with guests trickling in from the village. Maggie sighed. *It's just a coincidence, I'm sure it'll be another Tina... I hope...*

Chapter Four

The hexagonal log building was lit by lanterns dangling in the wind. The fire in the centre of the room roared and colourful outfits slowly moved around it, as if they were compelled to circle it like on a merry-go-round.

Her job taking portraits allowed Maggie to observe the guests without appearing rude. When walking around to see if Amy had arrived, Maggie came face-to-face with a tall thin woman. She had a yellow poodle hairstyle, a strict beige suit with the skirt well below the knee, low black pumps, and a large white bow on her blouse as her only eccentricity. That must be Aunt Maaike. She matches the description Catherine gave me.

"Hi, I'm Maggie. I understand that you flew in from Holland for the wedding. How're you enjoying it so far?"

In a thick Dutch accent, the aunt responded, "I am Maaike. Enjoying it? I just arrived. I have a jetlag, you know, just flew in from Holland."

"Oh, but did you have a good trip?" Maggie was already biting her lip for having started this conversation.

"Very tiring. Busy. Driving all the way here after the plane! And on top of it I wasn't allowed to bring my present of Dutch cheeses... I was forced to leave them at customs, such nice cheeses..."

Maggie nodded in support of her outrage. "A real pity, that's regulations for you... Will you be staying here for a while? At the lodge?"

Aunt Maaike sighed. "Of course! If I come all this way, I can't just stay a day or two. It's expensive, you know. Although my poor little Billy, I had to leave him behind. You see, I never do, it'll be so hard for him. I'm very worried about him."

Maggie assumed she was referring to her husband, and seeing the dark look on her face, asked, "Is he ill?"

"No, no, he's not ill, or I hope he's not if the neighbour doesn't forget to feed him. It always happens, you see. Who can you count on nowadays? I thought I could count on her until I found out she had let him out, and he isn't used to..."

"Oh, Billy's a dog?" interrupted Maggie, relieved.

"No, I once had a dog, poor devil, but he got run over. Alfred, or Alfi. Do you like dogs? I do, but I got a cat, Billy, after Alfi. Supposing it was easier to deal with until I found out my son was allergic to cats! He can't visit me now."

Maggie gently said, "That's a shame, but you can still pay him visits, your son?"

"Yes, but he lives far away. I have to take the train, and no deals for seniors."

Whatever topic Maggie picked, Aunt Maaike would find a negative view on it. No wonder the family members seemed to avoid her. She felt a little sorry for her, since she sensed she was intrinsically a good person. Her demeanour wasn't welcoming, which explained why aside from Ms. Miller, only the new arrivals, not knowing better, were seen speaking to her.

Maggie seized an unlikely rescue opportunity to get away from Maaike when Tina Partridge made her way over to speak with her. At first Maggie wasn't sure it was really her, since she had ballooned in size and had bleached her hair, but the unmistakable voice, a high-pitched shrill in her ear, erased any doubt.

"Maggie! Denis said you'd be here."

Maggie felt a pang as reality kicked in. Denis had married her. She felt goose bumps on her arms, just like when she was a teenager, at Tina's mere presence. She looked at her, trying to smile, and then saw Maaike's questioning look.

"Hi, Tina, you've chang...still here then. A journalist, I heard."

"Yes, nothing escapes me! I married Denis...and you still have your red frizzy hair, I see."

"You've not yet met Maaike, perhaps someone to interview, she's from Holland... I've got to go and take more pictures, I'm afraid."

Maggie left the pair, hiding a little grin at the thought of Tina having to listen to Maaike, although she felt sorry for Maaike.

Maggie could still see no sign of Amy, so she moved from one guest to another between the trays of canapés, taking portraits. She stood in front of a short man with thick glasses, elegantly dressed with blue cufflinks gleaming in the light of the fireplace. He was looking at her with a broad smile, his arms crossed on his chest, slightly balancing his belly toward the front. *Could that be? No, it can't, she thought,* but then he blurted out, "Prickles!" Only one person called her that, because she was like a cactus that couldn't be easily pushed in a corner.

Denis opened his arms wide and rushed to hug Maggie. Relieved to see that he didn't seem to hold a grudge against her for breaking up with him, she returned his hug. Overwhelmed by him planting two moist kisses on each of her cheeks, she moved back a step. Seeing his worried look, she quickly said, "Denis, I nearly didn't recognize you in a suit. Good to see you! I heard you've set up your practice here. I've just moved in and was planning on visiting you."

"You haven't changed a bit!"

"You need better glasses then." Maggie laughed.

Taking them off, he looked at her, then putting them back on again, he said, "No, I'm right. Still as beautiful as ever."

Maggie felt uncomfortable with his show of affection. She reminded herself that he was now married; he must be over their relationship. "It's really great, you're a dentist here. You always said you'd stay in Foxton. Do you have any kids?"

Ignoring her question, Denis said, "I read about the buyout of your company. Congratulations!"

"Oh that, I was lucky, that's all. But tell me about you. You married Tina?"

"So you know, I couldn't wait for you to come back, could I?" Denis laughed.

Hearing his familiar crackle of a laugh, Maggie couldn't help but giggle. "It's funny, I always knew Tina had a crush on you, even though she never admitted it." She looked around, and sensing that he wouldn't talk about Tina now, she added, "You must know everyone here."

"Yes, nearly. Go on, ask me who you want to speak with, I'll try to introduce you to them. Although I'd rather chat with you the rest of the evening."

Maggie pointed to a short, rotund man standing next to the trays of canapés, eagerly picking one sausage roll after another, as soon as he thought no one was paying attention to him. "Who's he? With his little moustache and chubby hands, he's harmless, that's for sure." She smiled.

"Oh him—be careful all the same. Humphries. He's the local constable—sergeant, actually. Yes, I mean it. He's fundamentally a good guy, likes his food. I see you've already picked up on that. I can still read your look. Careful, don't stare too much at his canapés." said Denis before carrying on. "He's a little, how shall I put it... He can't listen. Very stubborn."

"I see, and the one over there, the big woman with the pearl necklace. She seems to be making signs to...oh yes, over there, the thin man with dyed black hair."

"She's the new mayor, Ms. Stilton. Moved up a year or so ago, and interestingly enough managed to get elected. She wasn't the favourite, but after Peter Wigmott disappeared, I guess she was still ahead of the other candidates."

Ms. Stilton darted a dark look toward Maggie, moving from her head to her toes in a judgmental fashion before pushing herself, bust forward, across the room toward the man with the dyed hair.

"Oh my," exclaimed Maggie. "She seems to be the critical type. Somehow I think she doesn't like me." Having watched the mayor for a little moment, Maggie turned back toward Denis. "You mentioned someone disappeared. Did they find him? What happened?"

As Denis was about to relate the story, a tall man with hair carefully combed back and a salesman's grin, grabbed two glasses of champagne and abruptly positioned himself in front of Maggie, handing her a glass.

"I've not had the pleasure... Leon." He turned his head slightly to the left while smiling, as if he were presenting his best profile, and said, "I'm ready for my portrait."

"Leon, don't you see I'm talking with Maggie?"

Undeterred, Leon replied in a more pronounced Québec accent, "Come on, my friend, this is a party, we all get to talk to each other." In doing so, he pushed away Denis with one arm and towered down over Maggie. "I heard that you're looking for solar panels for your cottage... I'm your man!"

Irritated by Leon's behaviour, Maggie replied, "Leon, didn't you hear him, we're having a conversation, and I don't want to discuss solar panels this evening nor..."

Before she could finish her sentence, Maggie felt a little tap on her shoulder. She turned around and was for a moment speechless when she saw Amy in her mother's gown. She looked stunning. Leon and Denis looked at Amy with appreciation in their eyes.

Eager to send Leon away, Maggie said, "Leon, I see the lady over there doesn't have a glass, perhaps you should give it to her."

Leon retreated with his glasses, and smoothly, as if nothing had happened, handed one to the mayor, who was now standing next to them.

Maggie whispered in Amy's ear, "It looks great on you!" Then she smiled at Denis. "Denis, this is Amy, my best friend, and..."

Amy chuckled. "You must be Maggie's ex-boyfriend, then. We've spoken a lot on the phone..."

"Yes, I remember you, Amy. We had a long call about Maggie…" Denis grinned.

"You must have lots to talk about. Don't mind me, I'll leave you to it." Maggie retreated from the pair.

Although Maggie knew Amy would get back at her for leaving them alone, she felt uneasy with him. Ms. Stilton's overwhelming presence accentuated the feeling, her exotic perfume dominating the atmosphere. Using the cover of her photographer role, Maggie boldly walked toward the sergeant, who was tucking into the little cheese tarts while talking to a woman in her forties with black hair, bright red lipstick, and a flashy red dress to match.

Maggie wondered where she had seen her face before. All of a sudden, the image of a billboard of one of the county roads appeared in her mind. On it, an enlargement of her long face grinned at her with bleached teeth, and below it were the words *Fiona McLenny. Womax. Trust the expert, I can help you live where you play.* Maggie never understood the need for realtors to advertise themselves as models for toothpaste commercials when what they were supposed to be selling were houses. A picture of a house would do a better job, she thought.

Maggie smiled at the pair, observing that they both clearly shared a culinary appreciation. Beaming, a crumb dangling from his neatly cropped black moustache, Sergeant Humphries held the tray of little cheese tarts under Maggie's nose.

"Try these, they're really good, smooth on the tongue…and smell them, just out of the oven, the crust, yum, look at it… I wonder how they make them?"

The sergeant proceeded to inspect the tarts by lifting the tray to eye level, capsizing them into Maggie's outstretched hands as she tried to stop their fall. They both knelt down, Sergeant Humphries on all fours, the only way to keep his rotund belly out of his way, and Maggie swiftly gathering the tarts and back onto her feet.

Maggie heard Denis's characteristic chuckle in the background as the sergeant tilted his head up to Maggie while trying to lift himself clumsily up from the ground. Dusting his trousers, steadied by Fiona McLenny, the realtor, the sergeant rubbed his moustache with two fingers as if a hair had been misplaced while on all fours.

Wanting to make Sergeant Humphries feel at ease, Maggie placed another plate of canapés under his nose. "Did you try the salmon mousse? It's really good."

Perhaps in recognition of a fellow epicurean, he relaxed and happily accepted the entire dish.

The missing man, Peter Wigmott, was still clinging to Maggie's mind. She asked the sergeant, "I've heard that a man's disappeared—"

Before she could carry on, the sergeant interrupted her, seeming eager to talk. "Do you mean Wigmott? Eh…yes, in fact this was the last place he was seen before he disappeared into thin air."

Maggie looked at him, surprised; he straightened his jacket and went on. "It was after the Christmas party organized for the township last December. We always have the party at the Lodge, the food is so good… Where was I?"

"You were talking about Wigmott," said Tina, who seemed to have appeared from nowhere and was now looking at them with her eyes as slits.

Maggie instantly stiffened. "So what happened at that party?"

"Peter was very loud. Too much to drink if you ask me…"

"I saw him chat excitedly to everyone about the election. He was campaigning for the position of mayor. Thankfully, he didn't make it," said Tina.

"I agree. He wanted to reduce the police department up here, to cut costs. He had no clue of how much area we've got to cover. It's not a town here. Not to mention what we do for the community. Can you imagine?"

Struck by what she heard, trying to ignore Tina, who was about to speak again, Maggie asked in dismay, "What happened to him? How could he disappear with all those people around?"

Tina responded, interrupting the sergeant once more. "You know how it goes. Everyone has a little fun, and Peter Wigmott was bullying everyone into voting for him. You can't do that, he was spoiling the Christmas party. Not getting what he wanted, he left early."

"He didn't turn up the next day at the township meeting," added Sergeant Humphries.

Suddenly the bust of Ms. Stilton appeared, as if by magic, and positioned itself between Maggie and the sergeant, casting a shadow on the pair. To Maggie's surprise, Tina seemed to shrink in her presence, which was hardly possible, she thought, given her corpulence. Maggie grasped the opportunity to ask the mayor if she could take her portrait for the wedding. Tina mysteriously slipped away out of sight at the word "photo."

Like a proud turkey, the mayor wiggled her body and positioned herself next to the sergeant, one leg slightly forward and hips on an angle in a lost attempt to provide a slim front to the camera. Sergeant Humphries, under a sudden spell of sneezing, excused himself, stepping aside from the mayor, leaving her alone for the picture.

As Maggie took the picture, she said, "Sorry to ask, but you've such an unusual perfume. What is it?"

The mayor looked down at Maggie, flicking her head back to remove a mesh of hair from her eyes. "It's very special, and you'll not smell it anywhere else, I assure you. It comes from Peru, based on a flower found in the high mountains. They gave it to me to thank me for my help in building a school. I love it and can't get enough of it."

Maggie, still behind her camera lens, noted that the mayor must have been pretty when she was younger as she replied, "What an incredible story! This perfume is very strong and different. Another surprising story I just heard…"

Before Maggie could finish her sentence, Tina was back in the picture, barging in her conversation once again.

"Your opposition candidate Peter Wigmott's still missing. What do you think happened to him? Just before the election, how convenient!"

The mayor's throat reddened under her pearls as she spoke in a calm voice, still posing for the picture.

"It's very unfortunate. Perhaps he simply left. I think Peter already knew he wouldn't win, and there would be no other position for him. What else could it be? Nothing turned up from the extensive search efforts we did, no body, nothing. I believe he's still on the missing person list, but no one has come forward with meaningful information. Isn't that so, Sergeant Humphries?"

Having barely overcome his sneezing fit, the sergeant slowly looked up at the mayor, still rubbing his nose with his handkerchief, spellbound for a moment by the shiny pearls dangling over her breast, as if from a cliff. Sergeant Humphries blushed and looked away.

"Sorry, I don't know what I have. Yes, yes, we did all we could... And on top of that, a suitcase was missing from his home, together with valuables." He mumbled after having blown his nose away from the mayor, "Sorry. The strange thing is that he didn't use any money from his account, although..."

He stopped his sentence in midair as he eyed a tray of meatballs passing by. Maggie didn't have a chance to ask any more as a thin man with round-rimmed glasses, wearing a brown velvet jacket worn out at the elbows, walked up to them and introduced himself.

"I'm sorry to interrupt, but I couldn't help overhearing. I disagree with you. I think something's happened to Peter." Turning to Maggie, ignoring Tina, who had taken out a little notepad and was scribbling energetically on it, he put out his hand. "Sorry to barge in like this, but you see I'm Fred Wigmott, Peter's brother, and you can understand that I won't rest until I know what happened to him."

Maggie felt a sudden uneasiness experiencing his sloppy handshake. Her instinct was telling her he wasn't to be trusted. She scolded herself for judging too quickly; he must be deeply unhappy with his brother's disappearance. Perhaps that caused the negative vibes. He was in his early fifties, with dyed black hair similar to Leon's, trimmed eyebrows, and a skinny but athletic build.

Giving him a concerned, motherly look, Maggie replied, "Yes, I understand."

Seeing Ms. Stilton and Sergeant Humphries too happy to leave him in her hands, she decided to satisfy her curiosity and question him, in spite of Tina, who was still annoyingly listening in but surprisingly quiet.

Fred was a little reserved but outspoken about his brother. Fiddling with his jacket button, avoiding eye contact with Maggie, he said, "Peter was everything to me. He had such a drive; I couldn't keep up with him at times. He thought he could make a difference by becoming mayor."

Maggie, noticing the use of past tense, replied, "You shouldn't be so defeatist. He might still be alive, since some of his possessions disappeared with him. Maybe he ran away with someone? A love story, perhaps?"

Fred sighed. "Unlikely. He would have told me. I think something bad happened because of those elections. People are jealous. You know how it goes."

"No, not really. What do you mean?" asked Tina, still scribbling in her pad.

Fred shifted from one foot to another and looked toward the door as if he wanted to escape Tina's questioning. He had no need to do so, as Denis interrupted the conversation by poking Maggie from behind. Surprised, she jumped, turned instinctively toward Tina, half smiling, and instead of seeing a smile on her face, Tina pursed her lips and abruptly tucked her notepad into her handbag.

Denis laughed off her behaviour. "Come on, Tina..."

Tina swivelled on her feet, her handbag flying around her and hitting Maggie's arm as she marched off, each step reverberating through the floor. As swiftly as he had appeared, Fred disappeared among the revellers.

Maggie, eager to ease the atmosphere, chose to ignore what happened and asked, "Is Fred one of your clients? You seem to have frightened him away!"

"No, he's never visited me. Maybe a case of dental phobia, since you might have noticed his teeth look like a bicycle rack."

"Yes, I saw that. I wonder what type of business he would be in."

"Roof insulation, I believe. Anyway, a contractor of some kind."

"Must be hard for him, all the same, the disappearance of his brother..."

Their conversation was interrupted by the chiming sound of a knife against a glass and Amy joining the pair. The crowd shuffled around, turning toward the small stage. A set of drums and instruments promised some entertainment. Richard Miller climbed up, his long figure standing out like a tall white pine among the canopy of maples. He looked very cheerful, a little unsteady on his feet, having enjoyed one too many glasses of champagne.

He held on to the microphone stand as if he hoped it would provide some support as he announced, "And now that you all have itchy feet, what better than our very talented friends to shake it up for you. Please welcome our infamous country band, the Haystack Needles!"

He jumped off the stage and grabbed his daughter by the waist, getting ready for the first dance. Maggie put her hand to her mouth, surprised to see the sergeant standing behind the microphone, dressed in a leather waistcoat with frills swinging around his belly, pointy cowboy boots, and a large cowboy hat.

She laughed. "Now I see the moustache is perfect... Who would have thought?"

Maggie wondered where she had seen the drummer's face before...especially the eagle tattoo on his shoulder. She walked up to the stage to take a closer look and smiled as he looked down at her and winked. That wink was so familiar. Suddenly it dawned on her—it was Archie. He used to teach music at school, but in his twenties he had been very skinny, with long hair. He had certainly changed, with bulging muscles only steroids could explain and a Mohawk hairstyle. She wondered if he recognized her or whether he thought she was an admirer. At the mere thought of the latter, she rushed away from the stage to let the bride and her father open the dance.

After the first slow dance, the sergeant played his country repertoire with the guests joining the dance floor and singing along until late into the night.

Chapter Five

Already a week had gone by since Amy's visit and the wedding. A creature of habit, Maggie had decided that Sundays would always remain free to enjoy time outdoors. She had kept to it even during her busy research days behind the microscope. This was no time to change it, not on a sunny, warm April Sunday, with the goldfinches chirping and the wild turkeys' soft calls wafting into the room through the window.

Maggie wanted to check out the beaver dam again and investigate the mysterious handle, spurred by Amy, who had said it might be a case of illegal dumping. Maggie certainly wanted the water around the beaver dam to remain clean and was adamant about finding out what the object was.

The grass was turning green and seemed alive with robins hopping around in search of hidden insects. Bluebirds had also returned and were investigating the bird boxes she had set up on the shed wall. Her camera in hand and green hat pulled down to protect her fair skin, off she went into the woods.

The sweet smell of maple trees with their sap rising and the wild leek aroma filled the air. Chipmunks dashed under her feet with their tails up like antennae. She reached the dam, walking quietly, hoping to see the beaver, but this time no animal. Instead, Maggie saw half a snowmobile sticking out of the water. Amy was right.

As she carefully walked along the dam structure to get a closer look, she was startled by a deep "G'day" behind her, leading her to fall into the muddy embankment, one leg getting stuck. The silhouette of a tall man standing against the sun on the side of the road vanished in the wink of an eye. Feeling a tug on her leg she let out a shout.

"Sorry, I didn't mean to startle you. You're all right?"

Grasping the man's green uniform with one hand to steady herself, holding her camera up with the other, her hat floating on the water, she peered through her hair at the soft blue eyes looking at her from above.

Embarrassed, she replied, "Yes, I'm fine, I didn't hear you come...thanks for helping me out."

"It's my fault. I should've made more noise, but I was tracking poachers. The turkey hunting season has started, and this property is marked 'no hunting,' so I was inspecting it when I saw you move and thought you might have been one of them."

At the thought of poachers on her land, Maggie opened her eyes wide. In response, he went on with a reassuring voice. "I was tipped off there might be poachers around, but they're not after people, no danger there. It's just that often they don't have the licenses to hunt or they follow their prey from one land to another where hunting's prohibited. My job's to ensure rules are respected and animal cruelty avoided."

Her eyes scanned the man head to toe, verifying the information provided, until they rested on the nameplate: "Adam Clarkson," and below it the conservation officer's badge. A real warden then. Regaining her composure and her footing, she stood at his side, his strong hand still firmly holding her by the arm and tugging at her to help her back onto firm ground.

Although she liked his approach, her pride made her wiggle out of his grip, and with a laugh she said, "You can let go now, otherwise we might both end up like this snowmobile in the water."

With one leap, the man reached the side and turned around with his hand stretched out. Not wanting to offend him, she accepted it to shore and shook it with a chuckle.

"I'm Maggie, the owner of this property. Thanks for getting me out of the mud, or more accurately putting me in there in the first place."

He blushed a little. "Adam, at your service..."

Feeling the moment was a little awkward, Maggie pointed toward the snowmobile, explaining that it wasn't hers. "It must have slipped off the road onto the dam and into the water. Either dumped on purpose or an—"

As Adam looked at it closer, he finished her sentence, "—accident. It's a top of the range skidoo, judging by the new handle shape. Surprising no one picked it up."

"You seem to know a lot about those machines. Do you think you could help me pull it out? I can then contact the police if need be."

Adam pointed toward the road. "My truck's nearby. I'll get it."

Maggie put her thumb up in an approving gesture and looked around the area to see if she could find any other clue as to what had happened. Positioning herself on the dam between the snowmobile and the car, she steadied herself with a stick while stretching her hand out to Adam, who handed her the clip of the winch. With the snowmobile secured, she jumped up to the road to get a good vantage point of the muddy machine slowly sliding out of the water onto the road.

She wondered what might have happened; perhaps a joy rider had stolen it and wanted to get rid of it by driving it into the beaver pond. The seat was damaged, which could have happened upon impact or perhaps from ice over the winter.

"The license plate's still on!" exclaimed Adam. "That'll help to find the owner."

Maggie inspected the only ski remaining and the stub where the other one should have been.

"Perhaps it got caught in the dam and the snowmobile could've then flipped over...the rider must've had a big fall then...but I don't see any sign of that."

Maggie automatically lifted her gaze and scanned the surface of the water with her binoculars, looking for the missing ski. She smiled at the sight of the beaver slapping its tail in warning and diving out of sight.

Having wiped the license plate clean, Adam walked around the machine and knelt next to the engine. Finding it hard to see over his shoulder what he was inspecting, Maggie offered to take pictures hoping to be of help. Seeing she would not get any answer from him, her mind wondered back to the beaver. She lifted her eyes and jumped up, tugging at Adam's sleeve.

He sprang up from his crouched position, unfolding his long body as if the soil had been too hot to touch; his muscles seemed tense ready to pounce, like an animal, and he asked her while scanning the surroundings, "Did you see a poacher?"

"No, I don't see anyone. We make far too much noise for them anyway...but look! There. To the right, a piece of red cloth against the beaver dam."

Adam moved across to take a closer look, grabbing a long stick to reach the item in question. As he poked, a red and black mass floated up.

Maggie gasped as she saw what looked like an arm in a suit sticking out of a lumberjack jacket. "There's a hand! It's a body!"

Adam seemed to realize it at the same time and put his large hand in front of her eyes, shielding Maggie from the sight, only to be pushed aside. "Stay there, I've got to alert the police, don't touch anything."

Maggie stood motionless for a moment. The sight of the body in the water reminded her of the time Amy explained the advances in DNA analysis, allowing for the identification of highly degraded samples. Instead of triggering a feeling of disgust, the sad find spurred her scientific mind into action. She slipped on the working gloves she always carried with her to remove branches from the trails.

I won't touch anything, but if I'm far enough away from the body, maybe I'll find a clue...

She spotted a black lump at the far end of the dam. Only a few steps away from it, she saw it was a woollen hat. *Let me see.* She bent down slightly, lifted the hat out of the water with a stick and peered inside it. No label.

Hearing Adam call her name, she swiftly stood up, dropping the hat back into the water as if nothing had happened, tucking her hair behind her ear with one hand, the other throwing the stick away. She waved to him. "I'm here! Come and have a look." She pointed at the hat.

"No, you come over here. It could be a crime scene. You can't just walk around!"

"I thought I was far enough from the body."

"Maybe you are, but just in case, it's best to come next to me till the police arrive. I don't want you to get in trouble with Humphries. He'll turn up for sure. As soon as there's something happening, he's always the first on the scene. His constable, Raj Gupta, complains because he feels left behind, having to stay at the police station. I'd prefer Raj."

"I guess in a place where little happens, he'd want to be there when there's a sign of action, but why doesn't he come with Raj?"

"Raj is smart, and Humphries hates being outsmarted, especially by someone he regards as a foreigner."

"I didn't think the sergeant was like that when I met him at the wedding. I've not met Raj. His name sounds Indian."

"Yes, Raj arrived in Canada when he was little."

"He sounds interesting."

Adam laughed. "He's funny with his sayings, especially when they irritate Humphries, who doesn't understand what he's talking about."

"Seems harmless to me. No reason for Humphries to dislike him, really."

"Raj'd better watch out, though. He's too eager to please Humphries, because he's ambitious and wants to move up the ranks quickly. Humphries hates that and thinks you should spend decades as a constable before becoming a sergeant like himself. I tried warning..."

Adam last words were drowned by the sound of a loud siren announcing the arrival of the black police car, and out came Sergeant Humphries, adjusting his belt under his belly.

"Another accident...ahh, snowmobilers driving way too fast! We need speed limit controllers on those machines." Suddenly aware of Maggie standing next to his car, he raised his eyebrows. "And what are you doing here, ma'am? It's not a place for wom—"

Clearly he didn't recall meeting her before. Not a good attribute for a policeman. "You're on my property. I've the right to be here to see what's going on."

"I see," grumbled Sergeant Humphries, "but this is now an accident scene, so you have to stay away." Ignoring Maggie's attempt to respond, Sergeant Humphries pushed her away and addressed Adam. "What do we have? I see the skidoo. You mentioned a body...I don't see any."

Adam gestured toward the dam.

"Over there. If you stand on the beaver dam you can see it, where the red cloth is."

The sergeant walked along the dam, lifting each foot as high as he could with each step. He stopped as if he were scared to go any farther, fearing a snake or other creature might be lurking among the branches. "Where exactly?"

Adam pointed toward it. In attempting to get a better view by tilting his head forward without walking farther on the ridge, the sergeant's belly suddenly unbalanced him. He would have fallen into the water had it not been for Maggie, who was standing behind him and caught him by his jacket. Sergeant Humphries turned around, red-faced.

"I told you to stay away! Look you nearly pushed me in! Ah, women! Always in the way!" The sergeant walked back to his car, grumbling. "I need the constable to get the body out. Again an accident..."

Adam turned to Maggie and whispered in her ear, "He never

does the dirty work...you'll see, and don't worry about him. He can be rough, but he's not bad deep down."

"I'm not easily bullied! He doesn't even remember I met him before. Did you have time to see anything else on the snowmobile?"

"Nothing strange so far. The person must have skidded off the road. No tracks, though. The snow layer must've been already a couple of inches thick and the soil frozen, otherwise I would've been able to find something," replied Adam in a low voice.

Maggie took several more pictures of the snowmobile from all angles, having noticed that the sergeant couldn't see her, since he was busy speaking over the radio in his car. At the sound of the second police car arriving, Sergeant Humphries hailed Adam.

"You'd better take this lady back home. We'll handle it from here. And Ms...."

"Maggie Flanagan, Sergeant, we met at the wedding party."

The sergeant rubbed his moustache downwards, without a glimmer of recognition.

"Yes, ehh...Ms. Flanagan...although it's likely an accident, I need you to come to the station tomorrow for a statement. In the meantime, please let the police do their job."

"Yes, Sergeant. Before I do, though, look, over there I saw a hat that might belong to the dead man..." The sergeant grumbled. Maggie added quickly, "I'll get out of your hair..." She remembered the shiny scalp of the sergeant now hidden by his cap and added, "I'll drop by in the afternoon."

After Adam dropped her off, Maggie stood at her entrance door, still holding the piece of paper with Adam's phone number. She wondered if she had dreamed it all. There was a body in her beaver pond. What had happened?

Chapter Six

The next afternoon, Maggie arrived at the police station situated on the outskirts of the village along the main road linking Foxton to Algonquin Park. A bag of freshly baked carrot muffins was tucked into her big handbag. She was determined to befriend Sergeant Humphries, appealing to his liking for food, even though he didn't seem to have a good disposition toward women. Her choice of an afternoon visit rather than a morning one was driven by an article she recently stumbled upon. Judges gave out more favourable rulings after lunch than in the morning, with a correlation between hunger and a negative outcome.

Constable Raj Gupta greeted her cheerfully from behind the tall counter with a slight Indian accent. "How are you doing today?"

The constable smiled broadly at her, his arms outstretched, fingers spread out on the counter as if he needed a support for his body or wanted to fill the space with his presence.

Maggie replied, "Great, how about yourself?"

"Happy as a lark, with such a nice weather outside."

Maggie smiled to herself, thinking of Adam's remark about Raj's sayings; she lowered her voice as if she were sharing a secret. "I'm Maggie Flanagan, here to see Sergeant Humphries for the statement about the accident... Have you found out who it was?"

"Ah, you're the landowner. You wouldn't believe it... The snowmobile belonged to Peter Wigmott, and I'm sure it will be his body too." Putting his hand on his mouth as if he had let a cat out of the bag, he added, "The boss doesn't want to announce it yet."

Maggie whispered, "Oh, I'll keep quiet."

Suddenly a loud voice echoed across the room from the end of a corridor. "Gupta, is the report ready yet? I want it on my desk within the next ten minutes."

Constable Gupta stiffened and changed to an official tone. "Sorry, duty calls. I'll let him know you are here. Please take a seat."

Maggie heard a few muffled voices, followed by Constable Gupta reappearing and giving her a sign to follow him. She walked through the swinging doors along a narrow corridor to an office with a view of the woods. Sergeant Humphries was sitting in a reclining chair behind a large desk.

The sergeant looked grumpy, his moustache drooping downward as he welcomed her with, "Ah yes, you've come for the statement, eh. I don't know if I should bother about it, really, but since you're here we might as well take it."

Maggie, surprised by his slackness and sensing his irritation, replied, "Yes, indeed, I've come for the statement, as you requested yesterday. How're you doing?"

Ignoring her greeting, Sergeant Humphries carried on, "Constable Raj Gupta will take your statement after I've asked you a few questions. Right, eh, can you confirm you own the property along Lake View Road where the snowmobile accident happened?"

Maggie answered his questions with short responses. He seemed uninterested in details. She couldn't help but notice the use of the word "accident" and was surprised that the case would have already been concluded unless they had all the evidence they needed. She wanted to go to the bottom of what had happened on her land, and noticing the sergeant's questions were drying up, she concluded a direct approach would not work with him. Instead, she diverted the conversation to the wedding and the delicious meal they had had.

"It was a lovely wedding, and you were right about the quality of the food at the lodge, it was delicious."

Sergeant Humphries's eyes widened and his hand moved toward

his belly. She pulled out her bag of muffins, letting it clumsily fall to the floor, allowing the sergeant to pick it up for her.

Feigning embarrassment, Maggie said, "I'm so sorry, they're carrot muffins I baked them this morning..." The sergeant's eyes glowed, she went on, "I was about to bring them to Adam Clarkson, the conservation officer, for his help yesterday, but...would you like one?"

The sergeant stretched his hand briefly toward the bag he had placed on the table. Maggie stood up and said, "I'll see Constable Raj Gupta for the details of the statement. Thanks for all your help with this affair. I hope you solve this mystery fast."

Maggie had discreetly placed one muffin on his desk and walked out of the room, throwing a glance back at the sergeant, catching a glimpse of his smile at its sight. At the door she nodded toward him. "Bye."

This time he responded, "Have a nice day, Maggie."

Her approach seemed to be working. Perhaps it would with Adam as well. Nothing like home-baked muffins!

Constable Gupta pulled out a chair for her. "I hope he treated you well. He can be tough. So please, go ahead and tell me when and how you found the body."

Maggie repeated her story once more. Seeing the constable seemed focused on his task, perhaps afraid to make a mistake, she waited until he had finished typing to ask, "How did you figure it was an accident?"

Constable Gupta slid his chair back, relaxing in it as if he were preparing for a nice long chat. "Oh, easy, all the signs were there. He was a daredevil, and he was drunk and driving too fast, I'm sure of it, so it was obvious. Fortunately, no one else was hurt!"

"I see, not much proof, though. What about his suit? I can see he'd wear one at the Christmas party, but don't you think he'd then drive a car, not his snowmobile to the party? I remember seeing a black suit under..."

Constable Gupta shook his wrist, a gold name chain bracelet

sliding down toward his hand. "Mmm, I never thought of that. I've never been on a snowmobile. My wife thinks it's too dangerous. I know his brother is a fanatic snowmobiler, and I've seen him use his sled to commute. I think they both competed in races... If I had such a sled, I'd use it all the time!"

"But I don't get why he'd go by sled in a dress suit in the middle of winter." The constable raised his eyebrows. She added, "I mean, he just had his plaid jacket on top of his suit, isn't that right?"

"Yes, I see what you mean, and no gloves or boots either, and it sure gets cold here. That's why it was an accident. He must have forgotten to put on his boots and gloves. That's why he must have been drunk."

Grasping a chance to find out more about Peter, Maggie said, "I heard he left the party early. Maybe he had an argument with someone."

With another shake of his name bracelet, as if it were a foreign object newly on his wrist, Constable Gupta replied, "I did hear something about that, what was it...? Oh yes, something with the solar panel guy."

As the constable was about to add, out came the sergeant. "Gupta, we have the coroner coming now." This time Sergeant Humphries nodded and smiled at Maggie as she took her leave.

*

Constable Gupta heard a phone call coming from the office between the coroner and the sergeant, with only the sergeant's voice reaching him.

"So you can't prove he was drunk?" Silence. "I'm sure he was! I need that proof. Do your job properly. Do it again." The sergeant's voice trembled slightly as he said, following a long silence on his side, "I'm not an idiot, eh...I knew you can't measure it when the body was in the water, but..." A sound of a chair being wheeled back and forth drowned a few words until he said, his voice louder again,

"Can't prove it's an accident? Well, it has to be an accident. I'm sure he was drunk." Heavy steps could be heard walking toward the door of the sergeant's room as he said, "No, I disagree..."

Instead of the end of the sentence, Raj heard the door slam and could no longer distinguish the sergeant's voice. He shrugged with a shiver at the thought that this might not be an accident.

Chapter Seven

Maggie remembered it was Adam's day off and decided she would bring him her muffins, hoping to start afresh on better grounds than a dead body. Adam had told her he lived on a farm between Foxton and Algonquin Park. He lived there alone, since he had divorced a few years back; his ex-wife couldn't stand living in the countryside.

Maggie expected fields and maybe some animals, but not the llamas that greeted her as she drove up the path, running alongside her blue truck like two watchdogs. A tractor spurted smoke as it drove back and forth in the field behind the empty chicken pen. That must be him. She took her time looking around.

The little white house looked very neat with its yellow windows and daffodils already poking their heads out along its wall. The wood for the stove was evenly stacked against the house, not one log misaligned. A red barn a little farther down, stood next to a field with rows of fruit trees. The back of what looked like a vintage khaki Land Cruiser from the early seventies with a white roof poked out of its entrance.

As she walked toward the building, the vintage tractor headed her way, puffing like an old man. The inquisitive llamas were sniffing her hair, but as soon as Maggie reached out to touch them, they took a step back, ears flat, looking offended.

Adam pulled over and jumped out of his tractor with a broad smile. "G'day! Crikey! That's a nice surprise. No more bodies, I hope."

Maggie suddenly became aware of his Australian accent and

wondered why she hadn't picked up on it earlier; perhaps there had been too many things that day, or it was his outfit, shorts, low leather boots, and his leather hat that gave it away today. Perhaps it was the warden uniform he'd worn the day they met, making her assume he was Canadian rather than an Australian in the north.

She was brought back to reality by a loud "Scoot!" and the llamas taking off together in a dust cloud. Adam stood in front of her. Maggie would normally have been the one to start the conversation and ask questions; instead she smiled at him shyly, as if under a spell that was only broken when he started speaking.

"I hope they didn't bother you. They can be a bit nosy and very inquisitive…but they're good watch 'dogs.' They even scare bears away! You don't seem afraid of them, though. Do you like animals?"

Maggie's uneasiness was replaced by her usual keen observation as she studied the head of one of the llamas. "I love 'em. I've never seen a llama up close. Very strange-looking eyes with their horizontal slit pupils." She giggled a little. "Made up like drag queens with long fake eyelashes. I've heard they can spit or bite if they don't like you."

"You're fine as long as their ears don't start pointing backwards…" said Adam, lifting one corner of his mouth.

Following his eyes, she saw the ears of the second llama swivelling around and stepped back only a little, not wanting to look afraid. "Do you keep other animals?"

"I'm out in the bush often and not here enough for that, and besides, the orchard, the vegetable garden, and the hay field are more than enough for me to deal with. Do you like insects?"

She tried to look open minded as she could.

"I have beehives." He laughed.

Standing on tiptoes to look over a wooden fence in the distance to where he was pointing, she said, "I see them now. You got me a little worried for a moment, imagining what insect you would have had as a pet. I love honey. You must get other visitors then, especially bears."

"I've an electric fence. Keeps bears and skunks out. Would you like to try some honey? It could go with those muffins of yours."

Adam pointed with a wink to the plastic bag of muffins Maggie had been holding tight against her chest, away from the llamas. Welcoming his invitation, curious to see his home, she thrust the bag into his large hand. "They're for you, but your honey does sound delicious!" Following him through a small wooden door into a kitchen, she said, "You know, I saw the sergeant for the statement. I was a little nervous at first, but it all went well. I gave him one of those muffins..."

"He can be a little rough, but he's not a bad bloke. No doubt your muffin would've appealed to his sweet tooth. You were spot-on there."

Adam gestured to Maggie to take a seat at an old wooden table as he put on the kettle. She ruffled her curls. "Yes, I think he liked it, although he didn't say it outright. I just noticed a crumb on his cheek, so I know he ate it. Oh, and the body is Peter Wigmott's. The police think it was an accident and that he was drunk and driving too fast. But I'm not so sure."

"Why's that?"

"How does a snowmobile at high speed end up in a pond at the far left side of a curve bending to the left? The centrifugal forces should've made him slide to the right side, no? Very suspicious, if you ask me...anyway, have you noticed anything else?"

Adam seemed to think for a moment staring at the steam coming out of the kettle. The loud whistle broke his silence. "I saw a few scratches on the side of the sled, but that isn't surprising given the fall. There was also something around the handlebar..." He lowered his voice, slowly pouring the hot water into a round indigo teapot. "Something weird." With a brisk movement he placed the teapot in front of Maggie, a drop of water landing on the table. "The skidoo was still new based on the odometer. Powerful beast. No surprise there given that Peter was a fanatic and a real good snowmobile racer." Adam stopped pouring the tea mid air as if he were visualizing the snowmobile then carried on speaking, looking into Maggie's eyes, "I remember seeing him race his brother, Fred. They were always winning the local races. Peter seemed to care more for his sled than his brother did, though. Different characters, I guess. But I must be boring you with snowmobile details."

Maggie shook her head, her unruly curls hitting her cheeks. She had half listened to him, mesmerized by his two light-blue irises and how the pupil changed size as he spoke from a little dot to a large black hole. "Not at all, fascinating..." Realizing her remark might sound strange, she asked, "Does a snowmobile brake like a car? I remember as a child I didn't use the brake; just by decreasing the throttle, it stopped quickly."

"Yes, but you still have a brake in case of emergency. Say you're driving full speed and an animal's crossing, then you'd still brake using the handle brake like on a bicycle."

"I see. Do you have a snowmobile?"

Adam tightened his ponytail. "I do, I use it in winter to patrol parts of Algonquin Park and sometimes to track wolves for a study on their interbreeding with coyotes. It's less tiring than snowshoeing, although I do a fair bit of that, too. Great to get into the bush. Have you tried it?"

Maggie fondly remembered trying to follow her father across a frozen beaver pond, getting entangled in the cattails and refusing to move.

"Snowshoeing? Only a little, but I plan to pick it up now that I'm here. It must be really nice and quiet in winter. I've also walked on frozen lakes, but I was always afraid the ice wouldn't be thick enough and never went far."

Adam replied with a laugh, "Speaking of ice, the Wigmott brothers were mad. They used to cross a lake that was only partially frozen by going full speed across the open water with their sleds!"

Maggie widened her eyes, visualizing what seemed to her impossible, a snowmobile on water. "That's dangerous. It must have gone wrong at times? Well, sadly this time it certainly did go wrong for Peter."

Lifting the large teapot, one last drop making its way into Maggie's cup, Adam jumped up to set the kettle before she had any chance of leaving. She looked around the yellow-painted kitchen. A thick butcher maple countertop in an L-shape sat along the back wall, and an army of utensils were neatly lined up on a magnetic rack, with a row of spices sitting on a shelf beneath it. On the walls, pictures of a different kind of bush stood out: very red soil and sparse greenery, with a few vividly coloured birds that looked like parrots in the middle.

She enquired. "This must be Australia. Pretty birds, what are they?"

"Yep, all the photos are from down under." Adam walked to the picture Maggie was pointing at, bringing it down for her to look at. "Rainbow lorikeets, cute little things, but surprisingly dangerous, as they have a strong bite."

Adam lifted his large hand up, holding out his thumb in front of Maggie's eyes. A very long thumbnail caught Maggie's attention. Was he a guitar player? As if Adam had understood what she thought, he said, "No, the scar there, in the inside of my thumb. I was trying to rescue one when I was a boy. It bit me, and it would not let go of my thumb!"

"It looks like a little pinch. Did it survive?"

"Sure, I saved it, what do you think! The smaller the bite, the more dangerous it can be in Australia, with snakes..."

"Oh, snakes. I'm not afraid of them, no dangerous ones here."

Adam's Australian accent was coming out stronger. "Yes most of them, but you've just got to be careful, like with the salties...you know, the sea crocs that can jump out of the water. It's best not to swim when they're around."

"You won't get me in the water if there's the slightest chance of one being there! Are you trying to scare me?" said Maggie, feigning fear.

"Didn't think you'd be easily scared. Having said that, those animals aren't dangerous either as long as you respect them and their space, not different from us humans."

Sensing a kindred spirit regarding wildlife, Maggie replied, "I agree, we really can live alongside wildlife by understanding their behaviour, and the more I observe, the more it fascinates me." Not seeing any picture of Canada, she asked, "What brought you to Canada?"

Adam added a thick layer of honey to a second muffin he had just placed on his plate, making Maggie wonder if she had put enough maple syrup in them for the sergeant to like them.

Licking his fingers after taking a bite, he said, "Tasty…" and wolfed down the remainder, a few crumbs still hooked to his stubble of a beard. "My mum's an Aussie and dad's a Canuck. It was a case of too hot or too cold for either of them."

"What do you mean?" asked Maggie, scratching her cheek, signalling for him to remove his crumbs, to no avail.

"I was born in Canada, then my mother wanted sun in winter, so we moved to Australia. Australia was too hot for my father, so back to Canada when I was sixteen."

"I see, and what do you prefer?"

"I like it here, the diversity of plants, very green, lots of water, and a lot of space."

"But Australia is known for its space too, far views. It looks spectacular."

"Yes, but the liveable part is really around its rim, at the ocean; most of the rest is desert. I like the lakes here, and the lushness, endless forests with wildlife, seasons, mountains: a real variety."

Adam looked out the kitchen window at the field and woods. Maggie could empathize with him, sharing the love of her country and its wilderness and missing it when living in England. She hadn't been to Australia, still a place she wanted to explore, but she knew it would be too dry for her to live there, and she loved the changing seasons and real snow that lightened up the landscapes, unlike the British drizzle in winter that only added more shades of grey.

Adam moved his chin forward toward her, causing the crumb to finally fall down. His eyes transfixed on her red hair, he asked, "What about you? Your last name sounds Irish."

"Yes, my red hair, a preconceived idea, though, as you'll find more dark-haired with light eyes in Ireland than-red haired. I was born here, in this village, so I'm more local than you."

"I didn't mean to offend. I like red hair."

Maggie felt herself blush. "My great-granddad came from Ireland, and when he came to Canada somehow he dropped the O in the name; we don't know why. My ginger hair comes from my mother. It ran in her family, not from the Irish side as far as we know, since her parents and grandparents were Canadians." She laughed. "You see, it's not all what it seems to be."

"So you just moved from England back here, did I get it right? Why was that? You don't mind me asking...?"

"No, no, I get that question all the time."

"Oh, then you do mind! Sorry!"

Maggie, seeing Adam shifted on his chair backward, farther away from the table and from her, extended her arm across the table without thinking and grabbed his forearm.

"No, not coming from you. My move back happened so fast. A combination of circumstances. I was kind of lucky. I had a good offer for my stake in the company I had set up, which made me free as a bird after a long period of hard work. Sadly, my parents passed away at the same time, killed in a car accident, leaving me their home here."

Maggie wiped a tear with the back of her hand. She picked up her cup to hide behind it and took a sip to get rid of the knot in the throat before she could get too emotional in front of Adam, the last thing she wanted.

"It soon dawned on me that I really missed Foxton and that I wasn't made for the city life. I need fresh air...nature, so here I am. Enough of the past. You're a wildlife expert, so where can I take good pictures of wolves and other animals?"

Having steered the conversation to a safe topic, less emotional, she relaxed. Adam talked to her about the best places to view the animals she wanted to photograph and of a number of tree huts she might be able to use.

Maggie already felt as if she had known Adam for a long time. Her golden rule with friends and especially new friends was: do not overstay your welcome and leave on a positive note to keep the desire to see each other again. She rose to her feet. "Wow, look at the time. I intended to drop by, not interrupt your day! Besides, I've got to finish unpacking my boxes. I didn't have a chance yet with my first wedding."

Adam looked at her with alarm in his eyes. "Wedding? You got married? Where's your husband?"

"No, no, I was the photographer for the Millers' wedding. The daughter of the owners of Moose Lodge. By the way, I didn't see you there."

"I was invited, but I couldn't make it. Had to see my ailing mother. Would have liked to."

"Oh, sorry to hear that. Is she all right?"

"It was more a case of attention-seeking. Anyway, you're always welcome to drop by if you see my car. And don't worry about this incident at your place; those things happen. I hope it didn't spoil your return home?" He followed Maggie, who had meanwhile managed to take a few steps toward the entrance.

"No, I'm fine. But if you hear any news regarding the murder, let me know. I feel involved, as it happened on my land."

Seeing Adam's forehead crease at the sound of "murder," Maggie already regretted her slip of the tongue, although she had a strong feeling it wasn't an accident. She had no proof, just a hunch that would not go away.

"What do you mean? You said it was an accident. We're a small community here, and frankly nothing much happens, and even less murder, I tell you. At least since I've been here."

"That's what they all seem to think, but somehow it looks fishy to me. I can't help it; I sense it. Anyway, thanks for the tea. I'm curious to see the outcome of this story, so keep me posted."

She winked at him as she walked out the door. Instead of friendly reply, Adam had his back turned and grumbled the word "murder," shaking his head. She froze on the spot until he looked at her and waved goodbye with a smile.

Back home, Maggie regretted having told him her belief that it was murder. She didn't know Adam yet had been speaking with him like she would have with Amy. She imagined herself in his shoes; he might think she was a drama queen, worrying and exaggerating, definitely not the way she wished to come across to him.

Or even worse, perhaps he would think it a liar's slip of the tongue, and she was the murderer who wanted to cover it up as an accident. It horrified her. Looking out from her terrace at her yard, tears welled up, until she pulled herself together. The only way to get out of this would be to find out what really happened.

Chapter Eight

The plumber, Joe Johnson, had convinced Maggie to set up a meeting with the solar panel installer, Leon LeBreton. He had assured her he would be the best man to advise her on the chances of putting her cottage off-grid. At the same time, Joe had secured the installation of her new sink in the kitchen and this very minute had his head in her cupboard, trying to hook it up.

Maggie's home faced south, which seemed ideal, according to Joe, although Maggie had numerous doubts about such a setup. She wanted to join the green movement if it made sense. She didn't particularly like Leon LeBreton, given her first encounter with him at the wedding and his salesman's approach, but since then she had heard he was the best around for solar panels.

Before making Leon LeBreton's appointment, she had scheduled Fred Wigmott to drop by to discuss roof insulation. Although Maggie genuinely wanted to insulate her roof properly, her ulterior motive was to find out more about Peter's death. She felt she had to, not only for herself but also to face Adam again.

She didn't want the plumber to be able to eavesdrop on her conversation with Fred Wigmott about his brother, and was relieved when Joe got an urgent call from a customer to deal with a leak. That also meant she didn't need to spend an inordinate amount of time talking to Joe, thus avoiding his elaborate explanations about plumbing or making maple syrup. Both topics could have been interesting, but she was quick to note that in his bills he didn't discount for the time he spent talking.

Soon after Joe left, Fred Wigmott's black Ford truck pulled up with gleaming chrome bumpers, surprisingly on time. His handshake remained as moist and weak as on their first encounter.

He looked around and said, "How's it going? A good old log home, like they used to make 'em."

He still seemed to have trouble with direct eye contact, and his hazel eyes often shifted upward to look just above her head. Having lifted her hand to her head in response to find there was nothing wrong with her hair, Maggie felt a growing irritation. Her eyes landed on a chunky gold ring on his pinkie with an A carved out. He seemed unaccustomed to wearing it, as he rolled it around his finger with his thumb, slipping it on and off until it disappeared into his coat pocket.

Maggie walked around the house, pointing at the old roof until they reached the terrace overlooking the lake.

Fred had been taking notes and nodding sideways all the way when he finally announced, "The insulation, the way it is now is no good for winter. You really should replace the roof too. Spray foaming is the way to go after that, leak-proof and durable."

Maggie sighed at the thought of what it would entail. Fred continued, "I know it's a big investment, but I wouldn't guarantee my insulation for the roof the way it stands now."

"Really? There's no leak as far as I know. It looks fine to me."

"If you keep it like this, it'll cost you more to insulate…it's an old building, so it's difficult for us to squeeze into the attic, and I'm sure there're bats, aside from lots of mess making it hard to work…it'll require more time and…"

Seeing where he was heading, Maggie said assertively, "Just give me your best quote for a simple insulation. Replacing the roof will have to wait. Besides, your suit, the one on your picture on your truck, should protect you well. It looks like a space suit!"

"I don't know who advised you about your roof. All roofers aren't equal. I've got a good friend who could look at it for you, and

I'm sure he'll agree with me."

Maggie smiled at the thought that his friend would of course be in agreement with him and decided to go along with him for the moment, since an extra quote for the roof couldn't hurt. Besides, she didn't want to put him off, otherwise she might not get any information from him regarding his brother.

"Sure, let me know who he is. I can compare things that way. Do you have any clients I could speak with for whom you've insulated the roof recently?"

"Yes, of course, my brother's place...but..." He sighed. "I don't have access to his house yet, since the police still want to check it out. And the Millers, I did redo some insulation in the cabins."

Maggie, seeing an opening to ask about his brother, offered him a coffee, and said, "It must be hard for you. Were you close to him, your brother?"

A quiver of emotion twitched the side of his mouth. "Yes, very, he was my little brother. The best snowmobile racer around, he was...always pushing it more than me...too far this time!"

"You raced with him?"

"Yep, as kids and till now. It's in our blood. I don't get why the police are still holding on to his snowmobile. It's mine now, he loved it."

Maggie asked, "It mustn't be easy to be pitched against your brother. I don't have siblings, but I'd hate it. Was there any rivalry between you?"

Fred laughed. "Nope, 'cause I always let him win...he never believed I did it on purpose...we all promoted him in the family. I financed his studies..."

"So he was the favourite child then?"

His body language turned defensive as he took a step back, folding his arms against his chest.

"I miss him! I told him not to run for mayor; it was a mistake. I don't know why he drank and rode the sled. He never did that before."

"Was it because of this election that he drank?" Maggie asked, not knowing what had happened during the election but having the feeling that there might be a link between the two—if not the drinking, perhaps to his death.

"This election story, he would have won, I'm sure of it."

"Why's that?"

"He didn't want the huge solar farm next to the village on the municipal grounds. A real eyesore, that would've been. Who needs green energy here with the hydroelectric dams? Peter wanted a community swimming pool. Everyone was for it."

"But I heard not everyone liked him around here?"

"He was no angel, oh no, and spoke his mind too much. But I tell ya, he would've won. This woman, the new mayor, was against him with her solar panels. She'd do anything to win that one. It's only because he disappeared conveniently that she won."

"Really? That's a rather strong insinuation. Surely in such a small community a fair election would've taken place. And you said yourself that it was an accident..."

Averting Maggie's eyes with his upward look, Fred replied, "You're right, an accident, but it's so unfair!"

Maggie gently put a hand on his shoulder. Seeing him cover his eyes with his hand, she didn't have the heart to ask more questions about his brother. "That's for sure. Now then, are you still up for making me a quote?"

As if shaken out of his apparent state of grief, Fred smiled. "Yes, of course, you'll have it by tomorrow."

As the white van of the solar panel installer arrived, Fred Wigmott frowned at it and took his leave hastily. Leon LeBreton, with his usual loud demeanour, shouted out, "Hey, Fred, not chasing you away, I hope, no hard feelings on my side in any case!" Leon then turned to Maggie with a broad smile. "Hi, Maggie, can I call you Maggie?"

Maggie felt the animosity between the two men. They grinned at each other like two baboons baring their fangs to impress each other. Fred clenched his fist while Leon pushed his shoulder forward, slightly tilting onto the ball of his feet, attempting to increase his size. *Something must have happened between them, but what?* The first thing that came to mind was that they had worked on a building site together, and as so often happened between trades, there had been tensions, but somehow she sensed it was deeper than that.

Wanting to defuse the tension, Maggie welcomed Leon LeBreton. "Sure, Leon, Maggie's fine. So I hear that your solar business is booming. I hope you'll have a little time to give me a quote and perhaps do the job, if I can be convinced."

At the wedding party, Maggie had noticed that Leon LeBreton loved talking to women and couldn't help stroking back his long black hair. She had had to save Amy from his grip as he kept returning to her to talk about forensics, as if he were fascinated by the topic, while incessantly scanning her body in the yellow dress when she wasn't looking. It was understandable, though; the dress had been just perfect on Amy's slim figure.

Maggie looked at his neatly combed hair, thinking of the laugh she had shared with Amy when she showed her a picture of Leon staring in front of a mirror at the lodge, oblivious to his surroundings, focusing on slowly sliding a comb through his hair. She had seen him do it several times that evening and for the fun of it had counted the number of strokes from one side to the other: always three.

Maggie caught a whiff of his aftershave and giggled. What Denis had told her at the party was true—Leon always wore a lot of aftershave, even though it meant that the black flies and mosquitoes would swirl around his head, leaving the other people around him bug-free.

"Anything the matter?" asked Leon.

"No, no. Just a tickle in my throat," lied Maggie. *It's fortunate for him the black flies aren't out yet.*

Maggie wondered whether he would wear his pointy cowboy boots when climbing up a roof, or if it was just for the initial client visit. His tight jeans were held up by a leather belt and large silver buckle. In contrast to this cowboy style, he was wearing a fluorescent tricoloured bomber jacket, reminiscent of the eighties with yellow sleeves and the body half turquoise and half pink.

After exchanging pleasantries about her home, they walked around the house to the deck facing the lake to discuss the panels. For the next thirty minutes he spoke about the advantages of solar. Her house had the perfect exposure for it, and interestingly, there happened to be a program running with the current municipality sponsoring his work.

"Do you know now that Stilton's elected, you can get a credit on your local taxes if you install the panels. Imagine all the savings you'll make!" Leon LeBreton beamed.

"Well...only after a big upfront payment... I'd have to see the details. Since you seem to know the new mayor well, do you know if the large solar farm project is going through?"

"Sure it is, I'm the one that convinced her."

"What about the permits? And funding approvals? I heard most of the villagers are against it, as they won't directly benefit from it and it would be unsightly."

"All in the pocket already. The mayor's assured me she can convince all her colleagues."

Leon LeBreton lifted his chin, looking down at Maggie, his hands on his hips, attempting to increase in size as he spoke. This didn't sound right to Maggie; either he was lying or the new mayor truly had managed to turn the community away from the idea of a swimming pool. Another option was that Fred Wigmott was wrong about the pool, and the community was simply divided. In any case, she felt she had to dig further.

"I'm surprised. The locals wanted either to keep the field as it is for the summer games or have a swimming pool instead. I don't see how the panels would benefit them, since all the power generated would be sold back to the electrical company at an advantageous rate for the owner of the panels. You?"

"Yes, but I won't be the only one benefitting. The locals will get cheaper electricity!"

Maggie couldn't believe her ears. He seemed to be lying though his teeth. It was highly unlikely the locals would get lower electricity bills. Perhaps the municipality would, but that was it. Feeling angry, she said, "Really...had Ms. Stilton not been elected, this would not have gone through."

Leon LeBreton shifted from one foot to the other as he abruptly changed the topic of conversation. "Joe Johnson mentioned you wanted to see the solar panels. I can show you the home where I've installed them."

Maggie sensed there was no point asking more questions regarding the mayor. "I've already arranged with Joe to see it, thanks. Do you have a problem working with Fred? I was thinking of him for the insulation."

He raised his eyebrows. "No, why should I?"

"I overheard you asking about hard feelings, and I'd rather make sure everyone gets on when they work at my place."

Leon laughed nervously, peering down at his skinny fingers. "That? No, no, Fred was upset that he lost a bet we had on who'd win the elections. Only a few bucks, nothing serious."

Maggie looked at him sideways. She wanted to push Leon a little further and tried to provoke him by saying, "Fred believed his brother would have won the elections. Perhaps he was upset because his brother might have been murdered because of the elections..."

Leon's face grew pale. "Murder...? It was an accident. You shouldn't listen to the local gossip! He just had an accident with his sled, that's it, hit a moose or deer, happens all the time."

Maggie smiled reassuringly. "Yes, you must be right, but still..."

"He was drunk. I saw him at the party. He had a few too many. An accident, I tell you."

Maggie was silent, wondering how Leon LeBreton could have known the body was Peter's and that it was an accident, since the police hadn't officially confirmed anything. Was it from the local gossip, Fred having talked and someone overheard him?

The silence seemed to trigger a flow of words from Leon LeBreton.

"You probably don't know, but although Peter was the favourite, he was no angel. Did you hear about the scandal in Brampton, south of here, where Peter was an advisor to the mayor at the time?"

Maggie shook her head.

"In order to get his position, Peter discredited his opponent, Suzanne McLenny, by digging up her past and exposing it in the local newspapers. A sure way to get enemies."

"But surely this type of appalling behaviour is not a reason get killed, and you just pointed out it was an accident." Leon flicked his eyelids and shifted his eyes toward the van. "Is the realtor Fiona McLenny by any chance related to this Suzanne McLenny?"

At Fiona's name, Leon's eyes lit up.

"Fiona, no she's not related to her," he replied defensively.

She laughed inwardly and thought Leon and Fiona must be having an affair. In any case, he seemed to like her. Not wanting Leon to feel too much at home and settle comfortably on her deck, she ushered him gently up and out by focusing back on the quote that she was now expecting from him promptly.

As he drove off, Maggie couldn't shrug off the idea that Leon had all motives to want Peter out of his way, but would he kill for it? It could have been an accident, but the more she thought about the story, the more suspicious she grew.

Chapter Nine

Adam couldn't help thinking about Maggie, a very unusual woman, a tomboy, unlike his ex-wife. He walked around his barn and contemplated for a brief moment the red maple tree flowers colouring parts of the wood with a warm burgundy hue. As he gathered some hay for his llamas, his eyes fell on his snowmobile. He remembered what was bothering him about Wigmott's skidoo.

There had been something strange about the handlebar, and focusing his mind as if he were looking through a telephoto lens, zooming into the object, he suddenly saw it: the brake cable had been loose. Why had he not seen it before? Oh, yes, he had been distracted by Maggie showing him the body in the water. Feeling the urge to verify his vision, Adam remembered that the skidoo had been brought to his pal Barrie's garage for inspection; the police relied on him for outside expertise.

Adam rushed into his house, slipped on a clean T-shirt, and ran out, his llamas poking at him for some hay. His soft side took hold of him, so he ran back to the barn with the two llamas in tow, picked two carrots from the treat box, and piled a generous portion of hay in front of the barn. The llamas, having smelled the carrots, stood lined up a metre away from him, their big ears pointing toward him and nostrils flickering.

Adam had been training them using a horse-whispering technique, which seemed to bear fruit as they kneeled down in unison with one click of his fingers. He handed each one their treat and then jumped into his car, brushing the straw off his T-shirt.

Barrie Brown's garage with its blue façade was nestled between an old movie theatre that was barely able to sustain itself were it not for the little army of volunteers keeping it running, and a popular ice cream parlour that stood out from the other buildings with its pink ice-cream-scoop roof sitting on a cookie cone wall. Its prime gossip location ensured that Adam would get the latest village news simply by visiting his friend for a little chat between oil changes.

On his way, he stopped at his favourite hangout at the end of Foxton's main street overlooking Perch Lake, Heidi's Horizon Cafe, to pick up Barrie's special coffee, knowing his visit might take a little longer than usual.

Adam always looked forward to viewing the weekly art exhibit Heidi housed in her cafe. It was usually based around a theme; this time it was all about maple syrup and sugar maples, and any art form that related to it could be on display and sold. Heidi had encouraged Adam to pursue his chainsaw sculpture interest and promised to have a theme around it when he was ready to show his work. After a brief chat with Heidi about the exhibit, he walked out onto the main street toward Barrie's garage.

The garage was packed with shelves and metal storage chests, and yet it seemed that all the tools were sitting on the tables around. It amazed Adam how Barrie could find his bolts and nuts in such chaos and yet managed to repair engines in a wink of an eye.

Barrie had grown up in Foxton and taken over his father's garage when he was only twenty. Now in his thirties, he worked alone. Occasionally he would have an apprentice but complained that they were always hanging around Danillies ice cream parlour speaking to the girls and were never there when he needed them. This time he was alone. As soon as Adam entered, Barrie slid out from under a car as if the coffee aroma pulled him out.

"G'day mate!" exclaimed Barrie.

Adam was used to Barrie's attempts at imitating his accent and choice of words and often tried to improve his pronunciation.

"Nearly there, just the 'a' sound needs improving." Adam laughed.

"Crikey. That's grand. I can do with a coffee and a break. This freaking car is giving me a headache; with all the new electronics fitted in you can't just repair the machine. I can't figure out what's wrong with it."

"Can't help, I'm afraid. I heard you've been working on a police accident case, the Wigmott skidoo, is that right?" Before Barrie could answer, Adam added, "Here, thought you might like one of Heidi's pretzels fresh from the oven. Her *apfelstrudel* wasn't ready yet."

Picking up the warm pretzel with his hands still full of grease, Barrie replied, "Thanks, yum! Yep, I've been in there all morning and still need a few more hours." He pointed to a back room with a large sign on it: *Private do not enter*.

"All morning, still not done? Not enough electronics in it?" asked Adam, knowing full well if he teased him a little, Barrie would be too happy to chat away about cars or anything with an engine.

"Well, it's a brand-new skidoo. The engine wasn't tampered with as far as I could see, a ski missing and a few scratches, but I saw something weird with the brake cable. I showed it to Humphries this morning, but he said the cut in it was due to the accident, and the cable could've been torn by a branch."

Adam's curiosity was piqued. He followed Barrie, who waved a hand to show him along.

"Come and have a look. I disagree with the sergeant, I think the cable was cut deliberately. I'd like your view on it. The steel core of the cable has a straight cut like you'd get with a cable cutter, while the plastic cover is partly torn but also partly cut." Barrie opened the door and entered a second garage open to the back of the building.

In the middle stood the red skidoo, stripped open as if on an operating table with a large lamp shining above it. Sipping his coffee, Barrie pointed to the left handle with a black cable hanging down from it. Adam took a closer look and noticed a thin cut diagonally through the plastic cover and some fraying where it had been torn.

Barrie held up the cable under the light. "My guess is that the steel core was deliberately cut, while the plastic sheath kept it from breaking loose, and that part only ripped during the accident after the brakes failed…"

"Gee, you're right. This means that it was tampered with. And you tell me that the idiot sergeant thinks it was a branch!"

Barrie laughed. "He even mentioned a beaver. Can you imagine a beaver cut this so neatly like that? I think he wants it to be an accident, less paperwork, if you ask me!"

"I imagine you'll write this in the report, and he'll have to escalate it. Do you think this could have caused the accident?" asked Adam.

Barrie took a sip of coffee. "You know like I do that you don't often use your brakes on a snowmobile, and if you do, it means that you had to react very fast. Peter was a very good rider. He could've been trying to avoid an animal on the road."

Adam's mind was racing along. "Still, why would someone tamper with the brakes and hope that he'd hit an animal? The chance of that happening is still low. Wasn't his sled in tiptop shape for the race on Sunday that was only a few days before the Christmas party?"

"It was. I even checked it for him at his place. I'll leave the detective work to the sergeant. And you should too. I can only say what happened to the vehicle. He missed the animal, no hairs there, and no blood, not even a dent aside from what the ice did to the seat and the ski, and a few scratches."

Adam walked around looking at the damage and scratches. Barrie rubbed his hands on his towel, having finished the coffee, and said, "I better get busy, his brother wants it repaired. Not sure I'll be able to do so, the engine is dead because it stayed too long in the water. Can you imagine a new engine? A fortune, better buy a new sled, I said."

"I bet you Fred is superstitious, and he thinks riding this sled will make him win like his brother."

"Maybe. I tried telling him that it would bring bad luck. Look what happened to his brother!" Barrie changed topic unexpectedly, surprising Adam with his loud voice, "Hey...you asked me the other day if I knew of anyone who caught a turkey. Well, last night I heard Alfred's boys boasting they bagged two. Didn't they lose their hunting license because they trespassed on Peter's land? Didn't you catch them?"

"A bit of a murky story. I didn't catch them. Peter requested I take their hunting license away without any evidence of them having killed an animal on his land. I'm sure they tried, but you know they really need the meat for winter, so I gave them a fine this time. They're only kids and you know what it's like, just testing our limits... And Peter, well, he agreed to this but blew the story up, and you know how gossip goes...before you know it, it was a murder..."

Adam put his hands in front of his mouth, realizing that this time it might be true and thought about Alfred's two sons. Yes, they could be poachers, but why would they want to kill Peter or hurt him? Two teenagers thinking it a practical joke to cut a brake cable: that seemed unlikely...although they were notorious for not thinking of the consequences of their acts.

Adam walked out of the back garage with Barrie and thanked him for the news on the turkeys. Perhaps it could be the lead for his poachers, in which case he would have to visit the boys' home tomorrow and speak to them again. It had become a yearly routine visit, and this time would be no exception.

As Adam drove out of Foxton, his faithful Land Cruiser J40 seemed to be on autopilot as it went straight toward Otter Lake along Lake View Road. Without knowing why, he had ended up just in front of Maggie's home. He was still of two minds about Maggie. He had a good feeling about her and yet the dead body lay heavy in his mind. Adam was thinking of turning around when Maggie popped her fluffy head out of the door decorated with a hand-carved wooden sign, *Home Sweet Home*.

Chapter Ten

Maggie shivered under Adam's dark look and deep furrows. Eager to befriend him and ignore her fear, she welcomed him as if he were an old friend. She put her hand under his arm, leading him into the house through the living room, with its inviting red couches adorned with mismatched cushions, through a narrow corridor decorated with happy family photographs: Maggie waterskiing as a child on the lake, a picture of a group of kids around a bonfire roasting marshmallows, her father waving from his little plane on the lake.

Maggie entered a smaller room at the end of the corridor. "I'm glad you dropped by." Believing she had better be upfront about the accident instead of avoiding it, which could otherwise appear suspicious, she said, "It's as if you knew I wanted to speak with you, about the accident...as you offered?"

"Sure."

"It's been bothering me. I found something I'd like you to see on the pictures of the snowmobile."

Adam looked down at her from the doorway. "Funny you say that. I'm just back from Barrie's, and I saw the brakes had been cut! This means that you were right."

"About what?" asked Maggie innocently, not wanting to use the word "murder" again.

"It could've been a murder."

Maggie looked up to his piercing eyes, forcing her to tilt her head back to see at six foot five their spark framed by deep wrinkles. For a split second she wondered if he was testing her, to see if she was involved in anyway. After a closer look at him, not having discerned any hostility, she brushed aside her fear, opting to be completely open with him instead.

"It seems we're getting clues that tie together, the cable, but also possible motives since a number of people have voiced their strong dislike of him, perhaps to the point of wanting him dead."

Planted in front of the patchwork of photos hanging from floor to ceiling, he said, "Fun pictures, is this your father in the yellow plane?"

"Yes, he was a good pilot, and that's his plane." Maggie, seeing Adam had taken a few steps back into the corridor, looking at other pictures, waved for him to join her in her study.

Adam walked in and said, "I like your log home. I've always wanted to build one myself, maybe one day."

"But your home is very cute. A cottage has its charm too."

"Yes, for a little old lady maybe. The ceilings are so low, and I bump my head all the time, whereas here there's space."

"Perhaps we could swap?" Seeing Adam look around, taking in the place as if he were the owner, she quickly added, "Just kidding. Size-wise it might make sense, but I really like my parents' home. Still lots to do to make it my own, though."

"I already like it the way it is. And what on earth do we have here?" Adam made a swiping movement toward the camera lenses neatly lined up on the shelves, a microscope next to a large screen computer. "Is this your lab then? Can't see your white coat and safety glasses."

"No, not really. My photo lab now. I've told you I hung up my white lab coat when I sold my share of the company. I want a new deal, and this is it." Maggie pointed to her camera lenses, then reached for her desktop and brought up a blown-up image of the body of the snowmobile. "Speaking of which, take a look at this."

Adam was looking down the microscope, fiddling with its knobs, trying to peer through the lens at an image of unidentified clusters that beamed back at him. She continued, "I use it for photography now. It's nothing, just a bit of pepper, was testing if I could make an abstract picture. Look there." Maggie poked at the computer screen. "Do you see it?"

Adam uncurled his back, folding his legs down like an accordion to look at the image.

"See, when I zoom in, I can see the paint's been damaged, and there, see the scratches. Maybe from a collision with another vehicle. Can't be a tree or animal, none of them would have left such marks."

"Yes, I see what you mean. Strange...it certainly didn't have a scratch before that evening."

As Adam bent over her shoulder, she felt a little tickle on her cheek; thinking it was her hair, she brushed the area with her hand and caught his necklace.

"Oh sorry!" Looking at it closely she said, "The feather's pretty... does it have a special meaning?"

"I just liked the looks of it."

Maggie was a little surprised that he would choose to wear a necklace only for its decorative purpose, but then why was she judgmental? She wore necklaces when she liked them.

Adam laughed. "Don't worry, I'm not offended by your question. Actually, it does have a special meaning. A chief from up north gave it to me after I split up with my wife and spent some time in their community. It represents life. This is a turkey feather with a bear's tooth, and I just feel it's a lucky charm."

"I like it."

He stood back a little, his eyes staring into the void as if he were in another world, perhaps his time in the indigenous community or with his ex-wife.

With that in mind Maggie brought him back to reality. "What do you think?"

"You might be right. It looks like a scratch from a vehicle; it took off the red paint but didn't leave any other colour on it. Strange that Barrie mentioned scratches but thought nothing of them. He did say there was no evidence of a collision with an animal. On which side of the sled are they?"

"Right, I think."

As Maggie zoomed out of the picture, Adam mimicked what looked like driving the skidoo into a curve. Dropping his hands to his side, he said, "That adds to the puzzle. So he was driving into the curve toward the left and got hit on the right. The car or whatever it was must've been in the middle of the road or driving on the left side, and we're not in Australia!"

"Maybe he was driving in the middle."

"Why is there only a little scratch? Unless he managed to avoid it, and if that's the case then..." Adam fiddled with his necklace, then added, "We might be able to find the culprit, that is if we can spot a snowmobile or car with some red paint on it. But I don't think it's very likely, not much information to go by."

Maggie spun around on her chair. "But still, this together with the cut brake cable means it was murder, and we have to let the police know before they close the case." She stood up as if propelled by a spring and checked her phone for the time. "Shall we go to the police station? They should be on duty now."

"Not sure Humphries'll like this, and good luck convincing him to look into it."

"He has to know, it's his job!"

"He'll get Barrie's report, so no need for us, really. I thought of inviting you for an ice cream at Danillies. I know it's not summer yet, but they've just opened and you've got to taste the maple syrup one if you've not done so yet. Going to the police station isn't really my idea of fun, if you know what I mean."

"Just in case he doesn't get it, I mean considering that it could've been a murder, I feel it's my duty to tell him what I found out."

With a sigh, Adam replied, "Okay, so what about we first go to the station and then go for an ice cream?"

"How can I refuse?" Maggie smiled as she grabbed her bag and car keys.

"No, no, I'll drive, you can tell me all about your theories of what happened without the risk of causing an accident after your stay in England driving on the wrong side!" Adam laughed.

Maggie grinned. "Interesting comment coming from an Aussie. By the way, this Barrie, is he by any chance Barrie Brown?"

"Yes, why?"

"It's funny, I remember him as a little boy. A friend of mine used to babysit him. Strange to think of him as a grown man, although I'm not surprised he took over his dad's garage. He always loved cars, driving my friend mad making all those car engine sounds."

Adam smiled, shaking his head as they climbed into his car. She had never driven in a Land Cruiser and had always liked the looks of it. It made her think of adventure.

"Is this the same car that's used for safaris in Africa?" Rubbing her hands on the seat cover, she added, "The canvas covers look like the ones I've seen in a safari magazine."

"Those are from Australia, but you're right about the Toyota Land Cruisers. They're reliable all-wheel cars and easy to repair, so they've been used in the bush a lot in Africa."

"I'd love to go there and see a herd of elephants," said Maggie, settling in her seat. *This is a start, I'm in the car, next I'll go there with the little plane, oh that'd be so nice...*

Adam interrupted her reverie. "You're dreaming about elephants then? I've been to Botswana to work on a rehabilitation project. I loved it. You really should go."

A large metal cage, large enough for a bear filled the back of car. Maggie tugged at the contraption to test its solidity. A rattling sound filled the vehicle. "Is the cage for moving animals around?"

"No, for the poachers."

Adam waited for a moment, looking at Maggie. She looked at him in disbelief then burst out laughing.

"Stop pulling my leg! So it is for wild animal release then."

"It's not as exciting as that. It's mainly to transport lost dogs and cats. I've only used this for a raccoon and porcupine, once for a fox, but normally I've got a company truck for that type of job with the proper cages for it. Do you like dogs?"

"My parents always had dogs, and I loved them to bits, but when I moved to London I thought it was simply not a place for a dog. Why don't you have one?"

"Llamas are more than enough!"

"I always wanted a parrot. I imagined it would sit on my shoulder, and I'd take it everywhere I'd go. But now I feel the real place for a parrot is in the wild, free." Maggie sighed. "Although it is the perfect setting for a dog, actually two dogs to keep each other company. But no. No pets for me. I like to see animals in the wild. They come as they please and don't depend on me to survive."

"They're more fun than hassle, I find. I've had both pet animals and rescue animals."

"I want to travel, and you can't do that with a dog."

"I can always keep it for you."

Maggie wondered why Adam was telling her all this. Did he have a dog he wanted her to adopt? If so she would resist at all cost. She had promised herself not to be too soft. "I can also look after your animals while you're away."

"Here we are then," said Adam pulling up in front of the police station.

As they approached the main entrance, the sergeant stepped out with Tina Partridge. It was too late to turn back now that they were virtually in front of the door. Maggie would not be able to explain to Adam why she would rather go to the police station once Tina had left. Adam might understand the argument that Tina could be prone to gossip, being a journalist, but that wasn't enough, and she certainly didn't have the time to share with him her difficult history with Tina. She had insisted on speaking with the sergeant, and she had to do it, with or without Tina present.

Sergeant Humphries seemed a little surprised to see the pair, looking at Maggie then at Adam in turn. Likewise, Tina looked at Maggie then at Adam, and Maggie could see in her eyes that she was trying to figure out if they were together.

Adam whispered in Maggie's ear, "The muffins worked."

Maggie chuckled as she approached the police officer. "Hello, Sergeant Humphries. Hi, Tina, surprised to see you here."

"So am I. Have you come to give evidence? I understand that the body was found in your pond," replied Tina in a dry tone.

"Well, yes, no."

Maggie bit her lips for having responded in earnest at first because of the sergeant's presence. She thought it would give Tina just what she was looking for to spread gossip, just like she used to, always reinterpreting anything Maggie told her to the worst possible understanding. Maggie quickly added, "I'm here to speak with the sergeant, in private. Sergeant Humphries, may we go in the station?"

Maggie squeezed between Tina and the police officer to reach the door and enter. She turned around, holding the door, and noticing Adam's perplexed look, she knew she would have to explain it to him. Her behaviour must look suspicious to him, or at a minimum strange.

Tina left abruptly. "I'm covering this story, so I'll be kept informed by the sergeant anyway. And I'll be doing my enquiries... Have a good day. Sergeant, call me when you want me to publish the story as we agreed."

"Sure, yes. Eh...it's just an accident anyway, the file is about to be closed."

The sergeant entered the police station, followed by Adam, the glass door closing behind them. "Now Maggie, what on earth have you dug up or imagined this time?"

Maggie glanced around to see if there would be anyone else who could hear what she was about to say, and satisfied that they were alone, she said, "There's new evidence, scratches on the snowmobile that can only be caused by another vehicle, not an animal. I've got a picture of it."

"A picture? Who told you to take pictures?" asked the sergeant angrily.

Adam came to Maggie's rescue. "I was there, and she had her camera. It was before we found the body, so it was just of the snowmobile, nothing wrong with that."

"Ah, okay. But scratches, he was racing with it, so it could have happened then," replied the sergeant.

"No, Barrie had checked it after the race, no scratches, and the brake cable—" Before Adam could carry on, the sergeant, whose face had turned red, interrupted him.

"Not you too. It was an accident. If not…I've got to call the chief, and you know he doesn't like being disturbed for nothing. Come with me!"

All of a sudden, Sergeant Humphries pirouetted on his feet and propelled himself back through the swinging doors, out of the public space into the staff quarters, waving at them to follow. He bellowed at Constable Gupta, who was standing by the coffee machine out of sight but in hearing distance of the group. His mouth wide open as if he were caught in the act of doing mischief, Raj looked toward the trio with wide, round eyes.

"Gupta, no time for coffee breaks! Where is the garage report on the skidoo? I want it on my desk now! And get visitor badges for them."

The constable put his Canadian flag mug down, coffee spilling out of it on impact, raced to his desk and nervously shuffled his papers. Sergeant Humphries peered over Maggie's blown-up picture of the scratch in the skidoo's body. He leaned back into his chair, pushing the photo as far away as possible from him, as if he hoped it would disappear from the case. With a deep sigh, he opened the report the constable had handed him, his eyes running down the page until he found the picture of the brakes.

He rubbed his chin, scratched his head, and grumbled, "I'll look into it, but stay out of the case now. It's police domain."

Sensing the sergeant was on edge, Maggie rose to her feet and politely said, "I was only trying to help, and you said I should come to you if I had any other information."

"Yes, yes..."

Tentatively, Maggie asked, "As you can imagine I'm concerned and would like to know what happened. It was on my land, you see. I might come across other clues... May I still come to you with what I find?"

Sergeant Humphries looked up at her. She smiled at him, trying her best to look innocent. He softened.

"Yes, since you would otherwise be withholding information from a murder investigation!"

Maggie glanced at Adam when the sergeant used the word "murder," confirming their suspicion. Her heart was racing. She would definitely have to keep away from Tina before she spread any rumours, and make sure Adam was convinced she was innocent.

"Murder? That is serious..." said Maggie.

"Yes, well, we'll have to see though. It must still be an accident somehow," grunted the sergeant.

Adam walked toward the door. "We'll leave you to it, Sergeant, a difficult case, and I'll look after Maggie. Don't worry, she won't bother you anymore." Adam slightly pushed Maggie in the back in a protective way as they moved out of the sergeant's office.

Maggie didn't wish to linger talking about the murder case for fear of raising suspicions, unless Adam brought it up. It had been a very long time since she had tasted her favourite maple syrup ice cream. It wasn't yet a warm day for an ice cream, but Danillies was already open for the season, and the sun was shining enough for the locals to queue up in front of its little counter open to the street.

Seeing Tina in front of Danillies, Maggie stopped in front of a garage. "This must be Barrie's place, if it's still the same garage. I might ask him to service my car. I've got to get it checked, as it's been sitting for a long time."

"He always looks after my cars. He's really good with any engine, even planes, believe it or not. Mmm, strange, his door's closed. We might bump into him if he's gone to the Horizon Cafe for a coffee break."

Maggie glanced sideways toward Danillies and was relieved to see Tina wobble away in the opposite direction. Her desire to taste again her favourite maple syrup ice cream would be fulfilled.

"Did you see anything?" asked Adam, looking in the same direction.

"No, no, thought I recognized someone, but I was mistaken." Maggie made her way to Danillies, Adam at her side. "Planes, you say, that's interesting. I've inherited my father's plane. I'm not sure what to do with it yet, but maybe he could take a look at it and tell me what he thinks of it."

"I'm sure he'd love that. I'll ask him, and you just need to pop by one of these days. You normally can find him inside the garage or standing in the door frame keeping an eye on what's happening around." Maggie and Adam walked along the main street of Foxton, appropriately named The Street, tucking into their ice cream while admiring the colourful flower baskets dangling from the lampposts. Stopping in front of a knitting shop window, The Jolly Jumpers, Adam suddenly said, "Do you think the sergeant picked up that I mentioned Barrie told me about the brake?"

"He isn't the most perceptive person around," replied Maggie as she licked a drop of ice cream before it fell onto her blouse.

"That info wasn't official, and I just wanted to say I'd seen the brake cable without mentioning Barrie. I really don't want him to get into trouble because of me. Already you giving all this information to the sergeant was nearly too much for him."

"But, I had to...and I really want to know what happened."

"I understand. By the way, do you have a bit of time now?"

"Yes...why?"

"I want to show you something. It's not far from here, and I think you'd like it." Adam smiled broadly at Maggie with a wink of his right eye.

Maggie loved surprises and was curious to see what he thought she liked. She tried asking him where they were going, but he refused to give her any clue. She sat in his car in silence, trying to guess.

Failing to come up with the answer, she looked out the window.

Seeing a deer pop out from the bank of the road, she shouted, "Watch out! The deer! Phew, you saw it."

"Not as dangerous as a moose, though!"

"I'd love to photograph one up close. I was thinking of driving to Algonquin Park one of these days. I've heard that along the road that crosses the park you can see moose in spring in search of salt on the road. They're such strange-looking animals; they seem dressed in rags and tags, with their drooping skins around the chin. Is it true then? Have you seen them there?"

Adam nodded. "You still have to be lucky, but yes, it's possible, and most of the time it's best to be there early morning or before nightfall. I've seen many up there. I could take you on a canoe trip in autumn up at one of the distant lakes. I know a really good place to see them if you like, better than the road."

Maggie squealed with joy. "I'd love that." Unfamiliar with this route, she said, "I don't know this road. Are we really going somewhere or into the bush?"

Adam coolly replied, "Yes, don't worry, I'm not heading to a hut in the middle of nowhere yet..."

Maggie peered suspiciously out the window, seeing a sign for *Animal Shelter*. They turned onto a narrow path snaking along a lake and sharply up hill into the woods. She heard the bark of a dog and a strange grunting sound. They stopped not far from an enclosure. She took a step back, startled by the black bear sniffing the air, its black and beige snout pointed toward them.

Adam responded to her fear with a calm hand on her shoulder. "This is Linda. She was rescued as a cub and couldn't be released back into the wild because she's habituated to humans. She's only looking for food. She's friendly."

An Irish setter leapt toward Maggie's feet, braking on all fours, wagging its tail furiously. Maggie smiled down at the dog, patting it on the head. It quickly sat down on her foot, its head leaning against her leg, giving her a sweet, irresistible look. Then out came a small ball of energy, the origin of all the loud barking, on its way to Maggie as if it were jet-propelled, and squeezed itself between the pair. Maggie let out a cry of laughter as the two dogs swirled full speed around her, whipping up dust in closer and closer circles.

Adam looked on with a large grin. Maggie wondered if he had planned this. She would have to resist if the plan was an adoption. She had no intention of getting a pet now, let alone two.

A woman dressed in overalls came out of the house. "What's all this commotion?" Seeing Adam, she said, "Adam, it had to be you, but what's happening to the dogs? I've never seen them like that. I can't believe it. They were lethargic since you brought them to me, and now look at them!" She clapped her hands and came up to Maggie. "I've got to give you a big hug! You've made my day. It's you, I'm sure of it. They like you."

Maggie was slightly taken aback by her hug but was too overwhelmed by the little white bundle peering up at her with loving eyes, oddly highlighted by a brown patch around one eye and a black patch around the other, while the large red one was busy licking her hand, to react.

The woman added, "I think they've found their new owner, don't you, Adam?"

"You're right, Barbara..." replied Adam.

Maggie looked at them, feeling angry and betrayed, and yet she couldn't help wanting to touch the dogs.

"They simply have chosen you. I'm thrilled to see they can still be happy. Do you know these dogs?"

Maggie looked at Barbara. "No, they're certainly very nice. I'm not looking to adopt any pet, as I told Adam earlier..." Maggie gave him a black look and said, emphasizing his name between her clenched teeth. "So, *Adam,* you brought them here, I understand. Were they lost? If so, we should be able to track down their owners. I'm happy to help you find them."

Barbara came quickly to Adam's rescue. "Adam found them up at the trapper's hut. They've been abandoned, I'm sure of it. No collar. They were in real bad shape. You can still see they're skinny, but at least they're clean and no more fleas."

Both dogs were now sitting at Maggie's feet as she stroked their respective heads. She could feel her heart melting as she looked for ways to get out of this.

Barbara raised her hands in the air. "I've already got four dogs of my own, without counting the raccoon, skunk, and bear I'm taking care of. You see this is an animal shelter, but I finance it out of my own pocket, and I can't take on more dogs now, so I need to find them a home."

"They're cute for sure, but I really don't want to adopt them. I know it sounds hard. What about you, Adam? You already have two llamas?"

Maggie caught sight of Adam's index finger flicking from side to side in negation. Barbara once again took Adam's defence.

"Since they like you so much, why not have them over as boarders, and if we do find anything about their previous owners, or if anyone else steps forward, then you can hand them over and it'd be a real help for me. Besides, Adam is often away, and initially they'll need a lot of care and love."

Adam added, "I've already got them checked out by Matt the vet, so they're ready to go. And it's ideal for you, they can follow you when you take wildlife pictures. You've got enough space for them. Just try it a bit, look at them!"

Maggie bent down to what looked like a terrier, perhaps a Jack Russell or a mix thereof, now sitting with a paw on her thigh, imitated by the Irish Setter. She sighed. "I can take care of them temporarily until we find the right home for them. Adam, I'm counting on you to help me find either their owners or adoptive parents, as it won't be me."

Adam grinned at her, rubbing his hands together. "Sure. It will only be for a while. I'm sure you'll enjoy them and maybe you'll change your mind…"

"Adam! Don't go there!" Maggie feigned anger although she

could already feel an attachment to them. After all, they had chosen her. It was very special, and how could she refuse such a friendship?

*

Back home, Maggie had now to deal with two hungry mouths to feed. She opened all her cupboards looking for something to give them. She had the muffins she had forgotten to offer Adam when he visited her. Although it wasn't the diet she wanted them to have, it might calm them a little till she got the right food. At the sound of a plate breaking she turned toward the table where she had left them. There on the floor the muffins, were lying among the broken china with the Irish Setter standing next to it, wagging its tail, looking at the muffins then at her with expectation, while the terrier had run behind her legs, attempting to look innocent while drooling, a crumb on top of its nose.

"Come on, you two, this is not going to work if you behave like this!"

Both dogs, their tails between their legs and heads down, ears back, went to the corner of the room as if they were expecting a beating. Maggie couldn't bear to see them in such a state and called them back to hand them each a piece of muffin.

"I really don't know how this is going to work out... I've got to find another solution. What have I got myself into? Maggie, oh Maggie! Maybe Amy? I'll ask, but in the city, no..."

Finally, at the end of the day, the dogs were too tired to be excited. With a full belly Maggie watched them snuggle up to each other on one of the blankets she had laid out for them. She smiled briefly as she closed her bedroom door, leaving it ajar in case they needed her. Her own exhaustion took hold of her. Her whole body ached as if she had run a marathon. She had to find out what had happened to the dogs, to the body... confused, she crept into her bed.

Chapter Eleven

An engulfing cold draft woke Maggie as the little terrier tugged at her red and blue quilt, while the setter's red head appeared next to her pillow, flat on the mattress, looking at her with soft golden eyes.

She chuckled at the sight. "You'll have to become better behaved. This isn't how I want to wake up every day...but you're both so funny!"

As she jumped out of bed, the two dogs barked with joy and accompanied her to the kitchen. Maggie was wondering what she would name them if she needed to call them. She couldn't just call them both "doggy." She turned around, alerted by a scraping sound on the floor, followed by a white ball darting past her.

"You really have lots energy for an undernourished animal! What will it be once you're well-fed, scary... You're full of beans!" She reached down to pat the little head. "Beans, that suits you, short enough to call out the name fast... And you over there! No! You're not allowed on the table..." As she spoke, Maggie rushed to push the large dog back from the table. Instead of looking scolded, it put its head down, lifting its behind with the tail fanning away, ready to play. She looked down at it, trying to hold back a laugh, then mustered her deepest voice, her finger raised toward the dog in warning.

"No, I'm angry! Not playing! You have to learn. It's not all fun and games. You'll have to improve your manners if you want to stay here."

Surprised by her tone, both dogs froze and sat down, looking at her with the tip of their tails still wagging, their ears pointed forward with their drooping corners softening their gaze.

Although Maggie had a tinge of apprehension when she opened the side door to let them out, she wanted them to be free to explore the bush, and she would have to take the risk they would run away. To her surprise, they ran out but stayed close to the house, keeping an eye on each other. Within a few minutes, as soon as she sat down to enjoy her breakfast and think about the day ahead, they were both at the door, Beans jumping as high as she could until she reached the door handle to let herself in.

This will be fun, but more of a handful than I thought. They're intelligent animals, and they have lots of energy that needs to escape somewhere.

Her phone beeped, bringing her back to the day's agenda. This was the reminder for the appointment with Joe Johnson, jack-of-all-trades plumber, to check out his work on the house, together with the solar panel installation he claimed to have helped install. Maggie had meanwhile seen through Joe's appropriation of all jobs done; he might be a good plumber and all-round handy person, but he seemed to have a tendency to claim the credit for his friends' work, if he thought it could make him look good.

Maggie glanced at the time. It was too late to work on her photo website. If she left now she would have time on her own to walk around the house and form a quick opinion before Joe arrived. She packed the wedding photo book she had prepared for the Miller parents, together with photos of the dogs—the lodge being so close to the house, who knows, they might know the dogs and/or their owners.

She attempted to walk out, leaving the excited animals inside, but Beans managed to squeeze through, keeping the door ajar and allowing the other dog to escape into the yard. Maggie would have to bring them along, and perhaps that was best; the Millers would then get to see them and fall for them. Although she felt her heart melting by the hour in the company of the hairy pair, she was determined to find them a home, if only to prove to Adam that she meant it when she said she didn't want a pet. She wanted a free choice of when and what type of pet, if at all, she might get without being pressured.

The trio happily drove off toward the house. Maggie heard a strange noise of crunching coming from the back seat, where the Irish Setter was sitting. Through the mirror, she saw him with a carrot poking out of his muzzle, bits falling out as he gnawed it. She remembered that they were intended for the llamas but had forgotten about them under the spell of the Aussie, and to her surprise, this dog liked carrots.

She looked at him and said, "Okay, Carrot, at least you'll not turn orange. You already have a rust colour!"

Maggie pulled up the driveway of the dwelling. The garden looked new, meticulously planted with flowers and not a weed to be seen. The solar panels were gleaming in the sun. In contrast to this display of green energy, a large wakeboard boat with an overpowered engine was parked in its trailer, waiting to be launched into the lake below. Maggie wondered why people didn't opt for electric boats; they would not pollute the lakes, would be quiet, and would not require all the maintenance and fuel, especially if they wanted to be portrayed as being "green."

After letting the dogs out, she walked around the house, the dogs following her, afraid to lose her, seemingly keen to be liked by their new mistress. The building looked tidy and the finishing well done; however, that was neither Joe's work nor Leon's. The solar panels appeared well fixed, with all the cables disappearing into the side of the house.

Carrot sat half on her foot, enjoying a scratch behind the ear while Maggie stood looking at the view across the peaceful Deep Lake. All of a sudden, Beans darted toward the road, Carrot running after her as she barked at the utility van arriving on the driveway. Maggie sighed with relief that the dogs stayed clear of the road and Beans was now barking at Joe, who was looking down at her through the car window.

"Hi, Maggie! Does your dog bite?"

"No, I don't think so!"

Joe looked perplexed as he slowly inched out of the car while Beans intensely sniffed his feet.

"I've just taken custody of the dogs until they find new homes, but so far they're very sweet. I've only had them since yesterday. I'll put them in the car."

Reluctantly, Carrot and Beans climbed into her truck through the red door. At first Maggie thought she would paint the red passenger door blue to match the body of the car but decided to keep it, since she thought it gave Big Jay more character.

Joe regained his composure, and as if he were the owner of the place, he led Maggie around the garden to the back of the house, stating proudly, "I'm looking after this house for Mr. Bern. He trusts me with it, and I have the keys if there's anything wrong, since he isn't often up."

Joe appeared very at ease showing her around the house, after having carefully removed his shoes, revealing a pair of mismatched socks without a blush. Seeing the red and green socks, Maggie smiled to herself, wondering if he was colour blind. She followed him into the living room with its tall ceiling, cathedral windows, and flies gathering in front of its top window. A woman's scarf printed with red tulips lay on the couch. For some strange reason, the image of the cloth seemed to linger in her mind once she was in the utility room looking at the engines of the house.

Maggie's attention was pulled back to the machinery in the room by Joe's sudden loud voice as he pointed to a line of batteries.

"This is the powerhouse for the solar panels, ready to be hooked up. It could also fit in your house no problem!"

Cables linked a line of boxes, and a number ran out of the room to a control unit. It all seemed a little messy, she thought as she tried to figure out how the system worked. Suddenly Joe tripped on a bundle of cables half lying on the floor, half hanging from a hole in the wall as he turned toward the open door to the outside. Grumbling, he bent down, at first attempting to coil them up in a corner but, abandoning his pursuit, left them lying.

"Those electricians, always messy. They have to be careful. These wires can be live; they're hooked to the solar panel."

Maggie stepped back, looking at the mix of red and green wires, perplexed. She was glad to exit into the fresh air. The utility room felt very small for the two of them.

His hands on his hips, Joe rocked on his feet. "Now that you've seen my work and Leon's, what do you think?"

Maggie looked at him straight into his eyes. "It all looks good, and I was happy with your work on my kitchen sink. Now I'll only need to see a very good quote in order to decide. You know I'm comparing offers."

Joe glanced away, seemingly unable to withstand her gaze. "There's no other solar installer around. Leon took over their business a few months ago...and as for my work, you might get a cheaper quote, but no one, I tell you no one, does a thorough job like I do. I can assure you there will be no leaks, absolutely, and that can't be said for the others."

Maggie headed toward her car, the two dogs poking their heads out of the half open window in anticipation, and turned to Joe.

"I have to say, you seem to have done a good job. Supposing I decide to get solar panels, will you be working with Leon?"

Joe seemed to increase in size as he pumped his chest up like a peacock. "Of course, Leon can't work without me. You can count on me."

"I'm reassured, it's hard to find someone trustworthy..." Maggie waited a little before continuing. "I'm in good hands then." She glanced at her watch, knowing he had a tendency to linger on talking, and she was keen to move on to the lodge before lunchtime, when it would be busy for the Millers. Before he could open his mouth, she said, "Already that late! I've got to dash, I promised to bring the pictures to the Millers. I'll think about it. In the meantime I still want the quote for my bathroom!"

She really could have walked to all those places from her home, along Lake View Road, but jumping in a car seemed to be what everyone did here. She promised herself to walk more to shed the years of sitting, and now with the dogs she had no excuse.

Maggie was happy to find Richard Miller hooking up a sign with the day's menu. He was always easier to speak with than his wife, at least that was how she remembered it from when she was a little girl. Richard invited Maggie in for a drink.

"Sorry, Sue is out shopping for the restaurant. I hope I can help you. But anything to do with decisions regarding the photos will be up to my daughter or Sue, I'm afraid."

Maggie eagerly talked about the two dogs, hoping to find their owners, only to be rebuffed and cut short.

"Nope, never seen them before and don't know their owners. I'm not interested in adopting them either; in my opinion, anything that requires bending is not worth cuddling. Only Great Danes are my kind of dog."

Maggie hadn't expected his reaction. A little disappointed, she said, "The Irish Setter, I call him Carrot, is a big dog, not a Great Dane, but sizeable. Are you really sure?"

"Maybe big for you, but not for me! Besides, you can't separate them. They seem to have a strong bond."

As Richard spoke, he pointed toward the window to the yard, where the pair of dogs were racing after each other, playing. Seeing that there was really no hope with the dogs, she replied, "I can still show you the pictures. This is the one in the church."

Richard put his reading glasses on the tip of his large nose. After bringing the print closer to his eyes, he put it down, laughing with a deep guttural sound. Maggie couldn't help herself; feeling the contagion of his laughter, she started to giggle like a little girl. He exclaimed, "This will be the one we will have on our wall! That must be when your hat fell down as you took the picture. Your bewildered face looked so funny, we all burst out laughing! You managed to capture that happy moment. Everyone is smiling."

While looking through the printouts of the wedding pictures, the stack of photographs fell to the floor, a close-up of the mayor on top. There she was, staring arrogantly back at them. Richard handed her the prints with a look of disdain on his face, his lips turned down and eyes looking away.

Surprised, she asked, "You don't seem to like her. Strange woman. I can't figure her out. What do you think of her?"

"I don't really know her. I invited her because she's the mayor and we're such a small community. She positioned herself as the green mayor in contrast to Peter Wigmott but was new to this round of elections."

"Interesting...do you think she would have lost if Peter Wigmott would have still been alive? In other words, would she gain from his death?"

"I don't know about that! But I don't think she'd have won. People here don't like voting for people they don't know... I don't know, I find her a little scary I guess," replied Richard.

"The first time I saw her, I thought she was an opera singer. She has such a powerful voice and..."

Richard laughed. "You're spot on. Sue, who sings in the local choir, told me that the mayor joined and will be the soloist! I thought she was more the type to break windows than to sing like a bird."

"Does she have a family? I didn't see her husband or partner at the party."

"Not as far as I know. Tina mentioned, you know, the journalist..."

"Yes, I know, not surprised she'd have a story there!" Maggie lowered her voice a little so that he would not pick up on her sarcastic tone.

"I think she said she was divorced and moved up here to start a new life." Richard added with a naughty side look, "When I talked to Peter about her at the Christmas party, the only thing he said was that she was man-eater!"

"A handful!" She looked at the figure of the man standing next to Ms. Stilton in the picture, dwarfed by her imposing frame.

Feeling that more information would be hard to gather without diving further into the realm of pure gossip, Maggie stood up at the sound of a car arriving. This was her excuse to take her leave.

From the corner of her eye, she caught sight of Ms. Sue Miller arriving. Maggie thought it best to avoid the difficult question of payment for her work for now, noticing that Ms. Miller likewise had slipped away behind the house, clearly thinking she hadn't been spotted. Maggie had heard she had great difficulty parting with her money, but eventually, at the end of the month, a cheque would arrive in the letterbox.

As Maggie climbed into her truck, she shuffled around to find her camera. She didn't have it with her at the Millers. No, it must still be at the house with the solar panels. She rushed back. She parked her car in a cloud of dust and ran toward the back of the house overlooking the lake where she thought she might have forgotten it.

The door of the utility room stood wide open. *I'd better close it before critters get in.* Maggie nearly tripped with fright over a figure lying in front of the door. A woman lay on her side, her head in a puddle of blood. Maggie kneeled down to feel the pulse in the wrist. Nothing. She tried the neck. Nothing.

She sprang up and reached in her bag for her phone. With a shaking hand she called the police, wary of the possibility of a murderer still on the premises.

Chapter Twelve

At the police station, Sergeant Humphries had received a grilling from a homicide detective for his handling of Peter Wigmott's case. Assuming it had been an accident, he hadn't opened a proper investigation when the body was discovered, although he had followed up with all the appropriate paperwork as soon as he received the mechanic's damning report. Sergeant Humphries swore internally at himself for having assumed too much and not having focused on the facts. He was worried his boss would demote him—or worse, order his transfer to another station.

Imagining the worst, he clung to the thought that his spotless career would help, and perhaps he would be able to keep his position. Sergeant Humphries couldn't conceive of living anywhere else than in his beloved cottage country, where everyone knew him as an honest man, a little lazy, but fair. He could even gather a crowd when he took to the stage with his country band, The Haystack Needles. He had truthfully believed that a murder couldn't have happened in his community, having never seen one during his fifteen years of patrols around the area.

A knock on the door brought him back to the present. Constable Gupta poked his head through the door, presenting him with the printed report to review. Sergeant Humphries couldn't allow his feelings to get the better of him, especially in front of the constable. He asked the constable if he had the list of the Christmas party attendees, as he would have to speak to each one, all possible suspects.

With a bobble of his head, Constable Raj Gupta asked in a low, hesitant voice, "What about you, Sergeant?"

With a growl Humphries replied, "What about me? What a strange question."

Constable Gupta stiffened, a few beads of sweat trickling down his sideburns. "Sir, I was just trying to say, you were also at the party...do I need to put you on the list and question you?"

The sergeant tried to hide his irritation at his constable's fair question. The mere thought that his constable might see him as a possible suspect hit him in his core, even though he couldn't ignore that he was right to follow the rules.

"Eh... Yes, you're right to do things according to the book, even though it's a preposterous idea. You only need to add my name. And...while we're at it, where were you? You were not at the party."

Constable Gupta's thick eyelashes flickered very quickly, like little brooms, his eyes focused on his feet as he stammered, "B-but sir, I was at the police station on duty. You assigned me there as you always do..." His voice trailed off with the last words.

Sergeant Humphries softened but wanted to teach him a lesson. "That's right, so if you spoke to anyone while on duty, get their names. Come to think of it, look for the security camera recording, if we still have it. That should do. And please don't be such a... Well, assert yourself, you should've come up with this yourself, you can't hesitate like this. Be a man...if you want to become a sergeant one day, as you keep telling me, you have to suck it up, buttercup!"

As if under a spell, Constable Gupta straightened his back, his arms aligned to his trunk, feet clasped together like a little soldier, and replied with slight sarcasm in his voice, "Yes, sir! Actually I wasn't alone...perhaps you hadn't been made aware...I was on duty with two officers all night. It was a quiet evening, so we didn't have to go out of the station, sir."

"Okay, fine, I'll take down your statement as well."

The sergeant hated it when people pointed out what he had forgotten, and especially when it was the constable. Ignoring the constable, Sergeant Humphries glanced at the long list of guests, pondering where to start. Unfortunately, they didn't have any time of death; the only lead was when Peter Wigmott left the party and whether anyone left before him or just after him. All the while, Constable Gupta stood next to him with imperceptible breathing, as if frozen on the spot.

Feeling watched and already on edge at the prospect of a team of detectives sent over from the city to help manage the case and keep a close eye on his every move to evaluate whether he would keep his position, Sergeant Humphries roared, "Get on with it! Check the arrival and departure times of the guests and stop looking like a fish out of water."

Constable Gupta wobbled his head vigorously, with a chirpy, "Yes sir!" He swung around and disappeared from sight.

Sergeant Humphries sighed. *The only way I can get through this is one step at a time, and we'll see what happens. No point worrying about an outcome I don't know.* As he sat back into his reclining chair, dipping his hand into a bag of compensatory nuts, the phone rang with Constable Gupta on the line.

"Sorry to disturb you, but Ms. Flanagan's on the line…she found another body!"

Sergeant Humphries barked back, "What! Eh…put me through, what are you waiting for?"

Nut crumbs jetted out of his mouth at the shock of the news, sprinkling over his belly. He sat up on his chair, angrily brushing off the crumbs, one elbow on the desk holding the phone.

"Hello, this is Maggie Flanagan. I'm at the house number 22 Fairview Lane, just off Lake View Road, and I just found the realtor Fiona McLenny lying dead. I called 911 as well but thought you should be informed directly."

Sergeant Humphries shouted, "Don't touch anything. Wait there, keep everyone out aside from police, you hear me! I'm on my way."

He stormed out of his office, grabbing his cap and jacket, all the while ordering Constable Gupta to come along and get the car.

*

Maggie sat down, tightly grasping her phone, a shiver rocking her shoulders as she thought about Fiona. *The man in my pond and now this. How terrible.* She put her hand to her mouth and said out loud, "Oh, my camera!" She jumped up and ran on the wraparound terrace of the house toward the lake, her senses heightened like an animal being hunted. *Thank God it's there.* She hastily picked it up, its strap still caught on the corner of the garden table. A loud, metallic thump reverberated as the table came crashing to the floor. Maggie let out a little cry and pushed the table back, an eerie thought having crept into her mind. *They might suspect me.*

Her heart still pounding, she rushed back to where the body was lying next to the utility room and looked down at it in amazement, as if she had hoped it would have vanished and it was all a nightmare. She shook her head and cleared her throat, breathing heavily. She held her breath, wide-eyed, listening for human noises. It was just a branch in the wind.

She bent down toward Fiona, hoping she could do something. Still no pulse. She was dead.

Maggie stood her arms tightly crossed against her chest, a little farther away from the body, scrutinizing it. *I've got to wait for the police, think scientifically. Like Amy would.*

Calmness enveloped her as she closed her eyes, as if she had left her actor's costume and moved into the audience to watch the scene from the outside with a clear, analytical mind. She opened them again. Fiona was still lying on her side. One of her arms lay outstretched, with the hand turned toward the sky, as if it were trying to grab hold of something. *How strange*, thought Maggie as she noted red marks on the tip of the outstretched fingers and an unusual stiffness in them, as if rigor mortis had already set in, judging from the angle at which the fingers were kept up.

Why was Fiona here? The house isn't for sale. Her mind raced, trying to imagine what might have happened. Hearing the loud sirens of the police and ambulance approaching, Maggie stepped aside toward the driveway, relieved she would no longer be alone.

Only now did Maggie see it was Fiona's car, with her larger-than-life picture on its side as she walked up the other side of it. She looked down at the tire marks, comparing them with the ones from her own car. Large footprints that appeared to head toward the road caught her attention. It surprised her, since it had rained the night before. Could they be Joe's steps? He was wearing boots, not trainers.

Sergeant Humphries pulled over at the same time as the ambulance. He jumped out of his car in a blurred vision, surrounded by a cloud of dust like a sheriff in a Western ready to shoot, his hand on his gun, only to readjust his trousers that had the tendency to glide down, pushed by his belly. Maggie, mesmerized by the vision, stood looking at the sergeant growing in size as he approached her, gesticulating to the paramedics.

"Check if the victim is alive, quick! Maggie, did you touch anything?"

Maggie waited for a moment until the medics responded that she was dead.

"Only her pulse when I found her to see if she was alive and if I could help her," replied Maggie calmly.

"Gupta, where's the tape? Come on, cordon the scene, all of it, and call the homicide department. We can't rule anything out now."

"But last time you didn't—"

"Last time was different, " interrupted the sergeant. "Get on with it!"

Constable Gupta ran back to the car and dove into it, soon emerging with a large reel of tape, brandishing it as he ran back.

Sergeant Humphries walked around the body. "Yes, this time it's murder—the wound and the murder weapon." As he looked down at the bloodstained rock next to the victim, he continued, "They've even left it! We'll see what the coroner has to say."

He turned around and jumped back, as if he didn't seem to

expect Maggie right next to him, having followed him to the body in case he wanted to speak with her and still wondering why the victim's hand appeared so stiff.

"What are you still doing here!" Sergeant Humphries said. "Go back to the car and wait there. You always—ahh, it could be a murder scene with all the footprints, and you're adding yours everywhere!"

Recalling the sergeant getting out of his car and trampling over the trainer footprints Maggie had noticed a few moments ago, she thought he wasn't any better, and he was supposed to be the professional. She wondered how many murder cases he had actually dealt with. Very few if any. She walked back to the car, all the while looking at the activity around, not wanting to miss anything.

The scene was getting busier by the minute: a white cube-like campervan arrived with white-clad forensic men and women pouring out of it. It was surprising to see how many could fit in such a van. They spread out onto the crime scene like a group of ants.

Waiting for either the sergeant or the constable to tell her what to do, she remained next to her car, analyzing the situation, now and then popping her head into her car to calm the dogs. She tried to recall her encounter with Fiona at the wedding party, hoping for an insight of any kind. She remembered her gleaming teeth and plastic smile as she distributed compliments to everyone, as if they were sweets. Fiona had been wearing a red dress that seemed to attract a lot of attention from men, one in particular...

Maggie struggled to recall who kept lacing his arm around Fiona when she looked up to the sky, and the sight of the solar panels brought it back. It was Leon LeBreton. *She must have been having an affair with him,* thought Maggie, playing with her curls, twisting them around her finger, a habit she had acquired as a girl when she was thinking.

Constable Gupta called out "Ma'am?" He cleared his throat loudly and tapped on Maggie's shoulder. She jumped and turned around to face him. "Ma'am, I need to ask you a few questions before letting you go, and please don't leave town for the moment."

At first Maggie remained relaxed, in contrast to Constable Gupta, beads of sweat resembling a pearl necklace dripping down the side of his cap, along his thick sideburns as he struggled with his notepad and pen. The prospect of being regarded as a suspect came back to haunt Maggie now that the sergeant viewed the case as a possible murder.

She reminded herself that the more relaxed she could be, the better her communication and the more the other party would believe what she said. It also had the advantage of having a soothing effect on irritable men like the sergeant.

It had worked with one of her bosses, a scientist who had fits of rage. Instead of fearing him, she would wait patiently to discuss anything till the colour in his face died down and his voice came down. Her colleagues asked her how she did it, how he never seemed to raise his voice with her. She used to say jokingly, "I've had training, I've shared an office with such characters, and the only way to survive their fits was to remain calm and try to convey that to the person while avoiding absorbing their strong emotions."

She perceived it was happening now with Constable Gupta, whose tone had become a bit aggressive. *Perhaps he's imitating Sergeant Humphries to hide his insecurity.*

Careful to speak slowly and articulating every word to make sure he would correctly take note, she said, "I forgot my camera on the deck of the house. I only noticed after I'd been to the lodge to see the Millers so I came back to pick it up, when I found Fiona." Seeing the constable lift his eyes from his notepad, Maggie added, "I was here in the morning with Joe Johnson, viewing his installation work. We had an appointment, we were alone then."

A bead of sweat was now teetering on the tip of the constable's nose, and Maggie wondered when it would fall when the Sergeant Humphries call, "Gupta! Over here!"

Maggie was relieved that the constable had forgotten to ask her about her camera, or any other question that might make her look suspicious, before he ran toward Sergeant Humphries, who was speaking with the team of forensics. Adam was right; the constable still needed training. Sensing the tension in the air, she hastily took her leave, making sure she had the constable's approval.

As Maggie climbed into her car, she heard an engine noise behind her and a shuffling sound. She turned her head and was faced with a camera pointed toward her. Before she could say anything, the window had closed, and only once the car had passed her to park did she realize it was Tina.

Maggie was about to intercept Tina, but then she wondered what she would tell her. Asking her to delete the photo would only make her suspicious. Maggie turned back on her heels, jumped back into her car, and sped off, hitting the steering wheel with one hand and cursing Tina. The dogs hid as best they could, flat as pancakes on the back seat.

Maggie felt the need to share what had happened with someone before they might consider her a suspect. She didn't want to involve Amy yet. Denis was a good listener and level-headed and was very good at keeping secrets. But the vision of Tina's grin from behind the camera cast a dark shadow over his prospect as a confidant.

She sat in her car, parked in her own driveway, her two dogs sniffing at her and licking her hands. She felt her emotions creeping up; she couldn't fathom who would want to kill Fiona. She could imagine people getting irritated by her sales approach and marketing attempts, but that was certainly not a cause for murder. Looking down into Carrot's soft eyes, she thought of Adam and their talks. She liked his openness. He had told her she could speak with him whenever she wanted; he was, after all, already part of the first murder story. If Fiona's death had something to do with it, he would be the one to talk to. With the engine of her car still running, she put it into gear and drove away in search of his cheerful face weathered by the years spent outdoors.

Chapter Thirteen

The news of the suspected murder spread like wildfire across Foxton. All households were feverishly debating who did it. Joe, who had received a call from Constable Gupta to report to the police station later that day, was now submitted to Heather's dread. She expressed it with anger and jealousy.

"I knew it, you were with Fiona. I hate you. Did you love her?"

"Honey, no, how can you think that. I love you!"

"Why would you've been to the house then? It was to meet her. I'm sure. I don't want to speak with a murderer!"

"I promised Leon to keep quiet, but he was Fiona's lover, not me. Don't you see, he can't be trusted, but you can trust me! Please..."

"Now you're using your friend, that's horrible! Covering up your mess!"

"Heather, no, please believe me, I was at the house in the morning yes, with Maggie..."

Heather interrupted, stamping her foot on the floor, "And now it's Maggie. I can't bear listening to you." She covered her ears with her hands and turned her back to him.

Joe approached her from behind, putting his hands on her shoulders, attempting to calm her. "Heather, sweetie, I'm sorry I didn't tell you about Leon and Fiona. I couldn't have killed her. I wasn't there at lunchtime, and that's when they say it happened. I was only at the house with Maggie in the early morning."

Heather turned around with the speed of a tornado. "What were you doing with Maggie then? The new girl in town, is that it?"

"No, remember, you told her about viewing the house, not me, that it'd be a good idea to see my work. It was only business."

Joe held her hands tight, trying to pass over his feeling of love, desperate for her to believe him. He searched her eyes for any sign of trust.

With tears running down her cheek, Heather asked, "Why didn't you come back for lunch then? Where were you?"

Joe was bewildered by her doubts. Releasing his grasp and dropping his hands as if they weighed suddenly a ton, he replied, "I picked up pipes at the hardware store, and on the way stopped for a sandwich because I was running late for my next appointment."

He often did that, so he didn't see how that would have been out of character for him and why his wife would suddenly have expected him for lunch, unless it was a wedding anniversary or birthday. He quickly looked at his phone to check his calendar, knowing he typically forgot these dates.

Stamping her foot again, Heather cried out, "I don't believe you! Were you having an affair with Fiona or not? Now tell me the truth. I've asked you once, this is the last time I'll ask and then... Listen to me! I'm talking to you!" He was still looking down at his phone, her words slowly entering his brain. Having been subjected to such fits before, he knew it usually blew over and she calmed down on her own. She added, "I knew it, you're avoiding my look, so it must be true!"

She stormed out of the room, leaving him standing in the middle, his jaw pulled down in amazement as he mumbled, "No honey, you know me...I love you..." She had already left the room when his words came out, slamming the door behind her.

Ever since they had their first child, Heather was afraid that Joe would have an affair. From then on, she had been keeping a close eye on him, checking his pockets, looking over his shoulder at his emails, even when he had surprised her in the act and made her promise not to snoop if she loved him.

A cloud drifted through Joe's mind. *Could she have done it out of jealousy... No, she's not capable of murder.* He wasn't thinking straight.

Joe felt a pang to his heart; he loved his wife and knew he would have to fight hard to get the idea of an affair with Fiona out of her mind this time. It struck him that it was more than that; if he didn't succeed, he might be seen as a suspect in the murder. He looked for her around the house, but she was nowhere to be found.

He panicked and thought of Leon. *He has to come clean! I'll get him to tell Heather about Fiona.* The thought spurred him into his car to find Leon. As he approached Leon's house, knowing he usually did his paperwork at home in the afternoon, Joe was surprised his white van wasn't there.

He sped off, a cloud of dust billowing behind his rear wheels, thinking he might find him at the marina. Leon always liked sitting in his boat and soaking up the sun to top up his tan, whatever the temperature. He was always the first to put his boat out in spring. Sure enough, there he was sitting in his boat, staring at the lake.

At the sight of Leon hunched over and staring at the water with a drawn face, Joe concluded he must already know about Fiona.

"Leon, I'm so sorry about Fiona."

"What do you mean?" Leon looked up at Joe.

"You don't know?"

"What on earth are you talking about?"

"She's dead, murdered."

"What! It's not true, you must be mistaken."

Leon stood up, nearly capsizing the boat, if it were not for Joe grabbing his arm to steady him. Joe pulled him up onto the pier.

They both stood in silence for a moment until Joe broke it with a sigh. "No, it's true, it's hard for you I know, but..." His voice rose with fear as he added, "Heather thinks I killed Fiona because she is convinced I was her lover. You have to get me out of this and tell Heather you were her lover, not me!"

Joe held tightly on to Leon's right wrist. Leon freed himself, taking a step back.

His face grew pale, contrasting with his jet-black hair. "But then they'll think I did it!"

Joe tried to control his emotions, speaking slowly. "If you didn't do it, you have nothing to fear. You don't have a suspicious Heather to deal with...."

Leon looked Joe in the eyes. Joe could see fear but also anger as Leon said, "If you were my friend, as you claim to be, then you'd understand I've got to keep quiet."

Joe felt anger bubble up in him. He clenched his fists and looked away at the lake. Seeing a cottage like Mr. Bern's on the other side of it, he remembered a crucial piece of information.

"Leon, weren't you going to Bern's house at lunch to finish off the solar installation?"

"Yes...so?"

The idea that Leon might have killed Fiona suddenly overwhelmed Joe as he grabbed him by the shirt collar and said, "You bastard, you did it!"

Not wanting to hear one more word from Leon, Joe stormed away, inadvertently pushing Leon into the water. Blinded by his anger and running toward his car, Joe had ignored the splashing sound. He was too focused on finding Heather before she would talk to anyone.

Chapter Fourteen

Maggie waited for Adam's return, picking a comfortable spot in the yard while keeping an eye on the dogs circling around his llamas. She enjoyed basking in the sun, her back against a tree trunk, half daydreaming, half thinking. Problems always seemed to disappear, replaced by obvious solutions only a natural setting could foster. She wondered what linked the guests at the Christmas party. What were the real feelings under the cover of the public display of amiability at such a gathering? Who had a close tie to Peter Wigmott, a real politician, changing like a chameleon according to the crowd he wanted to woo? Fiona was similar in that respect, always smiling, appearing to like everyone. Likewise, the new mayor seemed to have many facets, pretending not to have known Peter Wigmott while the rumour ran contrary.

Then there was Peter's brother, Fred, a strange one, a secretive and jealous type, promoting his brother with a little too much ardour. What was he trying to hide? What about Joe and his passionate wife Heather? Joe had told Maggie jokingly that he often had to write down in his diary a man's name instead of a woman's when he had an appointment, otherwise Heather would question him through the night. When Heather pushed Joe into offering his services to her, it seemed out of line with what a jealous woman would do: arranging a meeting with another woman for her husband, even for business.

Maggie wondered whether Heather was more calculated than

she appeared. It could have been a test to see how Joe reacted to one of his female clients. She brushed away the thought as she remembered Joe mentioning that his wife knew he didn't fall for redheads. Perhaps she felt she had nothing to fear...

The warmth of the sun on her cheeks connected to the thought of solar panels. She couldn't explain her uneasiness about the entire business, especially Leon LeBreton. She didn't trust him. He boasted and liked himself too much. Normally that would be enough for her not to hire him, but she needed an excuse to speak to him again without raising any suspicion about her true motive.

She felt she had to help find out what happened, to clear her name of any possible suspicion on the part of the police—or Tina. She knew Tina was doing her own investigation, and if there would be a way to incriminate her, she would. Just like when they were kids, when she had pointed the finger at Maggie for the mysterious disappearance of the classroom's skeleton—still a mystery to this day.

What if the murderer thought Maggie had seen him or her when she found the body? She might then be the next target. Maggie shuddered. She had to get to the bottom of it. Although the local police were good people, they didn't seem the fastest around and could do with help.

She hated lying and concluded the way to trick herself into concealing her fear and views from Leon LeBreton when meeting him was to remind herself she genuinely was considering solar power for her home and was evaluating the option, even if she was doubtful of its viability.

She should not judge him yet; it might be a preconceived impression. This made her think of the relationship between Leon LeBreton and Ms. Stilton, the controversial solar panel project that no one wanted. Leon might have resented Peter, who was against the project, and had he been elected mayor, the solar plan would have fallen through. *Now that is a motive to get rid of him! He was at the party; he could have cut his brake cable.*

Although Leon could have wanted Peter Wigmott gone, Maggie

didn't see why he would want the same for Fiona. It even appeared they liked each other, judging from seeing them dance together at the wedding party, eyes locked, while Fiona's husband Patrick was standing at the bar, looking at the pair with disgust. Maggie had only briefly spoken to Patrick, who appeared closed like a clam, only answering her questions with very few words and shuffling from one foot to the other as if he wanted to run away given the chance. She hadn't caught any glimpse of humour in him or any interest in interacting with anyone. The only topic his eyes lit up for behind his glasses was computer programming.

At the time, Maggie had found it hard to believe Fiona and Patrick were an item and wasn't surprised Fiona would be looking elsewhere for attention. Perhaps they didn't get along, and Patrick wanted to get rid of her or caught her with a lover and killed her in his rage. He might be a boring man, but the angry look he gave his wife at the party was meant to harm; it wasn't just a look of disgust. His fists had been clenched.

Deep in thought, Maggie patted Beans, playing with her little black ears as she lay with her head on her lap. Beans sprang up and barked. The llamas were getting excited, and a moment later Maggie heard a car engine. She got up, brushing the leaves from her trousers as if she were brushing away her suspicions.

Adam poked his head around the trunk of a centenary maple tree and greeted her with a loud, "Hey, Maggie, you can't hide from me. Good to see you and your happy bunch!" He pointed toward the dogs.

"Not trying to hide. I was enjoying your peaceful place." She smiled as wide as she could, eager to hide her anxiety. "I just wanted to show you how well the dogs are doing and see if you had any news regarding their owners..." Her voice trailed off, and her eyes shifted downward as she tried to hide the real reason she was there.

"No news on the owners. You've only just got the dogs...but that's not why you've come?" Adam looked at her straight in the eyes.

She felt small again, as if she had told her parents a lie, looking for an escape and yet eager to tell them the truth that was weighing on her.

Confronted by silence, Adam added, "I don't mean to pry, and if you don't want to talk that's fine. I'm sorry, I can be a little forthright."

Maggie relaxed as he put his hand on her shoulder.

"I hoped I wasn't an open book. It's been a very strange day so far. The realtor Fiona Mc...not sure what her last name was."

"Was?" asked Adam. "What do you mean, not another death?" He looked worried, his forehead furrows bunching up together in a combination of horizontal and vertical lines.

"Yes, dead. I found her. Sergeant Humphries thinks it was murder this time, a knock on the back of her head with a stone..."

"Come on, that's crazy. Where did you find her—not at your place!"

The last word had a drier, harder tone to it, as if he was accusing her.

"No, at the electrical utility guy's home, Mr. Bern—you know, the big newly built cottage with the solar panels I talked to you about."

Adam led her into the house, a little colder than before, keeping his distance from her by walking a few metres ahead. As he put the kettle on, Maggie sat at the kitchen table, feeling uneasy and desperate to change the icy air that had just risen between them. She regretted having come, but now that she was here, she had to find a way out.

"I don't know if I should be telling all this to you. I feel I might be burdening you, and I don't want you to get in trouble because of me."

Adam looked again at her with his intense eyes X-raying her, then tilted his head sideways, his wrinkles around the eyes pleating upward in a friendly fashion. Maggie released a deep sigh of relief as he spoke.

"Nonsense. Of course you're not, and why on earth would I get in trouble with it. And even if I would, this is mad, you have to tell me all about it. Do you think it is linked to Peter Wigmott?"

"It might be." Maggie gathered her courage to come out in the open with the idea that she might be suspected. That way it could be discussed and dismissed. If she kept quiet, it would only lead to suspicion.

"I'm worried the police could consider me a suspect for this murder because I was at the house in the morning looking at Joe's work and Leon LeBreton solar panels to see if I'd hire them." Maggie didn't let Adam interrupt her, since she wanted to give him the whole story first before he made up his mind, her words flowing at high speed. "After the visit, I went to Moose Lodge but remembered I'd forgotten my camera, so I drove back, and that's when I found her. What I say might sound weird. I've the feeling all this has something to do with the solar power business and big money. It's a feeling, I don't know why."

Adam looked puzzled. "Why would a real estate agent be murdered because of solar panels? That seems a little farfetched, don't you think? Come on, you're in shock and you're seeing things."

"Maybe she was involved with the sale of land relating to the solar panel project and was against it?" retorted Maggie.

Adam shook his head. "Sorry, I still don't see the link." Then he carried on speaking slowly, as if he were thinking aloud. "Although you must have heard she was popular with the blokes around, but not really with the women, as you can imagine. The gossip goes that she had a fling with every successful newcomer. I think it is a little exaggerated. However, if I'm right, Peter Wigmott was one of them, when he first arrived shortly after she sold him his house. That is if Barrie got it right."

"You see!" exclaimed Maggie, her fist hitting the table. "I knew it, and there is a connection. Who is she seeing now—rather, was?"

"I don't know. I'd have to ask Barrie. Not only does he pick up the chatter, but he also sees things. You should show him the picture of the paint scratch you took. He might shed some light on it." They both were quiet for a moment, deep in thought, interrupted suddenly by Adam.

"Did you hear anything about the time of death?"

Maggie looked down at her large watch and lifted her head, recollecting when she had left the house. "It must have been between eleven thirty and one o'clock. I was away then."

For a moment the heavy silence fell back on them like a black cloak sticking to their bodies, difficult to remove. Maggie watched Adam nod, wondering what he was thinking and hoping he would believe her, until he lifted his head with a deeply concerned look, his eyebrows like two swords battling each other as he asked in a severe tone she never imagined, "Do you have anybody who could testify to seeing you during that time?"

Maggie shuddered and stammered, "You don't think I did it..." Then she pulled herself together with the thought that she had nothing to fear as she was innocent. "Yes, I do, for part of it. I was at Moose Lodge speaking with Richard Miller just after leaving Joe. Then I took the dogs for a little walk around his land and drove home and realized I had forgotten the camera." Maggie stopped speaking, having only just remembered that she had walked the dogs on her own without a witness. She added, "I guess there is a time when I was on my own aside from the dogs. No witness."

Adam sweetened his voice, extending his large hand to her arm across the table, the furrow between his eyebrows melting away. "No. Anyway, I don't see what motive you'd have. Besides, you only just arrived here." She frowned at him and he added with a smile, "Unless of course you liked Leon and were the jealous type..."

Still feeling under attack and not seeing the humour, given the circumstances, she countered, "And where were you, since we're talking about suspects! Just checking you're not one of them. Were you not at the Christmas party when Peter disappeared?"

Holding his two large hands against his heart and leaning back into his chair, Adam replied, "Okay, touché. You were the one to mention being seen as a suspect, after all. I was on duty writing boring reports at headquarters. What about Ms. Miller?"

Maggie wondered why he was suddenly directing the focus away from himself. Was it to hide something?

"It just occurred to me you were with Richard Miller at the time and didn't mention her."

"I'm a little edgy, sorry for that. Ms. Miller wasn't there, and for all we know she could have been out there killing Fiona. She seemed to dislike her; I noticed Ms. Miller avoiding Fiona deliberately with a tray of canapés when I was speaking with Fiona. My hand was left floating in midair as she passed them under our noses too swiftly and left me scratching my head instead, not to look stupid. She gave Fiona such a black look! A murderous look."

Maggie sipped her tea, waiting for his reaction, mesmerized by his shiny eyes for a moment. Her mind moved away a sordid thought, the blood pool around Fiona's head. She remembered the tulip motif scarf that lay on the couch when she viewed the house. She wondered where she had seen it before. Adam's voice interrupted her train of thought.

"Don't worry about all this. I mean, you merely happened to be there each time. Maybe you should forget about it. They'll find out what happened."

Maggie was stubborn, and once she had set her mind to solving a problem, she would hold on to it and not let go until she felt she had looked at it from all possible angles. She had learned from science that looking for answers usually created more questions, and it was a never-ending story. Mysteries were different; they often seemed to have simple solutions, usually rooted in human psychology—jealousy, fear, anger, revenge, far simpler than the imagination would speculate.

"Yes, I can't do much now anyway... What happened to the poachers? Did you catch them?" asked Maggie, eager to change the topic.

"Funny you ask, I met up with Alfred and his boys this morning: a lumberjack with two teenage sons who often get into trouble. They were still angry with Peter Wigmott, even though he's dead now."

"Why? What had he done to them?" asked Maggie, surprised.

"Peter had filed a complaint against them and requested they have their hunting license removed for poaching."

"Was the accusation fair?"

"Not really. They had trespassed on Peter's land while tracking a wounded deer, and Peter happened to witness it. They should have asked for his permission, but Peter didn't have a no trespassing sign on his land, and there was no fence, so it really was hard for them to tell the limit of the property."

"I imagine it's important to track the wounded animal down," added Maggie.

"Yes, it is a hunter's obligation to do so, but that doesn't mean trespassing. Anyway, I managed to let them get away with a fine. They took their revenge, though; they confessed only after I questioned them about Peter's murder to having dumped a heap of garbage on Peter's land and covering it with snow in winter for him to discover it in spring."

"That's a crime, no?" asked Maggie, always appalled by any illegal garbage dumping and its impact on the environment.

"In theory, I have to report it to the sergeant, but I know their father, he's very strict, and I'm sure he'll know how to make them regret what they did. I'm letting them simmer a little."

"Why?"

"I feel they know who the poachers are and are hiding something." Adam looked out the window for a moment, tucking some of the unruly silver blond meshes back into his ponytail. Lowering his hands back on the maple table, he said, "They'll talk. I just need to wait a bit."

Fiddling with her shirt buttons, Maggie caught a glimpse of her neglected fingernails. She looked at them for a moment, and seeing Adam's eyes following the same route, she buried her hands under the table. "Are you really so sure they didn't cut the brakes? You know, a joke turned bad, not having thought of the consequences?"

"That's exactly what Barrie said, but they're good guys, full of energy and testing their limits, but murder, never. And they're not dumb; they'll know what a cut brake would mean! Having said that, the sergeant might not see it that way if ever he gets hold of them. They've had issues with him, riding a dirt bike without license and things like that. He's always suspicious of them, he has that with teenagers once they hit sixteen."

Maggie could see Adam had a soft side for the boys. They were lucky to have such a man understanding their desire for exploration and testing the limit, which came with their age. She believed Adam; it was very unlikely they would have done it, and besides, there were already a number of suspects with a real motive—love, finances. She combed her flaming curls with her plump little fingers, and as she stood up to leave she said, "Thanks!"

"For what? I haven't done anything."

"I feel much better now, talking things over with you. But next time I'll have cheerful topics to talk about, I promise."

Walking out with Maggie, Adam laughed. "No worries. Maybe we should have a drink at Heidi's. She always has fun exhibits on."

"I'd like that, I love Heidi's cooking." Maggie smiled from her driver's seat.

*

The excited pair of dogs barked all the way till she reached home and let them out into her woods. The little terrier darted off, clearly pursuing a scent, followed by the setter and by Maggie. She noticed fresh moose tracks in the mud and followed those, hoping the dogs were on the same tracks. They led her to her beaver dam, and sure enough, both dogs were now barking on the banks of the dam, having lost the scent in the water.

Beans took off, nose down to the ground, across Lake View Road. Maggie rushed to her side, ready to scold her for crossing the road when she saw her sniff and growl at a purple fleece hat lying on the ground, slightly covered by leaves. Maggie knelt down, pushing Beans away to take a closer look, imagining someone had lost it when jogging. She picked it up and looked inside it to see if she could find a name.

A familiar whiff of perfume crept up her nose. An image of Ms. Stilton made out of a Peruvian cloud of perfume appeared, like a genie out of the hat. Given her physique, the mayor didn't seem the jogging type, so what was her hat doing there?

Maggie stood up and looked at the footprints around the hat, following their direction toward the dam on the other side of the road. She lowered the hat to Beans's snout to sniff in the hope she would guide her along a trail left by its owner, but Beans instead thought she was playing tug of war and bit the other end.

Irritated, not in the mood for a game, Maggie raised her voice, "Stupid dog, no, I thought you were a terrier, a sniffer dog!" Surprised by Maggie's tone, Beans whimpered, tail between her legs, looking sideways as if she expected a blow. Maggie reassured the little dog with a pat between the ears and lifted the torn hat to her eyes.

"It's not your fault, I should've known better." Maggie shook her head, looking down at Beans's pleading eyes. "How can I present this to the sergeant? Look at what you've done. It's all torn. It might be evidence! Even if it isn't, I can't possibly return it to its owner in this state."

Why would the mayor walk along this road, close to the snowmobile accident? She lived on the other side of Foxton—plenty of walks there. Perhaps Ms. Stilton had visited the crime scene and dropped her hat while retrieving incriminating evidence.

Or had someone planted her perfumed hat here to frame her? Maggie decided she needed to find out if the hat was the mayor's without confronting her directly. She didn't want to scare her. She just had to find the right DNA match with some of the hairs still in the hat. She looked inside it at the hairs to see if there would be enough of them, and to her surprise she saw what seemed to be different colour strands. Could they all belong to the mayor? If not, whom else could they belong to?

She walked slowly, thinking about the different scenarios, staring at the ground. She heard her dogs splashing in the water, playing in the dam. As she lifted her head to check the animals were safe on the other side of the road, her eyes were drawn to a shiny little object a few metres away from where Beans had found the hat. She bent down and picked up a small piece of aluminum-looking metal. She tucked it in her pocket in case it might be relevant, remembering that the police hadn't investigated this side of the road.

Maggie tried to reenact what would happen should she be riding a snowmobile down the road and imagined a moose crossing from the right. She would have turned left if the moose was poking its head out, and yet it didn't seem wise; the moose would likely have run across in panic. If, on the other hand, the moose had nearly completely crossed the road and only its rump was on it as it headed into the bush to the right, a swerve to the left could make sense but would mean crossing the dividing line into a blind corner, the road veering to the left. The reflex would have to be to quickly steer back to the right to stay on the road, even with a broken brake cable. If the moose were coming from the left side, it would make even less sense to turn to the left off-road.

There had been a snow bank on either side of the road from the snow clearing, which should have helped dampen the fall. In order to land in the dam, he would have had to be riding the sled fast and intentionally direct it to jump over the bank, otherwise the skis would have gotten lodged in it and prevented the sled from going any farther.

She shook her head. Perhaps it was an accident trying to avoid a moose or deer's rump...and yet why cut the brakes and hope for an animal to cross the road? The brakes had to have been cut that same evening of his death. Peter Wigmott would've noticed it the following day before the Christmas day race, always inspecting his sled before each race. It didn't make sense. There was another piece missing in this puzzle, and it wasn't a moose.

Walking back onto her land, Maggie whistled to call the dogs. After her walk, she would hand the hat over to the police and explain her ideas but doubted she would convince Sergeant Humphries to get it tested. Maybe she could ask Amy to run a DNA test on some of the hairs from the hat and compare it to a DNA sample from the mayor, and while she was at it, she could check the other suspects. The tricky part would be to retrieve useful DNA samples from each individual. Amy would surely have some tips on how to collect the sample.

She counted the possible suspects on her fingers, walking past her apple trees. Ms. Stilton, Leon LeBreton, Fred Wigmott, the lumberjack boys, no, unlikely to be involved, Patrick, Fiona's husband, Ms. Miller, and Joe. No, why him unless his wife Heather was having an affair with Peter.

Maggie ruffled her hair. What motive would Ms. Miller have to kill Peter? Perhaps the murders were not linked. At the same time, it seemed highly unlikely to have two unrelated murders in a village in such a short timeframe.

She stumbled on a rock, still absorbed in her thoughts. She steadied herself. *Maybe I should invite Amy over to see what she thinks of all this...or just call her. I need help before I get taken in for questioning. I'm sure I'll be next in line...if I don't figure out the culprit soon.*

Chapter Fifteen

Sitting at his grey desk at the police station, Sergeant Humphries struggled with his computer, typing with one finger at a time his report on the second murder. This time he couldn't afford any mistake and didn't want to delegate the task to his constable, even though he would have already typed it by now, having used computers all his life. Sergeant Humphries remembered the time before computers with nostalgia, when letters were mailed and everything seemed to move at a slower, more manageable pace.

He felt butterflies in his belly. This was the first time in his career he had to deal with serious cases of murder. He dreamed of recognition for his astute findings and perhaps a little article in the local newspaper, accompanied by his portrait, on how he solved the cases. He had already spoken with Tina Partridge in anticipation of solving the case so that she could write an article about him. It was a little premature, but she had seemed so eager to follow both cases, and he certainly didn't want to miss such an opportunity.

Sergeant Humphries briefly leaned back in his chair, picturing himself interviewed, explaining what had happened and how he made the arrest. Perhaps he could also put in a little advertising for the Haystack Needles. They needed some sponsors for the summer fair coming up in June; it would be perfect timing. Constable Gupta disrupted his elaborate vision, barging in his room with the coroner's report on Ms. Fiona McLenny's death.

The sergeant peered over his little blue-rimmed reading glasses at the constable. "I assume it is a confirmation of having been hit on the back of the head with the rock."

Constable Gupta wobbled his head in a circle, his eyes rolling around. "Sir, I don't know, I didn't look. You told me that you wanted to see the report first. Obedience to lawful authority is the foundation of manly character."

Sergeant Humphries wondered what on earth his constable meant and brushed it aside as unimportant. He was content that the constable appeared to have followed his orders: he would get the news firsthand that he was right.

"Good, good, any other news?" asked the sergeant in a slightly condescending tone intended to reinforce his higher position in the hierarchy of the police force.

The sergeant had taken many years to reach his level and relished his position of local authority. Unable to conceal his irritation, Constable Gupta replied with a curt, "No, sir…"

"No news then? What have you been up to all this time?"

"I've compiled the list of guests from the Christmas party, as you asked, but Alfred Patterson's boys weren't at the party. Do I still need to interview them?"

Sergeant Humphries stroked his moustache with his index finger. "Yes, they are troublemakers, and it wouldn't surprise me if they'd cut the brakes as a stupid joke. Up to no good, those two, I tell you."

"Aren't they just teenagers? I haven't heard anything bad about them. Why woul—dd they wan—tt tt—to kill Peter Wigmott, Sir?" Constable Gupta said daringly, pushing his golden bracelet up his sleeve with the other hand.

Sergeant Humphries's newfound confidence in his case-solving capabilities lifted his mood, since headquarters had told him he would not be demoted if he dealt properly with the cases. He wasn't the first police officer to misjudge a case in its discovery stage. Eager to turn it around quickly and show his constable how to do it, he chose not to counter the constable this time but consider all viewpoints.

"You're right, I don't see their motive to kill Wigmott, but sometimes boys don't realize the consequences of their acts, and for the moment we don't have much to go on. You've got to go out there and question people, find out who disliked the man. Go through the list of attendees at the party. I want to know their relationship to Wigmott and check out who was supposed to participate in the snowmobile race from that party. Yes...that would be a good motive, come to think of it. Get rid of your competitor to win, with a premeditated accident: typical! You see, Gupta, often it's that simple."

Constable Gupta replied hesitantly, "But it might not always be what it seems...although I agree that is certainly a good explanation."

As if he was afraid to hear the sergeant's response, the constable rushed out of the room before he had time to reply.

Sergeant Humphries's mood improved by the minute, having only listened to the words he wanted to hear from the constable confirming his reasoning. It was just a matter of finding who would want to beat Peter Wigmott or perhaps who had bet on him losing. At least he knew the realtor's cause of death; he'd already congratulated himself on his power of observation. He had found the murder weapon, the stone, until three words stood out at the end of the report: *death by electrocution.* He flicked back the cover, checking the name printed on it—yes, it was the report on the realtor. He was so convinced by his conclusion that he thought there must have been an error or a mix-up in the files.

He shouted angrily to Constable Gupta to come over, his voice crossing the walls of his room. "You got the wrong report. Do I have to do everything myself? How difficult is it to print out a report!"

Constable Gupta flickered his eyelashes with the speed of a hummingbird flapping its wings and mumbled, "Sir, that is the report. I can double-check, sir."

"Yes, you'd better—well no, eh...come here now and show me on the screen where you downloaded it. Incompetence!"

The constable came behind the desk and bent over the sergeant's shoulder, quickly moving his mouse around until the document appeared. To the sergeant's bewilderment, it was the same document, and the death was indeed by electrocution. He turned toward Constable Gupta, dismissing him with his hand and picking up the phone to speak with the coroner.

Sergeant Humphries argued with the coroner in vain. "But there was no evidence, no wire, nothing…just the stone, which obviously hit her, as you say it was her blood on it, and she could have been hit by it. What do you say? I can't hear you, the noise outside…better check what's happening. You won't get rid of me like that, check it again and call me back!"

The sergeant stood up to look through the venetian blinds at what had caused the commotion outside the station. He couldn't see anything from that angle, but still, hearing the shouts, he went back to the security camera system on his desk.

To his surprise, he saw what appeared to be Joe Johnson the plumber, pushed by his wife, Heather, gesticulating toward the police station entrance. The sergeant could just distinguish a few words from Heather. "Tell …sergeant…told me. Not lover…kill her."

His curiosity rising, he went to the window, opening it slightly to hear Joe's response that was now in a lower voice but still audible.

"I'm doing this for you. I wasn't planning on coming here until tomorrow. They're too busy anyway, and I've got nothing to do with all this. If only you could believe me!"

"You were told by the constable to come for the statement, and you didn't yesterday, see!" shouted Heather, still looking beside herself, as if under the spell of an unstoppable rage.

Joe gestured to bring down the volume of her speech and replied in a whisper, since he suddenly seemed aware of a few people looking at them. "It's your fault if they jail me for something I didn't do, just because you want me to prove to you I wasn't with her. Your jealousy…"

Bystanders looked at the pair with disbelief and pity, as if they didn't know which one they pitied most, the betrayed wife or the man obeying his wife. They entered the police station, Joe pushing his wife in.

Constable Gupta greeted the couple from behind the white counter with his usual, "Hello, how are you doing? What can I do for you?"

Joe's angry wife suddenly calmed down, brushing her hair back with both hands and smiling as if she only now realized there were other people around. Joe stood next to her, sulking, not saying a word. Heather seemed to transform from a nasty, jealous witch into a beautiful fairy with only good intentions. The constable appeared spellbound by her charm. Her full lips, large, innocent blue eyes carefully highlighted by black eyeliner, and auburn hair certainly had the desired effect.

She glanced sideways at Joe, stepping heavily on his toes while pushing him forward and telling the constable, "My husband here has to give his statement. He was at the house the day of the murder."

Joe rubbed his hands together as if he was trying to wipe moisture off. "I was with Maggie Flanagan in the morning, showing her the building work I did. She can tell you that. I've got nothing to do with the murder, and once and for all, Fiona was never my mistress, is that clear?" He then turned to his wife. "There, are you happy now? It's the truth."

Joe's tense frame eased as soon as Heather took hold of Joe's hand and looked at the constable, batting her eyelashes in her seductive mode. "Yes, it's true, we're happily married, and he could never be with such a...woman. He only wants to perform his duty and avoid delays by coming forth with his statement."

Constable Gupta stared at her for a moment then shifted his eyes to Joe. "Don't worry, if we need a statement, I'll tell you, but you're not a suspect for the moment. The prime suspect is Fiona's husband, a jealousy case. Besides, you were not present when the body was found, so you can go."

Listening to the conversation from his office, Sergeant Humphries was trying to understand how such a woman could change from an angry beast to this sweet-sounding angel. Hearing his constable's last words, he rose to his feet and rushed outside, forgetting that he had taken off his shoes and had his big toe sticking out from a hole in his left sock. The constable looked down at his feet with big eyes. The sergeant stopped in his tracks, still hidden from the public view. He looked down and fumed internally. He gestured to the constable to come to him.

"Excuse me for a moment, don't leave," said the constable to the pair.

The constable went around the bookshelves to a hidden second desk where the sergeant sat and pulled him down to his level.

The sergeant whispered in the constable's ear, "Gupta, no, no. What on earth are you doing out there? You didn't hear them outside shouting?"

"No, why, what have I done?"

"First, go back and get a statement from him, and I also want to know their whereabouts during the time of death."

As the constable was about to stand up, the sergeant pulled him down again. "And stop giving out information about the cases, you understand?"

"But you did to the journalist, I thought…?

"No, no!" interrupted the sergeant, now boiling with anger. "Enough, let me do this."

The sergeant rose to his feet, still in his socks, and pushed the constable back, nearly knocking him over. Sergeant Humphries walked to the front desk, facing Heather and Joe. A smile on both faces made him aware of his feet as he tucked them out of sight as best he could.

The words he had heard coming out of Heather's mouth outside the police station reinforced his conviction that Fiona had been killed with a knock on the head out of jealousy, already forgetting about the coroner's death report. He stared at Heather in an attempt to apply his silence technique, determined to get a confession out of her.

After a few minutes of silence, still looking Heather in her eyes, the belief she could have done it had disappeared into thin air when she asked him with a smile, "Sergeant, are you all right?"

The sergeant shifted on his feet, tearing himself away from her eyes toward Joe, with whom he felt more confident. "Yes, fine. I want your statement. Gupta will take it. But first, tell me where were you between noon and two o'clock?"

Joe shot a side glance at Heather, then sighed. "I had lunch on the go, picking up a sandwich at the deli, then I had a number of clients to visit." Omitting to mention his visit to Leon LeBreton, he added quickly, "And of course in the morning I was with Maggie Flanagan, as I already told the constable. Can I leave now?"

"No, as I said, I want a statement and the names and details of your clients."

"I don't have them with me. You're not going to ask them, are you? I mean, what will it look like?"

"Only to check if you're telling the truth," replied the sergeant.

"Can I come back tomorrow with the details?"

The sergeant, irritated with Joe's behaviour, remembered having given Joe a fine for speeding with his snowmobile in the village. "Yes, that's fine. And by the way, did you participate in the Christmas snowmobile race?"

"What has that got to do with the case?"

The sergeant replied in a matter-of-fact tone, keeping to himself his growing suspicion, "Nothing for the moment, but we need to know it in relation to the death of Mr. Peter Wigmott."

Joe looked at the sergeant, his eyebrows arched. "Oh, but I thought it was an accident."

Feeling he might be accused of jumping to conclusions, the sergeant added, "We don't know; we have to check things. His sled brakes were cut."

As he said those last words, the constable's jaw fell. He would have to explain that he said it to get more information out of Joe. It was calculated.

Joe, wide-eyed, replied, "That's bad... Yes, I raced, for fun."

Heather jumped to Joe's rescue. "He isn't into competition like the Wigmott brothers. He prefers the camaraderie and an excuse to use his snowmobile."

The sergeant pulled a stern face and looked at the pair. "Okay, but tomorrow you have to come in, Mr. Johnson, and provide the details for your whereabouts, including on December 16. And while you're at it, before you leave, can you give all the names of the competitors in the race on the seventeenth of December? Do you think any of them would be capable of foul play?"

After a moment of silence, Joe said, "No idea."

"But, Joe, you told me the other day that Fred was bragging that he would win if it were not for his brother? And you should have won the other day, but he c—"

Joe squeezed Heather's arm. "Heather, this has nothing to do with it, and Fred's always been supportive of his brother. Sorry, Sergeant, she can sometimes imagine things, you know women..."

The sergeant laughed, thinking that it mustn't be easy to live with a jealous Heather, but on the other hand she was really attractive, and he imagined himself for a moment being the one putting his hand on her shoulder. Before the sergeant could say anything, Joe had whisked Heather off, saying he would come back with the names of his clients, and they could always ask more questions then.

The sergeant stood for a moment, looking at the pair walk away, unable to prevent the growing coldness creeping up his toes. He swivelled on his red socks and stormed back to his office.

*

Joe kept his hand around Heather's shoulder, directing her to the car, and only once on the road did he tell her, "Heather, my sweetheart, I love you. You have the proof you wanted. Fiona wasn't my mistress, or anyone else for that matter. But please, oh please, promise me one thing!"

Heather seemed to feel a little ashamed of her overreaction as she replied in a mellow voice, "Yes, darling, anything…"

"Don't speak to the police again unless I'm with you, and don't speak like a headless chicken about things you know nothing about."

Heather blushed. "What do you mean? I was only trying to help."

Joe replied, "There are times when keeping quiet is the best you can do! Anything to do with this case and in particular snowmobile racing: stay out of it. Don't you see this idiot of a sergeant is desperately looking for a scapegoat for both murders, and now he could see me as a suspect? First, because you broadcasted I had a relationship with Fiona, shouting like that for everyone to hear. Lucky he mustn't have heard it, otherwise he would've been a real pain. And now because of the snowmobile race you start telling him that I've an issue with the Wigmott brothers and their ways of winning, and before you know it I've cut the brakes!"

Heather narrowed her eyes. "Have you?"

Raising his eyes to the sky, Joe sighed. "Gee, no, of course not, why even ask! You see what I mean? You will get me in trouble with your overly suspicious attitude about everything I do. Enough is enough…"

Joe accelerated abruptly, as if he were trying to escape the cloud of trouble that seemed to be expanding by the minute. Heather broke the silence, adjusting her skirt over her knees. "You have a lot of explaining to do. I won't take it. You know where the spare room is."

Joe grumbled, avoiding eye contact, unsure of how he could turn the situation around this time.

Chapter Sixteen

In the comfort of her log home, Maggie carefully selected a number of hairs with their root sheath from the hat her terrier had found. Amy had told her it was essential to have the root with the hair to be able to ascertain that the DNA came from the suspect with a high degree of probability when comparing DNA samples. Maggie carefully placed the hat into a clean bag to bring to the police.

She made a list of the people she would need to somehow get DNA samples from in order to check if there was any match with the hairs in the hat. The mayor's unique perfume was a good giveaway as to its potential owner, but someone else could also have sprayed it onto the hat without it belonging to her.

Maggie lifted her fingers from the keyboard. Amy had a tendency to go out of her way to help her, so she was of two minds about asking her to do the DNA testing, let alone telling her that she might be seen a suspect in a murder case. The last thing she wanted was to compromise Amy in any way. At the same time, it would be impossible not to tell her. Amy would certainly not forgive her if she could have helped her out when she was in trouble.

They had always been soundboards for each other, even with an ocean between them. Maggie cherished their friendship, and now wasn't the time to wreck it. *I've got to take action to stop my mind from spinning around. I'll talk to her...maybe I'll first try to get hold of one or two just to see if it works out...*

Having a plan eased Maggie's anxiety a little. She would start with the mayor. She found Ms. Stilton's address online; her home was, as she had thought, not far from Adam's farm, and it would only take her ten minutes to drive there. This time she left the dogs behind, not wanting them to get her into trouble by poking their snouts where they shouldn't.

Ms. Stilton lived in a cottage on a small, dark lake with only a few houses around it, only a few kilometres from Foxton. Tall pine trees gave the place a spooky appearance, casting long shadows on the road, accentuated by their creaking as they rubbed against each other in the wind.

Maggie parked her faithful truck at the beginning of the road, where the mailboxes were stacked. Should Ms. Stilton be home, she could always hide in the bush or pretend she was going for a walk, although that would not make much sense since this was a dead-end and there was no convincing reason for her to be there. She brushed aside her concern and counted on her improvisation skills to wiggle herself out of such a situation, if it arose. She looked around and sighed with relief. No car, just a gleaming silver Airstream trailer parked next to the house.

Reassured, Maggie walked around the house, peering through the windows to see if there was a dog or any other pet. The garden was overgrown and the house looked messy. This surprised Maggie, as Ms. Stilton always appeared very neatly dressed. Maggie had counted on the mayor storing her rubbish outside, in a shed perhaps. She would not want to be caught trespassing in her house.

She bent over slightly to check under the wooden terrace a metal container that looked like the bear-proof containers for garbage. This is easier than I thought it would be. *I'll be out of here in no time. Quick...* She lifted up the heavy lid and peered into the bin. A strong smell engulfed her nostrils. Had she doubted she was in Ms. Stilton's home, the smell of her flowery Peruvian perfume was even in her rubbish, exactly the same smell as in the purple hat. Smells could be even stronger than images to trigger one's memory, and this perfume brought her straight back to her first encounter with the mayor during the wedding party.

She thought, *If only the smell would mean that it comes from her makeup cotton pads or something like it—a perfect source for the sample.* She moved a few bags aside, and there through a clear plastic bag tightly shut she saw old clothing, which explained the smell. This was ideal.

She busied herself untying the tight knot. She pulled out an old black tank top with a few hairs still hanging on it. She quickly put it into her coat pocket then stuffed the rest of the clothes back and tied the knot again as she had found it. She thought the mayor was likely to be perceptive, so she had to be very careful. She didn't want to linger for fear of being caught red-handed.

As she stepped back, the lid fell down with a loud, metallic clunk. Her heart beat fast, as it had when she and Amy had crept into the laboratory at night, unlocking the door to carry out their DNA test. She listened, and reassured, she looked around, walking under the cover of the terrace toward the side of the house where she could reach the road.

She felt a sudden tightening of her chest, the flight instinct taking hold. She rushed out and hit her head on a plank sticking out from the terrace. Slightly dazed by the pain, she stood frozen on the spot. Something had frightened her. An engine noise grew louder. Her mind raced for an escape route, her eyes scanning her surroundings until they landed on the shiny Airstream trailer. She sprinted to it, hoping it would be open.

Just as the car pulled slowly up, Maggie managed to slip into the Airstream, and catching her breath, her back against the door, she listened to the engine noise stop and two doors slam. She could faintly hear Ms. Stilton's voice and that of a man. She couldn't tell who it was. She slowly bent her head, trying to catch a glimpse of them through the small window. In doing so, an old bottle of beer fell to the ground and rolled across the floor with a hollow sound.

Alerted by the noise, the mayor interrupted her conversation and said, "Did you hear that?"

"What? No," said the man.

"It came from my Airstream. Wait a minute, I want to check it."

Maggie panicked; what if Ms. Stilton found her there? It would be hard to get out of such a tricky situation; she was no longer a young student, let alone a child. The only solution was to disappear somehow. Maggie saw a small closet and squeezed into it, pushing the clothes hangers to the side. Barely able to hold the door closed, a small slit remaining, she held her breath as the mayor entered, followed by the man. Maggie could now see through the slit that the man was Leon LeBreton.

Ms. Stilton looked around and picked up the beer bottle, her back toward the cupboard. "Probably those awful little creatures again. They keep coming in and hiding their nuts everywhere. Outside it's fine, but I don't like squirrels inside. They can do so much damage."

Ms. Stilton leaned her bottom against the little cupboard, closing the door on Maggie, who withheld a scream as one of her curls was caught in the door. Maggie felt quickly in the dark to find a handle she could turn to get out—none, just a protruding cold piece of metal with what felt like a slit in it. She nearly called out that she was stuck but stopped herself in time. She heard a throat clearing coming from Leon LeBreton, then a few steps, probably down the outside staircase.

Maggie heard Ms. Stilton's heels pounding the floor, moving away from her, and the sound of a door closing, her voice still audible. "No windows open this time. I'll have to check it out later, as I heard some strange noises, but I don't want to keep you waiting."

Maggie gently pulled at her lock of hair to free it, relieved that no one spotted it, while pushing on the door in vain. She waited a little until she couldn't hear any voice and took out the pocketknife she always carried with her. After a failed attempt at fitting the blade into the little slit, thinking it would move the handle, she thought of how easy it seemed to open doors with a knife in movies by sliding the knife along its side, but even this flimsy one didn't want to budge.

She would have to find another way. Leaning back among the clothes hangers, she tried to gather momentum to push the door open with her shoulder. That too didn't work, and her shoulder was now hurting and bruised. Afraid of making too much noise, she waited five minutes, a claustrophobic feeling slowly taking hold of her. She sat at the bottom of the closet, her knees against her chest, cursing herself. She would have to call someone for help.

Her feet propped up against the door, Maggie called Adam and felt like a fool when the door moved under the pressure of her feet. She hung up before Adam picked up, and with all her might pushed the door with both feet while leaning against the back of the closet. The door swung open, and her phone flew out with it. A frog-quacking sound emanated from it. Adam was calling her back. She scrambled out of the closet on all fours to stop the noise.

She sat still on the floor of the trailer, her phone in her hand, listening for Ms. Stilton, her heart pounding. To her relief, all seemed quiet. She looked around at the damage she had done. If she were lucky, Ms. Stilton would think a raccoon caused it. She peered out the window—no sign of the pair. Ms. Stilton and Leon must have entered the house and were out of hearing.

Maggie carefully tiptoed towards the Airstream door, checking she had everything. She had to move fast, afraid they might be able to see her from the house. The camper was parked only a few metres from the house. As she opened the door, she heard Ms. Stilton's voice slightly covered by the hissing of a kettle. They must be in the kitchen.

Instead of sneaking out straight away, her curiosity got the better of her as she stood next to the open door, trying to hear their conversation. Leon's loud deep voice reached her. "The subsidies you've approved, together with the ones from the province, will already apply once I start building the solar installation. But we'll only get the payback once it's working, of course. Is it all okay on your side? I mean, you don't see any issue with the final approval for this?"

"It's all clear, at least it should be, and I'm also counting on it. I want to present your project to the conference on clean energy coming up. I was planning on having a poster showcasing our village with its solar farm, a good example of having all the odds against you and still making it. The locals will come around to it once they see their village is seen as a role model for the region, you'll see."

"You'll be seen as a leader of the green…"

Maggie couldn't pick out the last words; instead she heard what could have been a window being shut, followed by silence. This would be her moment to escape. Fortunately for Maggie, the conversation in the kitchen lasted long enough for her to slip out of the trailer and close the door behind her, catching a glimpse of her own dishevelled appearance in the mirror-like body of the Airstream.

To her horror, she noticed that she had a pink polka-dotted piece of clothing stuck to her shoulder. She removed it and held up a large bra in front of her eyes. *I can't run away leaving this on the ground or take it with me. She'll look for it, an unusual silk bra. She wouldn't believe a raccoon could have taken it either.* Maggie laughed at the idea of a raccoon wearing it, perhaps as a hat. A hat for two raccoons, walking side by side!

Hearing a noise coming from the house, this time a door, Maggie jumped back into the Airstream, stuffed the bra quickly back into the closet where it must have come from, and dashed back out of the trailer, running into the woods for cover until she reached the road via the neighbours. Out of breath, moisture building up on her forehead and cheeks flushed, she climbed into her truck and sped off as if pursued. Only when she reached her driveway did she lift her foot from the accelerator pedal and finally control her breathing.

She made a mental note to get fit; she really had to lose some weight. It would be hard to cut down on the homemade cakes, so perhaps taking up jogging might be the answer. The dogs would like that. She felt her pocket. The piece of clothing discarded by Ms.

Stilton was still there, and if she had any doubt she could still smell it: the risk taken had been worthwhile. She tried to recall whether there was any security camera at the mayor's home, carefully going over the place in her mind, and dismissed it, thinking it was too late anyway. She should have thought about it sooner.

The next person on her list of suspects was Leon LeBreton. Even if she got a match with Leon for the hat, it was still possible that Leon might have handled the mayor's hat, given their frequent interaction relating to the solar panel project. He could have picked it up for her if she'd dropped it and not necessarily have placed it alongside the road on purpose. The presence of his DNA on the hat couldn't be conclusive, whereas the other suspects might not have the same access to Ms. Stilton and her hat, and finding their DNA on it would be surprising.

She felt strangely energized, emboldened by her stint at the mayor's house, adrenaline still pumping in her veins. She checked the time on her father's oversized watch. He called it his flying watch. He always wore it when he flew his floater plane in the skies above the lakes and explained it was a backup for the instruments, indicating pressure and height.

Maggie was always excited when he allowed her to climb into the two-person cabin beside him and they would taxi the plane to the middle of the lake. She used to wave to her mother, who was standing on the dock overseeing the event. Her father would ask her to look out for boats and canoes before they took off above the sea of trees dotted with islands of lakes. She would ask him to fly low over Algonquin Park so she could see what the moose or bears were up to.

Flying meant ultimate freedom for her, no need to ask permission to take off or land. It seemed he was like a bird, a loon, and could go wherever he wished. She decided she would fulfill another of her dreams now that she had changed her direction in life: learn how to fly, and what better place than here. She already knew the basics, having been taught by her father at a young age, without ever having gotten her license.

Suddenly the hands on the watch popped out at her. Already four o'clock, still time to do some work on her photos, but speaking to Amy would have to wait. She knew she was procrastinating; she wasn't sure how Amy would react. First she would get the samples, then once she had them all she would tackle her friend. *That's a feat in itself, if it will be all like the mayor's sample. No use Amy knowing about it if I fail...*

Chapter Seventeen

Fiona's shy husband, Patrick, sat in front of Fiona's dressing table, tears in his eyes. He caught sight of a large makeup brush, remembering her applying it to her cheeks; he tried it on himself to see if it would help conjure an image of her. Instead, the powder on it made him cough. Anger took hold of him. In a wild gesture, he swiped all the products off the table.

His sadness was more self-pity than real mourning for her. He wondered who would take care of the house for him. He had believed she would always be there for him and couldn't accept or understand this loss.

The thought of his mother haunted him, how hard it had been losing her. She had betrayed him by leaving his world when he was a kid. He had found in Fiona another mother, which was not the recipe for a balanced marriage and often resulted in fights, Fiona refusing to take on that role and eventually seeking attention elsewhere.

He sat on the chair, rocking his upper body, clasping his head with his hands. Jumping up violently, he slammed the dressing table with his fist and cried in pain as it landed on a small metal box. Calmed down by the jab of pain, he stared at the box, applying a piece of his shirt to his wounded hand to stop the bleeding, when out rolled a strange-looking ring. He had never seen it before, a large ring with a letter A carved out.

He picked it up carefully, turning it around, looking for an inscription. He tried sliding it on his finger, only to find it could barely fit on the tip of his pinkie. That reassured him; this meant it belonged to Fiona and would have fitted on her slender fingers. It couldn't have belonged to one of those men, given its size…although the style reminded him of university rings, and she never went to university. He knew she had had affairs.

At first Fiona had told him she nearly slept with their son's hockey coach, hoping this would trigger a reaction and he would pay attention to her. Instead, Patrick told her to go ahead; he didn't care. At the time he even thought it would be good. He wasn't interested in the physical relationship side and thought she would leave him in peace while they would live happily together. Initially, Fiona couldn't believe him and thought it was out of spite, like a teenager challenging someone to something they don't want and think the other person incapable of.

His attitude toward her didn't change over time. Patrick never shared anything with her. He was always absorbed in his computer, day and night, while promptly gobbling her meals. Out of desperation, Fiona had her first lover. Feeling appreciated again, she carried on speaking until she met Leon, who was all her husband was not: outspoken, cheerful, and confident.

A second fit of rage took hold of Patrick, remembering her words: "I want a divorce. I'm leaving you, this time for good." He had thought he would always find a way to keep her, even when she threatened him. Those had been her last words to him the morning of the day she died.

He muttered to himself that it was all his own fault; he had leapt toward her, grabbing her and shaking her like a tree. He should never had done that. Fiona might have changed her mind and certainly not be dead. She had accepted a lot and tried to make their marriage work for the sake of their son.

They married when they were very young; it had been a fling, and she became pregnant. Patrick had provided for their child, Damien, and for her during the first years, thanks to his programming skills being in high demand for new websites. Fiona was grateful of his support, but as soon as she had her own income as a realtor, found new love, and their son was out of the home, she no longer saw any reason to linger in a doomed marriage. Patrick couldn't grasp the notion she was gone forever, in spite of the police notifying him of her death.

He had to break the news to Damien, but had always been very clumsy in communicating with him and relied on Fiona to take care of that. He had postponed the moment as long as possible. He looked at the clock and slowly picked up the phone. He felt an urge to hear a familiar voice.

Damien's voice filled the room with questions, Patrick breathing down the line, was unable to utter a word. "Dad, I know you're there. It's your number. Answer! Speak, for once in your life!" Damien paused, the silence still present, and asked with fear in his voice, "Did something happen to Mom?"

"Your mother's d—" sobbed Patrick.

"No, Dad, it's not true, it can't be. Did you have a fight with her again?"

"Yes, but that's not how she died."

"I knew it, you never cared. She was right to leave you, but too late. Was that it, then? You didn't let her go, and now—"

Patrick couldn't bear it any longer and hung up. The doorbell rang. He got up like a robot and opened the door to Sergeant Humphries and Constable Gupta. Patrick felt miserable and distressed at the sight of the police. Constable Gupta whispered into the sergeant's ear that they might want to speak with him later. The sergeant waved his index finger in negation and went in. The phone rang. Sergeant Humphries asked, "Shouldn't you answer?"

Patrick shrugged, looking at the phone, fearing his son. Sergeant Humphries signalled to Constable Gupta to pick up the phone in the hall while he guided Patrick away to the living room, his hand on his shoulder.

Constable Gupta, as calmly as he could muster, picked up the receiver and confirmed to Damien that Fiona had died. This was the first time that the constable had to convey a death to a relative of the deceased. Raj carefully explained that they were not there to arrest his father, while quickly scribbling on his notepad, *Patrick possible killer according to his son.*

In the dark living room, Sergeant Humphries asked Patrick bluntly, "Where were you between 11:30 a.m. and 1:30 p.m.?"

"At home, working on my database project." His son's words echoed in his head until the angry eyes of the sergeant froze him on the spot with a dreadful thought as he managed to utter, "You don't think... No, I didn't kill her, I was home!"

The sergeant used a calm, soothing voice in contrast to his threatening eyes. "Did you speak to anyone at home, or was there someone with you who could testify?"

A tight knot took hold of his throat as he shook his head slowly.

Constable Gupta came over from the other room, having scribbled notes on his pad, and held it up to the sergeant, pointing silently to a sentence on it while looking at Patrick sideways. Sergeant Humphries looked up at him, "This is serious." He turned toward Patrick. "Your son was on the phone."

Patrick looked up at the sergeant. "Yes, I just spoke to him. I tried telling him, but he didn't want to listen."

Constable Gupta burst out with a high-pitched voice, "Your son mentioned your wife wanted to leave you. Why didn't you tell us that when I asked you on the phone if you were having trouble with your wife?"

Sergeant Humphries turned to the constable with darts in his eyes, enough to pin him in his place, wide eyed.

Turning back to Patrick, the sergeant asked, "Is that true?"

"She said that. She often threatened to, but it wasn't serious. You know what it's like," replied Patrick with a sigh.

"No, I don't," the sergeant harshly replied.

"She was having an affair, but that never lasted," added Patrick, feeling the need to explain himself.

The sergeant's eyebrows drifted upward. "Is that so? Did that not make you angry? Enough to kill her?"

Patrick, feeling trapped, already regretting his disclosure, replied, "No! I told you, I didn't! I want a lawyer, I won't talk anymore."

Sergeant Humphries took out his little notebook and reached for his handcuffs. "If that's how you want it! I'm arresting you on suspicion of killing your wife, Fiona. It is my duty to inform you that you have the right to retain and instruct counsel without delay. Do you understand?" Having read the charter of rights from his booklet, to which Patrick uttered a small yes, the sergeant ushered him out of his house.

Patrick protested in vain, feeling his entire world had collapsed as he was bundled out of the house into the police car to the station. He caught sight of the sergeant in the rear-view mirror with a strange grin, a contented look, or was it something else? Giving up, he tucked his head into his hands, hoping to hide from the world.

Chapter Eighteen

The following morning, Maggie woke up having dreamed she had mistakenly put on the purple hat she had found near her beaver dam. The police, accusing her of withholding evidence, had taken the hat away and identified her as a prime suspect, having found her hair in it. She sat up in her bed, Carrot and Beans running around, tugging at her pyjamas.

She had to go to the police station first thing to hand over the hat and suggest they might want to check it for DNA. Feeling the weight lifted from her chest, she slipped into her sheepskin slippers, followed by the cheerful duo, and headed to the kitchen. As a backup, she had kept a few strands of hair from the hat for Amy to test. She had made sure there were enough hairs left in the hat for the police to do their job if they wanted to.

Maggie arrived at the police station. As soon as she walked in, she noticed a young, bearded man sitting in a corner, his head sunk into his chest, playing with his phone. He barely lifted his eyes when she approached, smiling at him on the way to the counter. Constable Gupta waved at them from the back of the room, where he was pouring himself a coffee, and offered them one. Seeing the young man hadn't heard the constable, his music playing in his ears, Maggie relayed the question. He simply shook his head in response.

Maggie walked up to the counter, where Constable Gupta handed over a warm cup of coffee.

"If you want to speak with the sergeant, he's busy with a suspect."

"Oh, I don't want to disturb him, but I've got something that might be evidence for the snowmobile case," said Maggie in a low voice, wanting to keep her reason for the visit as confidential as possible.

"I'm sure the sergeant will want to speak to you about it, but if you're happy to wait, I think he should be soon done," replied the constable, shaking his wrist to reveal a golden watch.

"And is he before me?" Maggie pointed with her chin at the young man.

"No, he's waiting for his father to bail him..." Constable Gupta looked down nervously, then took off his cap to scratch the back of his head.

Not wanting the constable to feel uncomfortable, Maggie said quickly, "I'll wait, that's fine. I've got time this morning. Nice coffee!"

She lifted her mug up as she walked back to the chairs along the wall, where the young man she guessed must be Fiona's son was still sitting. The only suspect with a son that age was Patrick McLenny, from what she knew.

Maggie carefully positioned herself next to the young man. The constable was back behind the counter and had just picked up the phone that had been ringing for a while. Sensing her neighbour needed to talk, Maggie pulled some mints from her bag and offered him one. She looked at him, imagining how hard it must be for him to have just lost a mother, keen to make him feel better if she could. Perhaps if she just talked about herself, he might open up.

Maggie said, trying to determine if he was indeed Fiona's son, "I'm here to bring evidence. Well, I'm not sure it's evidence, but just in case, I want the police to know all I know. Often they need a lot in order to say if someone is guilty, not just a hunch. Anyway, this has nothing to do with you. I'm sorry to bother you with it." She waited a little while, observing from the corner of her eye a tinge of curiosity. Now that Constable Gupta had left the room, she decided it was the moment to be direct. He had to be Fiona's son; he had her nose and eyes. "I'm so sorry about your mother. I found her, you know. Please accept all my condolences. You might have heard my name. I'm Maggie, Maggie Flanagan."

He stiffened at the news and looked at her, tears welling in his eyes.

Maggie asked softy, "You're Fiona's son? Am I right?"

"Yes. Damien." He sniffed a little, wiping his tears away quickly with the back of his hand, regaining composure. "She was really great, my mom."

Damien's face changed to an expression of anger, his fists clenched on his lap as he looked down at the floor. "I'm here to get my dad out of jail. Don't know why, he must have done it!"

Maggie gave him the softest look of motherly concern she could muster. "You mustn't say that, they don't know yet. Why do you think that?"

"Mom wanted to leave him. Dad spent his time on his computer, ignoring her, and this time she was going for it. She told me, and I can't blame her. The only time I get to speak with him is when he asks me for something, just like the other day when I had to help him with his open-source computer program over Skype. Skipped my lunch to help him, it was so urgent...the same goddamn day Mom die..."

Maggie asked, "That must've been just when I found her. Or maybe? Noon or one o'clock?"

As soon as she asked her question, she regretted being so nosy, but Damien didn't seem to mind, at least for the moment. "I'm off work at twelve thirty for an hour, and Dad took all that time. Pfff, he can be slow, I tell ya!"

Maggie's mind was spinning. She felt happy for him. His accusations were too premature—his dad couldn't have done it. "Maybe you should tell the police what you told me. It's important, I think."

Damien shrugged, sinking back into his chair, ready to close up like a clam.

Maggie insisted, "Your dad might not have done it. Don't you see you might be his alibi..."

Damien sat up a little. Maggie waited for him to think about what she had said. Perhaps the idea would germinate in his mind, and he might view his dad in another light. Some colour returned to Damien's cheeks, just above the thick beard. Before she could say anything else, the constable called out his name to follow him through the swinging doors.

Damien rose to his feet and directed a little smile from the corner of his mouth toward Maggie just before he marched toward the constable. Maggie wondered whether Damien would tell the police his story, and hopefully the history of his Skype call would still be there to prove it.

She had only met Patrick once at the wedding party and could hardly say she knew him. It had been difficult engaging in any form of conversation with him, aside from computers. To each question she asked he would give a short response and then remain silent.

Maggie had wondered if he would have found her too inquisitive at the time, but without asking questions, it would have been total silence. She had had a very different experience with Fiona, who was talkative and seemed to relish her questions. At the time Maggie had wondered how they could be together. She stared into the void, thinking about Damien. A bit like his mother, perhaps, and might have sided with her over the years. Maybe Fiona had a lover and was leaving her husband for that man. Hard on her husband: the type to close up. *He has an alibi now, maybe, but jealousy can be so dangerous. I wish I could speak with Patrick. Did he know about her lover?*

Maggie ruffled her locks with the tip of her fingers, a habit when she was thinking, as if the rubbing would stimulate her brain in coming up with the answer. A shiver snaked its way down her spine. Or maybe Patrick did it, like his son said. *Oh no, then I might have pushed him to defend his father*. Still, if he Skyped from his home, it wouldn't have been possible for him to go to Mr. Bern's house and kill Fiona after the call—it's a thirty-minute drive at least! Or for that matter before the call, either. *That leaves us with another suspect: the lover...Leon LeBreton. It has to be...*

The door opened, and out came Patrick, followed by Damien and the sergeant, warning, "You're off the hook for now, but only for now thanks to your son. I'll keep an eye on you, and you can't leave town, you hear me?"

Patrick, head down, shoulders drooping as if he were carrying the weight of the world on them, responded, "Whatever you say."

Damien looked defiantly back at the sergeant, putting his hand across his father's shoulder. "I'll be with him, and you'd better find what happened. Come on, Dad."

Damien marched his father out of the police station as Maggie followed them with her eyes, relieved for Damien. A dead mother was already a lot to bear, but being suspicious of your own father, that must be terrible.

The sergeant was standing just behind the swinging doors and appeared to be looking down at a paper bag Maggie was holding. She caught his glance and grasped her bag tighter in response.

Sergeant Humphries greeted Maggie. "Maggie Flanagan, more evidence, I hear. Come with me!"

She couldn't help but notice his tongue on his lips, followed by a deep swallowing sound, as if he had had too much saliva—perhaps he was anticipating muffins...hence his pleasant greeting. *I should have bought some.* Once in his office, eager to dispel any ideas he might have, she placed the paper bag on the table. "I've brought you new evidence in this bag, or at least it could be." She pointed to it.

The sergeant sat back in his chair as if he wanted to increase the distance between him and the bag out of disappointment, and in a hardened tone he said, "Evidence? Why now, what is it?"

"It might relate to Peter Wigmott. I found it yesterday and brought it to you as soon as I could. You mentioned I should tell you if anything else turned up."

"Yes, yes, what is it now."

"I found it on the other side of the road, opposite the beaver dam."

"We've already combed that area. If there was something relevant we would have seen it. Must have ended up there afterward, whatever it is."

"Yes, you're right—"

The sergeant put his hands on the table and stood up. "Then why bother me with it—irrelevant!"

"Maybe not, if I may… It's a hat, a purple hat. I think it might belong to the mayor, Ms. Stilton. Smell, it has her strong perfume." Maggie opened the paper bag and placed it under the sergeant's nose, hoping he would recognize her perfume, but it triggered a sneeze. "You see, it's her perfume, you're sneezing again like at the wedding party. There's no reason for her to be walking there. Maybe she came back to pick up something that could incriminate her."

Maggie waited a moment to see the sergeant's reaction. Seeing he was quiet, she added, "Either someone placed it there to implicate her, or on the other hand, of course it might not be important and could belong to anyone who would by chance wear the same perfume as Ms. Stilton. Highly unlikely, though, given she told me that it was made for her in Peru. No one else would have it. You can check it with her."

The sergeant peered into the bag. Holding his nose with a tissue and taking a plastic glove out of his drawer, he asked, "Did you touch it with your bare hands? Maybe she just lost it, nothing special there."

Pointing to the inside of the hat, Maggie retorted, "But look, there're hairs in it. You can still check the DNA and ask the mayor for her DNA."

"You've watched too many movies. For a hat like this, a bit farfetched, no?"

"Why, maybe there's DNA from other suspects. Patrick for instance. It would help prove your case."

Contemplating her view, the sergeant smoothed his grey moustache with his index finger as if he were checking that all hairs were in the right place.

"Well, yes, people can lie and have alibis. His son can lie for him. Maybe..." Then, angrily, the sergeant added, "Anything else you've got to complicate things?"

Maggie shook her head vigorously, her curls bouncing off her cheeks like little springs. She stood up, feeling it best to leave before the sergeant might get too grumpy; being muffinless, it seemed to be the safest move.

Out in the fresh air, Maggie closed her eyes and took in a deep breath. She was determined to find a way to speak with Patrick. She needed more information to rest assured he wasn't involved, although her gut feeling told her he couldn't have done it. An idea germinated in her head: *A website, yes I need a website for my photography business, and he builds them, I think. That's it, I'll ask.*

Chapter Nineteen

Leon LeBreton sat up in his bed, drenched in sweat as if he had run a marathon, rubbing his eyes, trying to get rid of the nightmare. His head was hurting from a heavy night of drinking, and slowly he ordered his thoughts. Images clung to his mind of him being locked up with the mayor in her Airstream trailer with police knocking on its door shaking its entire body. He felt trapped and had a bad taste in his mouth. He shook his head. It was only a dream. Then Fiona's smiling face appeared in his mind, and he wondered whether he had simply dreamed her death. *It must be.*

He made his way to his kitchen, switching on the coffee machine, feeling his unshaven beard. His head was pounding. He poured himself a glass of water and swirled the water around, looking at it mesmerized until it seemed to morph into a wineglass. Where had he been—yes, he had gone to the Horizon Cafe. As usual, he must have had too much to drink.

Putting his hand into his pyjamas pocket in search of a tissue, he pulled out a tulip-patterned scarf. He stood at the kitchen sink, holding it up, perplexed. It belonged to Fiona. He had given it to her on their first secret date, when he was working at a remote cottage on an island, where she had joined him. He had no recollection of how it got there or of having spent the night with her. He looked around for evidence of her clothing just in case. He had a bad feeling in his stomach—something had gone wrong, but what?

Burying his head in her scarf, he cried, struck by the memory of her death. He didn't want to believe it. The image of a solar roof and Mr. Bern's house slowly brought him back to reality. The coffee was taking effect.

He spoke out loud, as if he had to convince himself. "Last night... I went back to the house, where I must have got the scarf... I had to. No one can know I had an affair with her, otherwise..."

After the late night, he had insisted on driving back home, in spite of Heidi's attempts to stop him. He remembered this far and that he had been lucky not to have had an accident or any encounter with the police. He had driven very slowly, his chin on the steering wheel, trying to stay on the road that seemed to move like a snake in front of him. The house—yes, he had stopped there, now he remembered.

There had been bright car lights that dazzled him. His heart sank as he vaguely recalled that it was stationary. Maybe someone saw him. He reassured himself that nothing was wrong; he had just picked up something he had forgotten. He had the keys and always looked after the house. What he obliterated from his mind was that he opened his car door, rolled out of it, and staggered onto his feet. Walked straight into tape, irritated by it, ripped it apart with one hand as he had done many times with building tape, and walked to the front door.

Fiddling for a long time with his key. Ripping more tape off, he finally entered the building. He stumbled to the living room looking for the scarf, the image of which dominated his mind until he put it into his pocket. He managed to walk back out and lock the door behind him, as he had done so often recently when they had met there in the evening.

What a perfect excuse, keeping an eye on someone's home and doing some work; no one would know they spent some time there together. Fiona would tidy up after, she was good at that. No one would know. Just the scarf. He patted his pocket, reassured that he had dealt with it, and staggered back to his car.

He put his hand in front of his eyes, dazzled by a car light that slowly drove by. He remembered that now. If it was the police, he could explain. He just wanted to pick up her scarf to remember her. He would have to deny being drunk, and there was no proof anyway. As far as he knew he hadn't given a blood sample or blown into any breath analyzer.

Standing under a cold shower to sober up, reality hit him. He saw it was police caution tape, not a simple building tape. It was where Fiona had died. He had trespassed that night, but he was drunk, they might understand...he hoped.

A mix of self-pity and sadness for Fiona released a flow of tears that fused with the water from the shower as he stood, his head tilted back, his hands slowly stroking back his hair. He didn't see a way out. He could ask Joe for advice; he knew about their affair and always had ideas, but then he remembered their fight. Swallowing his tears, drying himself, a glimmer of hope came to him. No one knew he had been there. Why would he tell anyone? He could always deny it. He could focus the police on what Fiona had told him that day.

He had disagreed with her for the first time and was worried for her. She had told him she had uncovered important information that could have a big impact on the local elections. She wanted to challenge the person with it before going public. She mentioned a name. He tried hard to recollect, but his head was still hurting from the hangover.

As he dressed, he tried to remember her words. Only her face smiling at him kept coming back sadly to his mind. In the kitchen, he hit his head with the palm of his hand as he heard the ten rings of his cuckoo clock in the kitchen. *My appointment, I forgot, I'm running really late...*

Leon hurried out of the house into his car when he noticed the flag on his letterbox was up. He thought he might have forgotten to pick up his mail, but that didn't make sense. He vaguely remembered having picked it up the day before. He drove up next to it and retrieved a folded piece of white paper. Leon opened it and stared down at the collage of letters. *I saw you. You can't escape.* He crumpled the note and stuffed it into his jacket pocket.

He would revert to his preferred tactic, burying his head in the sand, despite that never working and getting him into more trouble than facing an issue early on. He could always talk himself out of any situation. Needing to regain his confidence, he looked into the rear-view mirror, combing his shiny hair back with his comb and giving himself an encouraging wink.

Chapter Twenty

Sergeant Humphries told Constable Gupta to go question the mayor, Ms. Stilton. He had to ask her about the hat, and in any case about the Christmas party. Constable Gupta had pointed out to him that the mayor could have stood to gain from Peter Wigmott's death, thus defeating her only opponent. She would have never become mayor otherwise. Sergeant Humphries felt uneasy about it, not having spoken to her early enough in the enquiry, assuming it had been an accident.

He felt intimidated by Ms. Stilton and didn't want to admit it. He would conveniently use the training excuse to let his constable speak with her in his place; delegating was part of his role to teach the younger generation.

Constable Gupta pleaded in vain with the sergeant to come with him. "But Sergeant, she's an influential person here. Is it not better for you to speak with her?"

"I thought you wanted to get out of this building. You told me the other day that I don't give you enough assignments outdoors. Well, now you have one!"

"Yes, that's true but…"

"And it's on your beat. It's about time you did your village tour regularly. After the visit you can do that too. You said you liked it."

"I do like that."

"Off you go then, on the double!" exclaimed the sergeant, tapping his desk with his hand.

Lethally Green 155

*

The municipal brick buildings were very close to the police station, only a block away on foot. They overlooked Perch Lake, just opposite Horizon Cafe with a public beach and marina just below The Road, the main street of Foxton, leading to it. Raj usually enjoyed his patrols along the lakeshore and back up through the village streets, stopping to chat with the locals. He often stopped by the cafe, checking with Heidi that all was in order as an excuse to enjoy a coffee before carrying on with his round.

Two cheerful ladies greeted the constable from behind a low, long counter, wheeling themselves from one corner to the other, stacking green papers. Curious, the constable peered down toward the hands of the fair-haired clerk with her large glasses and flower-printed blouse generously open in front. The paper was an open invitation to the public to hear about the solar panel project and its benefits to the community hosted by the mayor. Sandra, rose-cheeked, looked up at him, parting her thin lips into a sweet smile.

"What can I do for you, Constable?"

"I've come to speak with Ms. Stilton about a police matter. I believe she's expecting me, or rather the sergeant. Sergeant Humphries sent me."

So far, he felt at ease. The constable was about to say he was a little early when the door swung open and Maggie Flanagan entered. The constable felt comfortable with her and had even mentioned to his wife that she might like to meet her, since they both had a bubbly disposition. He was keen for his wife to make new friends; he was worried she might feel lonely at times, having just arrived in Foxton and left her friends behind. Maggie greeted the group.

The constable picked up one of the green leaflets and was about to hand it over to Maggie, asking if she was planning on attending, when a strong scent filled the air, and all heads turned in its direction. Ms. Stilton stood in the doorframe, her dotted white silk blouse highlighted by a long, beaded green necklace. She clapped her hands in delight.

"I see you have already found my leaflets. I do hope you'll come. I'm keen on explaining to the community how we will all benefit from it and how each person can contribute to making our village greener. Recycling will be the second topic. I'm eager to hear your opinion on how to make it easier to meet our recycling target and reduce the garbage thrown on the roads. I believe in involving everyone in the decision, you will be committed to it, and we can be a showcase to other communities."

Constable Gupta hadn't anticipated the mayor would have taken centre stage with her monologue. He had lost all his self-assurance, and even his uniform didn't help as it had in the past. She reminded him of someone who had this effect on him, but who? He stood there, motionless, his mouth slightly agape, the green pamphlet about to fall out from his hand, until he was saved by Maggie.

She seized the pamphlet from him as it slowly slipped from his fingers. "I'm interested in recycling and how to reduce the garbage thrown on the roads at least. It's really needed. Are you considering fines for littering and putting the police in charge of enforcing it, like in BC?"

Ms. Stilton played with her necklace, rolling the beads around her index finger. "That's an idea. There're a number of possibilities, and I'll be there to listen to suggestions at the meeting. If you attend, you'll hear about it."

Ms. Stilton turned to the constable, who had just remembered who she reminded him of—a pair of round glasses was all that was missing to be a copy of his math teacher, his nightmare! Knowing whom she looked like didn't help him. As if he had done something wrong again, he looked down at his shoes when she addressed him.

"And Constable Raj Gupta, I hope you'll be joining us too."

The constable lifted his eyes to meet hers. "Yes, if I'm not on duty."

"I hope you're all taken care of," said the mayor, hinting to her clerks.

Sandra replied, "Actually he wanted to see you, Ms. Stilton."

"Oh, why's that?"

"Ma'am, Ms. Stilton, I'm here on a police matter. I believe you know why," whispered the constable, rubbing his palms against the side of his trousers.

"Oh yes, about the disappearance of Peter Wigmott and what happened on that Christmas dinner evening. I expected the sergeant, not you." She looked at him from head to toe. "You don't need to whisper. I've nothing to hide from my colleagues nor from...?" Ms. Stilton turned toward Maggie.

"Maggie Flanagan. I can come back later." Maggie turned away as if she were about to leave.

"No need to go. As I said, I have nothing to hide. So what do you want to know, Constable Raj Gupta?"

The constable regained a little composure now that he felt supported by Maggie's presence. He straightened his back and in a clear voice said, "As you wish, ma'am. Where were you between 5:00 p.m. the night of the Christmas dinner till 9:00 a.m. the following morning?"

"I was at the party. I arrived, let me see, at six, and then—well, as Sergeant Humphries, if he'd been here now as he said he'd be, might recall—I was at the party all evening. I even spoke to him. I think I must have left around midnight, and then I went home like everyone else." She waited a little moment and added, "And yes, I did speak with Peter Wigmott at the party. Who didn't speak with him?" She laughed. "He made sure he talked to everyone that evening, as always, even to Leon LeBreton, even though he disagreed with his solar panel project. That's all. I'm afraid I can't help you any further."

Maggie asked, "Yes, but after midnight?"

The mayor stared at Maggie as if she had been insulted. Although the constable was taken by surprise by her remark, he had a soft side for her, and his male protective instinct took over. "She's right, yes, were you alone at home? Had anyone seen you go home or could witness that you were there the rest of the night?"

Ms. Stilton seemed to change her stance and became defensive. "I don't have a bodyguard, if that's what you're asking, nor am I married any longer, nor do I have a boyfriend, okay? I was on my own. No one saw me, like half the village who was at the Christmas party, going to bed."

Her tone pierced the constable's ears. He felt the humid tickle from the sweat forming on his forehead. She had to be hiding something; he had to question her to find out what it was. Why react like that? He pulled himself together, while still not in control of his voice, which he could hear had a slight crackle in it as he asked, "Did you notice anything particular that evening with Peter Wigmott? Was he behaving in a strange way or anyone interacting with him in a strange way? Did you have an argument with him?"

"No, I didn't. Why would I anyway? He seemed a little upset after speaking with Leon LeBreton, which is unusual for him. Peter normally doesn't display his emotions in public. Now, is that all? I'm very busy. Can I go now?"

"Yes, but we might have more questions for you," replied the constable, having regained his composure.

Ms. Stilton didn't linger and disappeared from the room, leaving behind her a cloud of perfume particles. Raj's eyes fell on a notice posted against the counter. *No perfume allowed please, this is a public space.* He was about to jokingly comment that the mayor might not be aware of it but decided it would be inappropriate.

For the first time he noticed dimples dancing on Maggie's cheeks as she spoke with the clerks. He was thinking of his wife and how to make them meet.

Maggie interrupted his train of thought as she came up to him and in a low voice said, "Strange, don't you think, she pretends not to know him but talked about him as if she knew him well."

"Not sure I get you? Who?"

Maggie whispered, out of hearing distance from the clerks. "Ms. Stilton, about Peter Wigmott." Then added quickly in a normal voice, "Has the sergeant had time to look into what I brought him?"

The constable understood straight away that she was talking about the hat. "Yes, I've even dealt with it myself, sent it out, but we doubt anything useful will come out of it." He raised his hand to his mouth and stamped his foot. He had forgotten to ask Ms. Stilton if she had lost a hat.

"Is everything all right?" Maggie put her hand on his arm with a concerned look in her green eyes.

"No, nothing, thank you. I've got to rush."

The constable walked out briskly, leaving Maggie behind with the two clerks. Maggie casually chatted with them about how the garbage system worked and the lack of pickup service, which in her view was a good thing, as it forced people to see for themselves how much waste was produced when they visited the dump. Maggie moved on to the mayor and her role in the solar panel project. Both clerks shifted in their chairs, looking uneasy about the topic and glancing at each other.

This was enough for Maggie to sense that contrary to what Leon LeBreton had proclaimed to her, the project might not have received all the green lights. Ms. Stilton's backing might not be sufficient, hence the upcoming event hosted by her. She felt there was more to the project than met the eye, and it might have something to do with Peter Wigmott's death. She would have to speak with Leon LeBreton again and find a way to corner him into telling her the truth, not an easy task with such a slippery fish.

Chapter Twenty-One

It was a beautiful day, and Maggie looked up at the sky, trying to spot the little propeller plane she could hear. She promised herself to properly learn how to fly, and perhaps she could help Adam with his wildlife tracking from the air.

Having left the municipal building, Maggie walked along the sidewalk, past the garage and Danillies ice cream parlour. Her eyes still scanning the sky, she bumped into Fred Wigmott and stopped short as he said, "Hey, look where you're going!"

Maggie could smell the reek of smoke on his clothing and stepped back to look at him. He was unshaven, his hair ruffed up, a thick padded shirt hastily buttoned, his jeans folded into accordions toward his ankles, and a hollow look in his eyes, as if he were looking through her.

This is a very different man from when I first met him. Of course, his brother's death must've shaken him and yet...his anger and roughness seem out of character. A cigarette was nestled in-between his bony fingers. This might be her opportunity to get his DNA sample, if only she could get hold of one of his smoked cigarettes. His hand trembled as he lifted his cigarette to his mouth, but his nails weren't yellow, the sign of a heavy smoker. Was he in disguise? She even doubted it was him until he spoke to her.

"Oh, it's you, Ms. Flanagan, sorry."

"It's me. I wasn't looking where I was going! Are you okay? You look troubled."

He threw his cigarette away and said, "Yes, fine, just all the stories about my brother, you know, and now this realtor."

Maggie didn't want to interrupt him, hoping to hear more regarding Fiona, the possibility of the two deaths being linked having crossed her mind.

"If you ask me, there's something fishy about this Quebecker solar man." Fred looked around as if he were checking whether anyone was listening but overlooking Barrie behind him, standing in front of his garage, wiping his hands. Maggie mimicked Fred's body language, coming closer to him.

Fred cleared his throat. "He can't be trusted. My brother didn't like him. I heard LeBreton'd be broke without the municipal solar panel deal he worked out with the new mayor. I wouldn't be surprised to hear he was involved in my brother's death. He could've cut the cable and caused the accident. I'm sure him and the realtor…" He intertwined two fingers while looking around constantly.

Fred stopped short, seeing Barrie, who had stepped closer as if he wanted to catch more of his words and now turned around, scratching his head and pretending to pick up a paper from the pavement.

Fred changed the topic, pulling out from his jacket a quote for the work to be done at Maggie's house. "I was going to email you this. Take a look. Let me know what you think. I've got to go."

Maggie was still digesting his words, and her mind raced, thinking about Leon and Fiona as he disappeared as quickly as she had seen him. Barrie startled Maggie out of her reverie when he nudged her gently.

"Hey, Maggie! Good to see you! It's been a while…but I can still recognize you."

Maggie smiled, taking in the image of the young man. Barrie still had in his eyes a glimmer of the young boy she knew, despite his beard and broad, stocky figure. Barrie laughed and enveloped her in a strong, friendly embrace.

"Barrie, gee…you've…" She was about to say he'd grown, but feeling it might not be what he wanted to hear, she finished with, "done well for yourself, taking over your dad's garage. I heard you're a great mechanic! You always liked your cars...and playing the bassoon, right?" She looked up at the garage and back at him with smile, remembering the little boy with a huge bassoon wrapped around him like a boa.

"Yup...still like both. I heard you're the new photographer in town. I could do with some car pics to decorate this place a bit..." Barrie swung his arm back toward his garage. Without giving her time to reply, he added, "And what's all this about finding bodies? You really should be careful."

"What do you mean?"

"For one, not sure what's your business with Fred Wigmott, but he's not to be trusted."

Worried by Barrie's serious look, Maggie asked, "What makes you say that? If I were to listen to the gossip, no one would be trustworthy in Foxton! I can say the same of Leon LeBreton. I don't trust him for one second."

"You might be right."

Maggie looked at the street from his vantage point, perfectly positioned to have an overview of the village's main street. "I heard you know what's going on in the village."

Barrie looked at her, seeming clueless.

She spread her hand out toward the street with a sweeping gesture. "You must see a lot from here."

"When I'm not working, not that there's much happening, though—well, until you came back...and you're the one finding things!" Barrie laughed.

Hoping Barrie might have witnessed interactions between the villagers, she asked, "Have you seen Leon LeBreton and Fiona together? Like lovers?"

"Oh that, old news. They didn't show it openly, but only that fool Leon thinks no one knows about it. Fiona always bragged about her conquests. At first it was Peter, and then it was the pharmacist, and now Leon. She even approached me! Pretty woman, but I don't go for married women, too complicated." Barrie stared at Maggie, then added, "You're not married, are you?"

Maggie felt a little awkward because she still saw Barrie as the little boy surrounded by toy cars. But how much a boy could change. A real teddy bear figure with his thick brown beard, warm brown eyes, stocky build, and friendly smile, he must attract many hugs. She avoided his question by asking, "Really, was it serious between them? Between Leon and Fiona?"

"I guess so. Fiona talked about divorce just the other day."

"Somehow I think the police aren't aware of it. Surely it could be relevant to her death. Don't you think?"

"You mean Humphries? He's blind to that kind of thing until you put his nose in it. A link, you say...killing the lovers, mmm..." Barrie scratched his beard loudly.

"You think either Leon or Fiona's husband could've killed both Peter Wigmott and Fiona, but that'd only make sense if they were still together, no?"

"I've got no idea. Don't listen to me. So Adam said you wanted to show me something?"

"If you've got time? Or am I interrupting your street gossip scan?" said Maggie, looking at a group of people walking by.

"No, I can do two things at once!"

Maggie laughed at the naughty twinkle in his eyes. She could see why Adam would get along with him. He had certainly turned into a likeable young man. They must joke a lot. Pulling a photo from her pocket, she said, "I just want to show you a picture and a piece of metal I found. Did you see any bumps or markings on the snowmobile when you looked at it?"

Barrie thought for a brief moment, his head turned toward his garage as if he were reviewing the snowmobile, then looked at her. "Only a few scratches, and the seat was damaged, not a surprise there; it spent a long time in the water and ice."

"And those scratches, what do you think caused them?" Maggie pointed to the blown-up image of the scratches on the snowmobile.

"Branches, anything really. I gotta admit I didn't pay a lot of attention to them once I'd seen the brake cable had been cut."

Standing closer to him, Maggie could smell the oil and diesel fumes that impregnated his overalls as he looked over her shoulder at the photograph. She pointed at the corner of the picture. "You see, there, on the right side, the marks."

Picking up the photo with his rough, cracked hand, washed too many times, he rubbed his chin with the other. "Paint scratches, mmm. What you'd see when a vehicle grazes another. The other car or whatever it was must now have red paint on it."

"I don't get it, why?"

"Because this doesn't seem to have any paint. The silver you see is the undercoating of the paint. So the red paint must have gone somewhere..."

"And what do you think this is?" Maggie pulled out of her pocket the small metal piece she had found near the road next to the beaver dam.

Barrie looked at it, turning it around between his fingers, puzzled. "Not sure, it looks like aluminum or chrome. Could be part of a bumper. Would have to take a closer look at it and compare it to pieces in my workshop. Can I keep it?" He flipped the piece up in the air like a coin and made it disappear by holding his pocket open to receive it.

"Yes, but don't lose it. It might be evidence, who knows," warned Maggie with a smile at his trick. "Could it have caused the scratches?"

Pulling the piece out again, Barrie tried to bend the metal a little. "It's kind of flexible, so I'm not sure it could. Adam was right."

"About what?" asked Maggie, worried about what Adam might have told him about her in relation to the murders.

"You never let go...so did I get it right? You really found both bodies?"

Maggie felt the blood drop from her face. "Yes, that's why I want to understand what happened...before they suspect me." She laughed without conviction.

"You, a suspect, never!" replied Barrie with a smile.

Maggie sighed with relief, sensing he was genuine. Wanting to lighten the atmosphere, she asked, "I heard you also fix planes, is that right?"

Barrie lifted his head and took a step closer. "I love planes, sure, why?"

"My father's old plane has been idle for a long time, and I was wondering if you could take a look at it, tell me what you think, if it's safe to fly it."

"Sure! So...you fly?"

"Not yet, but I need to think about what to do with it. I'll show it to you, then. Well, you'd have to go see it really."

"No problem, anytime, just let me know! In the meantime I'll look at the metal piece, but you be careful, you hear?"

"Don't worry about me! I really appreciate your help." As she spoke, Maggie waved at Barrie and walked away down the main street.

Looking at a bunch of red tulips decorating the counter of Danillies, Maggie suddenly remembered Fiona wearing a scarf with red tulips at the wedding. She had seen a similar scarf at Mr. Bern's home. Perhaps it belonged to Fiona. She must have met Leon. There was no other reason Maggie could see for Fiona to be at the house. She felt the puzzle was coming together, and yet she couldn't tell whether the two cases were related. She wondered how Ms. Stilton might be related to Peter Wigmott.

Maggie climbed into Big Jay, thinking about the rest of her day. The murders seemed to take hold of all her time; it was impossible for her to keep her distance until she believed she could no longer be suspected and the murderer needed to be found before something else happened.

She could kill two birds with one stone: getting a website done for her photography business while finding out more about Fiona's widower, Patrick.

Maggie retreated to her study after a brief walk with Beans

and Carrot doing their best to gain all her affection. She had never encountered such smart animals as those two dogs. Every day she discovered a new trick they had come up with. Beans knew how to open doors, that was clear very early on, but she could also open cupboards and access whatever she wanted. The surprising aspect was that Beans didn't leave the doors open as other dogs would do. Items went missing from the cupboards, without a hole in them for a mouse to slip through.

One morning Maggie saw Beans very carefully clasping the knob of the door between her teeth and backing slowly away, one paw behind the other, opening the door. Beans then poked her head in the cupboard, sniffing at the items, and not finding anything edible, walked behind the door and pushed it shut with her nose. Meanwhile, Carrot sat at the other end of the kitchen, watching her, and whimpered as soon as Maggie stood behind her, as if warning her friend of the danger. Sure enough, Beans turned around to face Maggie, her tail wagging as she jumped onto one of her toys as a decoy.

Maggie could only feel admiration for the little dog. She decided to ignore the deed and placed locks on the doors she didn't want Beans to access, leaving others open now and then with a treat. Perhaps Beans was a guide dog.

Maggie sat at her computer to interact with the web developer, and instead had the urge to do a quick Internet search on Ms. Stilton. She found the mayor had been to university with Peter Wigmott.

Using Google photo search, Maggie marvelled at the software recognitions tools at hand. There on her screen was what looked like a party photo from the eighties. Ms. Stilton stood to the right, Peter Wigmott in the centre, and to the left, hiding under a mat of hair, a pair of high-waisted jeans and loud shirt stood a man.

The man had to be Fred; the hair was different but the figure was the same. The mayor was grinning, in very high-heeled pink shoes matching the colour of her painted nails and necklace. Ms. Stilton had a nice smile and had been slim then, with the typical perm of the time, looking very confident. Peter Wigmott looked proud with his arm around her shoulder, his hand dangling down. Attracted by the shine on his finger, Maggie saw what resembled the ring Fred had been playing with. Perhaps a university ring. With a similar large letter A. The mayor was wearing one too on the picture. It must be a graduation party picture.

She printed the photograph, intending to show it to Ms. Stilton. This would explain why she seemed to know Peter's habits. Had the mayor been his girlfriend? It was hard to tell from the photograph—both men seemed to lean toward her. Maybe she would first show it to Adam before confronting the mayor.

She suppressed her urge to see Adam straight away. She had to build her photography business and really needed a website. She already had an idea of what she wanted it to look like. It was just a matter of outlining it to Patrick McLenny.

Could he have killed his wife? It was in any case hard to fathom; it could have been premeditated. Both his son and father appeared to suffer from the loss.

Maggie wanted to trigger a visit to Patrick's place, and for that she wanted to sound very keen and perhaps a little naïve, ready to spend a lot of money on the website. It had to be a big enough hook for him to come out of his current state of mourning. She told herself that her prime motive was for business; he had all the credentials she was looking for and was the only one local for the job. She would tread carefully when asking personal questions; she didn't want to arouse any suspicion on his side.

The email sent, Maggie felt energized and ready to test her dream of flying. Nothing would stop her today. Perhaps it was the wonderful spring day, the goldfinches and pine siskin chirping outside her window, tucking into her freshly topped-up bird feeder, that filled her with vigour, or was it her two new friends poking her to go out and play in the garden, eager to distract her from the screen?

The decision was made: she would visit the local airfield to take a look at the state of the little plane her father had left her, and perhaps investigate learning how to fly.

Chapter Twenty-Two

To her surprise, Maggie heard a calm, melodious, familiar voice behind her as she poked her head through the hangar doors where the planes were neatly lined up.

"Can I help you?"

She turned around and recognized the Reverend John Smithers from the wedding. For some reason, when the reverend explained to her that he was the local flying instructor, she couldn't believe her ears. At the same time, she could see he would be good at it: a relaxed, reassuring, and cheerful person. He might also have the added benefit of a good understanding of character, given his ministering role to listen and advise his flock.

They walked around Maggie's father's yellow Cessna, John pointing out a few things that needed to be repaired before the plane would be safe to fly.

"You seem worried. It looks like a big job, but it isn't really. It's a very good little plane."

"I don't know if it's worth it. I liked flying with my father, but I'd have to learn, and I'm not sure it can ever be repaired to the standards of today's regulations so that I can learn to fly in it."

"Look, why not just come with me for a test flight? It's the perfect day. You'll decide afterwards what you want to do. Besides, the plane isn't in the way here."

Maggie felt joy overwhelming her, but then, concerned, she said, "But Reverend, in that case I must pay you for the flight, the fuel, I mean it's quite something, not like going for a spin in a car."

"Call me John. There's no charge for an introduction. Besides, I was heading out myself anyway. I've got to keep my mileage up to keep my instructor level. Look over there, that's my plane." He pointed to a little red-and-white propeller plane gleaming in the sun on the tarmac in front of the hangar. "It's a two-seater, so really if you want to test if you want to fly, come along! And I see you have your camera, perfect."

John suggested they fly over her property so she could take pictures of it.

Excitedly she replied, "Okay then, I can't refuse. I've got to start somewhere."

John's passion for flying, just like her father had, transpired in the way he spoke about his plane, with respect, as if it were alive. He had taken good care of it; it looked new, while it was from the seventies. He explained her what he was doing, the commands and a bit about how to navigate. It was all coming back to her; she had learned a great deal just by sitting next to her father and continually asking questions, as she always used to.

"Good. We're at cruising altitude now. Take a look around, you see the cell phone towers. Those are important to avoid crashing into and memorize as beacons. Take hold of the command for me. I just want to write something down."

Maggie grabbed the yoke with both hands, holding it steady, her eyes glued to the horizon gauge.

"Good, now just feel it, pull toward you...that's it, but not too much. We don't want to end up in a spin!"

"I can feel it, as if the wings were an extension of myself. Dad let me do that sometimes. I love it!"

John explained that he alternated between planes with floaters to land on water and ones with wheels to keep the reflexes fresh for each. He also mentioned skis and landing on frozen lakes and even up rivers. Intrigued by his skills, Maggie questioned him on his story and how he ended up flying.

Before becoming a reverend, John had been a bush pilot in British Columbia, bringing equipment to remote locations and for rescue operations. He loved Beaver planes and explained how on one of his survival bush flying lessons, his instructor had patiently guided him through numerous landings on lakes and even on rivers, telling him what to do when he hesitated. It went very smoothly, and he felt pleased with himself, planning to return to the airport as usual when his instructor said that the session wasn't over yet.

Maggie was hooked by his story, imagining what it must feel like to land up a river; it seemed an impossible feat to her. She didn't want him to stop and said, "And what happened then?"

"He asked me to fly high, higher than we are now, and cruise a little, then he'd help me with the landing, but instead..." John suddenly opened his door.

Maggie gasped and sighed, "You scared me, but I know it's not an issue. Even my dad flew without doors." She was keen to appear courageous and up to becoming a pilot.

"Yes, well, I was scared that day when my instructor did the same thing."

"Why? It's not dangerous since there's no pressure issue with a Beaver plane, just like this one, and you must have both had your seatbelts on?"

"I did, but I hadn't seen what he was wearing. I must have been too excited with the whole experience. Anyway, he had a parachute!"

"What?" She checked if John was wearing a parachute, and in doing so she inadvertently pushed the yoke away from her, and the plane dove suddenly.

"Be careful, steady now...level it again," John said calmly.

Maggie corrected herself, steadying the plane, focused entirely on the task, while John, his hands on the commands, was ready to take over any moment. Releasing his grip, his hands now on his lap, he said, "Good, you caught up well, but you shouldn't have such brusque reactions. You'll learn."

Maggie nodded, feeling her cheeks warmed by the emotion. He

waited till the plane was again cruising at the desired altitude before continuing. "Before I could say anything, the instructor informed me that this was it, my first solo trip in the bush."

"But how can that be?"

"I'll always remember his words: 'You're ready, John, you no longer need me. Have a good flight!' And then I only saw his back with the parachute and then an empty seat next to me."

"That's crazy! How did you react? Your first solo flight is already a big thing."

"I expected my first solo flight and knew they had the habit of not warning you ahead when it would be, but never with him jumping out of the plane! I had to sing to relax." He started to whistle, taking over the commands from her.

Maggie stared at him and whispered, still holding on to the yoke, "No way to escape! Exciting but hard to know how one would react. Just the thought of a solo flight would be enough for me to sing, and that'd be on the tarmac where I could always back out... but this...do you practice the same teaching?"

John laughed, throwing his head back. "No, don't worry. I won't jump out of the plane! At the time I had asked my instructor to land on a river to see what it felt like and see if I'd be cut out for what I wanted to do. I wanted the experience before going solo, for my own sake, as a reassurance. I think he thought I might have been a daredevil who needed to be cooled off a little. Before you can learn how to land on a river, you have to have many hours flying. It is a long course to become a bush pilot. Lots of extreme situations are explored."

"A bush pilot, a dream, to fly in Africa and see the wildlife..." Maggie imagined herself for a moment at the helm of her father's plane on a photo expedition.

"If you're up for it I've got the qualifications to train you all the way, but I don't approve of the extreme teaching I got. It'd be safe."

Maggie looked at the dials on the dashboard, dreaming of adventure, and in the spur of the moment she replied, "Yes, I'd like it, my father would have loved that."

"Your name is Flanagan, right?"

Maggie nodded.

"I remember a Mr. Flanagan on the logbooks here. I knew the yellow plane was his; I even dusted it the other day, hoping to see it fly again."

They remained silent for a long while. Maggie looked out of the window and noticed the familiar shape of the hexagonal log building of Moose lodge. She followed Lake View Road and spotted her house along Otter Lake and behind it her woods and the beaver dam. She asked John for a flyby so she could take pictures.

He flew low, following the road, and made a 180-degree turn, allowing her a better look at her house. Maggie pointed down, asking him to do another flyover, since she had spotted what seemed to be tire marks on the road running diagonally on the right side of the road and on the left side toward the beaver dam.

It was strange not having noticed any when she walked there, and the police clearly hadn't seen anything either. From above Maggie could clearly see a pattern, although it wasn't well defined, as if a car had driven across from the right to the left toward the beaver dam, making a U-turn there, a dangerous manoeuvre whether in a curve or driving across.

"Got it, thanks."

"We're heading back now, all right?"

"Of course, you're the pilot." Maggie laughed, enjoying every bit of the trip.

He turned the plane in the direction of the airport and pointed out the different cell phone towers as reference points and the horizon, both on the instruments and ahead.

"I won't let you land. It's the hardest part, and I am expected alive and kicking at the service on Sunday." John winked at her.

The flight was over before Maggie could come to grips with what she had done. It felt so easy, so natural to her. She was eager to start her flying apprenticeship as soon as possible.

Feeling lightheaded from the excitement, she headed back home to savour her experience by viewing the pictures. There in the middle of her emails a response from Patrick popped out.

The hook had worked; he seemed interested in discussing her project. Although Maggie was curious to visit him at his place, and seeing someone's home could give her clues, she felt it appropriate to have him come to her home, thinking he might need to be away from the house he had shared with Fiona. To quell her apprehension at being alone with Patrick, still a possible suspect, she would let him know that Adam was aware of her visit.

The following day would be perfect. Maggie busied herself with preparing for the meeting all evening, identifying websites she liked, only interrupted by Carrot and Beans chasing each other around and hiding under her desk.

Chapter Twenty-Three

For the first time, Damien cooked dinner for his father. They had never spent an evening together, just the two of them. Sadly, it had to be the dreadful loss of Fiona that brought them together. He wasn't prepared for his father's undivided attention. He might have longed for it but had gotten used to living without it. He was uncomfortable with his father staring at him, trying to read him without knowing what to say. He started to feel desperate for a diversion when he heard the ping of a new email coming in on his father's computer.

"Dad, you've got mail."

"It can wait. It's not as important as us now."

"But Dad, maybe it is. I can look!"

Damien hoped there would be something to spur him out of his gloom. He knew how much his father enjoyed his work, and for once he thought he would welcome a new project for him. In the past he had hated when his dad seemed never to have time for him; work, always work came first, but now it might be the solution.

Damien couldn't have hoped for a better distraction when he clicked on it: an email from Maggie. He liked her for some reason, felt he could trust her and that she was on his side. It took some convincing to make his father read the email and then respond reluctantly when he said, "Do it for me, Dad. I think she's a nice person, and it might be a fun project. You need a distraction."

"But I thought of taking time off to be with you."

"That's a nice thought, but I'm busy too. Besides, you can always ask me if you need my help for it. I'd find it fun to work with you on a website."

As they sat back in their recliner armchairs, with bottles of beer in their hands, having responded to the email, another ping sounded from the computer. Damien jumped up, as if expelled by the chair. It was a reply from Maggie, just what he had hoped for to pull his father out of his gloom. Nothing like having him focus on work, like he always did.

*

The next morning, Maggie was playing with Carrot and Beans in her backyard when Patrick pulled up. The dogs barked at the car as he slowly brought the window down to speak with her.

"They're all right, you should be okay." A little puzzled by his pale face, she whisked the pair away from him. "I'll put them away."

As he shook her hand and stroked his shaven chin, it dawned on her that his beard was missing; it can alter a man's face tremendously, perhaps a sign of desire for change.

Patrick seemed shy, not daring to look at her in the eyes, clutching his computer bag awkwardly, although they had met before at the wedding party. Maggie had prepared scones with jam and tea, hoping to ease the atmosphere.

Maggie could tell Patrick wasn't used to face-to-face meetings. He waited for her to ask questions and make conversation, otherwise not uttering a word. Sitting next to her on her couch, a little colour appeared in his cheeks as he sipped his tea with a mouth full of scones, clicking through websites he had made.

Perhaps he was simply hungry and hadn't cooked for himself. A sliver of jam dripped onto her keyboard. Flustered, Patrick dug into his pocket for a tissue, and with it a ring fell out onto the floor, rolling under the couch. Maggie dove down on all fours to retrieve it while Patrick noisily attempted to clean the keyboard.

Pulling a large ring from behind the sofa skirt, she recognized it straight away. It was the same chunky ring with an A she had seen Fred Wigmott playing with. Pushing herself back up with one hand on the couch, still kneeling on one leg, she held up the ring between her index finger and thumb and looked at Patrick straight in the eyes to capture his reaction.

"Patrick, you dropped this." She noticed his hand fidget when she evaluated his finger size quickly. His left eye twitched as she asked, "A bit small for you?"

"I found it in my wife's things. I've never seen it before. Probably given to her by one of her—"

Maggie interrupted him, noticing the bitterness in his tone. "Doesn't look like that sort of ring, more like a college ring. I've seen a bigger version elsewhere, on Wig—" She stopped short when she saw Patrick turn red and hold his fist tight. Afraid that he'd get angry with her—and who knew what he was capable of?—she softly said, "I'm sorry. I didn't mean to pry. It must be hard for you."

Patrick seemed to soften, like a child reassured by his mother.

"It's okay, it's just the name Wigmott. I can't stand him. All his fault."

The affair between Fiona and a Wigmott brother might be the missing link between the two cases Maggie was looking for. Fascinated by the ring she had just handed back to Patrick, Maggie remembered where she had seen it another time: the photograph, on the mayor, and on Peter Wigmott, not on his brother.

"Could it be?" she muttered.

Patrick looked at her. "What?"

"An idea, sorry, I should explain. I'm interested in what happened to your wife. It's just that I found her and can't get her image out of my mind. Her death is a mystery."

"Yes, it sure is. If only I could get hold of who did it!"

"Did your wife know the mayor, Ms. Stilton?"

"No, not more than I do, just by name. Fiona never spoke about her, but she didn't tell me everything, and I wasn't very receptive anyway." Patrick sighed.

"But she knew Fred Wigmott?" Maggie hesitated with her question, fearing she might upset him again, but she wanted to confirm the relationship.

"Fred Wigmott? No, his brother Peter Wigmott, the one who died."

"I see." Maggie couldn't help staring at him, wondering if he could have killed Peter.

"Fiona had nothing to do with his death, I'm sure. Or me, before you get any ideas. And it was years ago!" he exclaimed.

"I'm not suggesting anything, I just—well, Fred Wigmott had the same ring, you see."

Patrick looked puzzled, not understanding her. She asked, "Do you mind if I take a picture of the ring? It might be useful to find out who killed Fiona."

"You can have it. I don't want anything to do with it, especially if it has something to do with Peter Wigmott!" He threw the ring back at her with a disgusted look.

Maggie felt unsure; on the one hand she wanted to keep the ring, but on the other she might be getting into trouble by taking it. She put it on the table so he could pick it up if he wanted. "So Peter was, errr, her…"

Patrick nodded, looking away from her and picking up the computer. Maggie felt it would neither be wise nor considerate to try to get more information out of him. She still hung on to the belief he wasn't responsible for his wife's death, although a question remained for Peter Wigmott's death. She somehow had to confront Ms. Stilton with her relationship with Peter Wigmott.

She followed Patrick's gaze to a series of little bags lined up on her desk with names on them. She had forgotten to put away the bags ready to receive the DNA samples she planned to collect and give to Amy—if she would test them. Maggie still hadn't spoken to her. She quickly said, afraid he'd ask about them, "Oh, those are milkweed seeds I was planning on giving to cottagers who want more monarch butterflies to visit their garden."

She piled them up, hoping he hadn't spotted his name on one of them. With his thick glasses hopefully he would not have been able to read her writing from that distance. She had to divert his focus just in case.

"I'm sorry, I mustn't bother you with my questions, and I should be trying to make you think of other things! I met your son, Damien, a nice young man. I hope you're spending time together."

Patrick's frown disappeared, and his face softened. "Yes, he is, and I try to. He sent me here, though, when I wanted to spend the day with him." He nodded as if he didn't understand the reason.

If Damien sent him, he must have been trying to cheer his dad up, which meant that her asking for a website was a good idea after all. She was relieved that her email had been taken the intended way. She liked Damien. She felt he was a genuine and kind person. Keen to appear enthusiastic about him to his father, she said, "Really, that's nice of him!"

"Would you be okay if he'd also work on the website? He's good at design."

"Sure, and I imagine it'll be fun for you to work together. I'm impressed by the selection of sites you sent me. Did Damien also work on those?"

"No, but he's really good, you'll see."

Seeing a smile on his face for the first time, she added, "When can you start, and what do you need from me for it?"

"Right away, I think you've told me all I need for now. I'll get Damien to contact you for the design."

"Great, we have a deal!"

Maggie heard a commotion outside; her dogs were barking at something. This was the perfect interruption to usher Patrick out. She felt excited by her findings.

The thrush singing melodiously from the top of the spruce tree seemed to send a message to her. "You need a walk to clear your mind, listen to the birds, they will sort things out for you." She could always use as an excuse that the dogs needed it, but in reality, she needed to be in nature to relax and put perspective into her thoughts. Her heartbeat slowed down, and her ideas drifted and reorganized themselves on their own as she walked, looking around at the new buds on the maple trees.

There it was, the entire chain of events. It all fitted together, but how to prove it was another story...

Chapter Twenty-Four

Leon LeBreton felt cornered. His anxiety was gnawing at him. He had to confide in someone, share his burden. Once again he thought of telling Joe about the scarf, in his mind the only person aware of his relationship with Fiona and therefore the only option. He could tell him he had been foolish to retrieve the tulip scarf. He couldn't tell him about the letter; Joe might jump to conclusions, already having accused him once of her murder. Before he could implement anything, Leon heard a knock on the front door.

"Police. We need to talk."

Sergeant Humphries's voice hit Leon like a blast and urged him to run away from it. In a panic, he looked around the room at the nearest escape and raced to the window, lifted the double-paned window and slipped out. In the rush, he hadn't taken into account Constable Gupta, who had been walking around the house to see if there was another entrance.

Leon bumped into the constable and froze on the spot. Overwhelming fear made him feel cold. How could he explain his behaviour? Constable Gupta looked behind him as if he were looking for someone chasing him. Leon was unable to utter a word. Sergeant Humphries ran with difficulty toward them and stopped, out of breath, looking around.

"Nothing the matter, no one is chasing him. Not sure why he is in such a state," said Constable Gupta, his hands on his belt, still standing in front of Leon.

Leon followed the sergeant's eyes as he scanned the area and fell upon the open window he had just gone through. The sergeant walked up to it and knelt down, pointing to a large footprint at the bottom of the wall in the soft soil.

"Now, what do we have here? A big footprint…" As he said those words, he stood up and walked toward Leon.

Leon was desperately thinking of a reason to explain his behaviour when Sergeant Humphries confronted him, lifting his trousers as far as they could go under his belly. He spread his legs to steady himself and tilted his head backward.

"Why were you running away from us?"

Leon looked down without responding.

"I'm asking you again, why were you running away from us?"

Leon mustered what was left of his courage to hide his emotions. "Why are you here?" He knew the best defence when under attack could be a counterattack. This time, however, it didn't seem to work as the sergeant's moustache trembled at its sides, just before he thundered in his ear.

"Why did you withhold important information from us relating to Ms. Fiona McLenny? You knew her better than you let us believe…"

Exhausted from holding back his secret, he feared it was too late; they must have found out about the scarf. It had to be the reason for their presence. Leon broke down in tears.

"I panicked. I only wanted to pick her scarf up as a memento. You see, I gave it to her. I wasn't thinking straight, I was drunk when I broke into Mr. Bern's house after you'd cordoned it off."

Leon was confused by the surprised look on the sergeant's face. Had he spoken too soon? They didn't know about the scarf, that was it. He felt miserable and betrayed by his own fear.

Sergeant Humphries replied, "I knew it! You returned to the crime scene to retrieve evidence. Why else would anyone in his right mind break into a crime scene?"

"But I didn't do it, I just…"

Before the sobbing Leon could say anything else, Sergeant Humphries announced, "Leon LeBreton, I'm arresting you on suspicion of the murder of Ms. Fiona McLenny and breaking into police investigation grounds, thereby attempting to deviate the course of justice." Flicking open his little black notebook, the sergeant read the charter of rights. "It is my duty to inform you that you have the right to retain and instruct counsel without delay. Do you understand?" Leon nodded, a large knot in his throat building up. The sergeant continued with his reading. "You are charged with breaking into a crime scene. Do you wish to say anything in answer to the charge? You are not obliged to say anything unless you wish to do so, but whatever you say may be given in evidence."

He gestured to Constable Gupta, who stood a few metres away with his jaw agape. The constable seemed to pull himself together and approached Leon, who was now wailing like a child.

"I didn't do it. Yes, she was my mistress, I loved her, I couldn't have killed her ..."

Leon's voice disappeared into the car, his head pushed down softly by the constable into the back seat. The police car sped off toward the station.

*

Back from her walk, Maggie tried calling Amy at work, hoping to have her view on the situation and of course ask her about the DNA sample. The phone rang for a long time without an answer. Maggie sat back in her armchair, and then hitting the armrests with both hands, she stood up, thinking of Adam. It's so easy to talk with him. She stopped for a moment to consider her idea. He won't mind, I hope... She used to talk daily to people in her former life in the city and even had longed for a time when she didn't have to do that. Now she smiled, looking forward to sharing thoughts.

When Maggie arrived at Adam's farm, she was happy to see his broad smile framed by the pair of llamas as they enjoyed a stereo rub. He waved to her to come over.

"Hey, Maggie, nice surprise. Look, if I cuddle one, the other gets jealous." Adam pointed with his chin to each llama, both appearing to enjoy thoroughly a scratch behind the ear. "This is the best way to keep everyone happy. You can help me if you like and scratch Harry. He'll love it."

Adam looked at the llama with the Beatle-style hairdo. Maggie walked up to the biggest llama, pushing her curls away from her eyes. As she approached, Harry sniffed her hair.

"It's not hay, Harry!" She laughed, pushing his head gently away and reaching up to scratch behind his ear. "What's her name then, it is a she?" She pointed to the other llama, who had a white curly bonnet of hair around her head, as if she were a cross between a sheep and a llama.

"Sally."

Maggie looked at Sally and laughed. "Yes, it fits her, why did you call her Sally?"

"Sally rhymes with Harry… What brings you this way? No more murders, I hope?"

"No, not as far as I know, but maybe some clues."

"Glad to hear that, and don't think I'm not working. You always seem to catch me at home. I've some reports to write for the wolf study, which I prefer writing when I'm not in the office. But I was taking a break, perfect timing! Want a cuppa?"

"Yes, that'd be nice. Mmm, they all say that, just working from home eh?" joked Maggie as she followed him inside the house.

As he prepared the tea, she walked around the kitchen, looking at the photographs on the walls and down at a black-and-white picture of a man in full aviator outfit standing next to a silver plane from the fifties. The fuselage looked very similar to the Airstream trailer she had seen at the mayor's home, not as polished, though. "Who is he? Nice plane!"

"Uncle Elliot. Yes, he was a pilot and a real good one, a bush pilot out in the Australian outback. He became a pilot during the war, and then he went on to become a mail courier for small communities in Queensland. You like planes, don't you?"

"You could say that... I went for a flight with John. You know the reverend? It was great!"

"Ah yes, he sometimes helps me with animal counts."

Maggie loved the idea of tracking animals by plane and helping out with conservation. "Maybe I could do that too! Once I get my license..."

"So you're going for it. Better be careful, here she comes! In that case I know a very nice place up north next to a lake, a little cabin I have that you can only reach by plane. When can you take me there?" Adam smiled, rubbing his hands together.

Maggie chuckled. "Hold on, I still need to get the license. So seriously, you think it's a good idea?"

"Sure thing, I'll have my parachute ready!" He waited a little. Maggie felt a little offended until he added, "But I'm sure I won't need it with you at the yoke."

Maggie giggled and told him about John's parachute story. Their conversations always drifted effortlessly from one topic to the next without uneasy silences, balanced between listening to each other, commenting, asking further details, and joking. Maggie swiftly moved on to Patrick.

"I think he's innocent. Okay, he's not the best communicator, to put it mildly, but I believe him."

"Really, and why's that?" asked Adam.

"I don't think he'd be capable of it. He's shy and—"

"That's not a reason. Is he immune to jealousy and has no fits of rage?"

Maggie wondered if Adam was speaking of himself there. Could he get angry like that? "Maybe, some seemingly quiet people are like that in private, but still he has a strong alibi with his son. And Damien seems like a good person."

"Maybe. It might leave him off the hook for Fiona's death, but what about Peter then? You said Patrick hated him."

"Yes, but what if the two murders are linked? Fiona had an affair with Peter, and I think so did Stilton, or at least she knew him from her student days. Don't you think it strange she would turn up like that, and only a few months later Peter disappears?"

Adam was silent for a moment, then replied, "Supposing you're right. Patrick didn't kill Fiona, then who would benefit from her death, and why? It doesn't make any sense. Why on earth would the mayor kill her?"

Maggie excitedly replied, "Jealousy, perhaps?"

"Mm, the Fiona and Peter fling was a while back. No, I don't think so."

"A crime passionnel. Leon LeBreton could've done it. He had the means; he had the keys of the house where she died, and maybe they had met there. That would explain her scarf!"

"Yes, carry on..." said Adam, leaning forward toward Maggie as she spoke.

"Maybe she didn't want to marry him after all; Fiona only said it to get a divorce from Patrick. Leon, with his fiery temperament, might have overreacted." Maggie felt she was on to something, and speaking with Adam was helping her organize her thoughts.

Adam looked absorbed for a moment, then added, "Leon could've had a motive for the other murder: he wanted the solar panel project to happen. Without it he'd be broke. Perhaps you're right about the mayor. I don't like Leon, but I don't see him committing a murder in cold blood or cutting the brake cable."

Maggie looked at her watch; she had promised herself to speak with Amy and wanted to catch her during her lunch break.

Adam looked disappointed. "Does this mean you can't join me for lunch?"

"Sorry, I've a call I can't get out of. I'll be back, and besides, you said you had work to do! Can you do me a favour? If you see Barrie, ask him about the metal piece I gave him. All this aluminum—the plane, the Airstream—not sure, but I think there's a link. I forgot to mention, from the plane I saw strange tire tracks that can only really be seen from above. They appear to start on one side of the road on the soft shoulder pointing toward the dam. There's another pair on the other side again toward the dam. I took pictures of them."

"Not sure I get it." Adam looked at her with his eyes round like beads.

"It'll be easier to explain when you see them. I'll email them to you."

"Sounds strange. I'll ask Barrie and get on with your pilot license. I've got lots of places to go to!" Adam smiled.

Chapter Twenty-Five

With Maggie gone, Adam felt like company for lunch. His good friend Barrie was always up for a bite, and Adam could ask him about the metal piece at the same time.

Adam was glad to see Barrie taking his usual lunch break. When the weather was good, he would stand or sit on a chair outside his garage, enjoying the sun. Faithful to his habits, Barrie sat in a foldable camping chair with a large coffee nestled in one of the cup holders in the armrest. Barrie jumped to his feet, propping up a second chair he kept close by for such occasions. They both sat for a few minutes like two schoolboys, looking at the passersby chatting away, when Constable Raj Gupta walked by on his way to buy lunch, as he usually did.

The constable greeted them and was easily dragged in by the pair like a fly to a cobweb for a quick bite at the cafe, Adam having noticed an unusual smile on the constable's face, radiating a sense of contentment. Something must have happened, and he was curious.

The trio entered the cafe, which was already loud with customers sitting at the wooden tables, tucking into Heidi's famous homemade sausage on a bun, a bratwurst nestled in warm freshly baked bread, with a little sauerkraut on the side. Heidi was a very good cook, and Adam enjoyed indulging in her motherly urge to give him large portions; it allowed him to skip meals afterward. The locals affectionately nicknamed her Mutti because she always made time to enquire about their family and children and would never let them go hungry if she had a say in it.

Heidi had a soft spot for the trio. Adam and Barrie, both single, definitely needed her motherly attention and cooking, while Raj was such a sweet boy, always complimenting her on her cooking, that she could never resist them. She kept the bar stools in the corner free in case they turned up.

The three stools at the far end of the bar away from the crowd were still available, as always. Barrie and Adam sat on each side of Raj, keen to hear his story.

Although Raj endeavoured to keep quiet, he had a tendency to let the cat out of the bag when pressed kindly by his trusted friends. As he climbed onto the bar stool, his little booklet where he wrote his daily reports slipped out of his pocket, opening to the page where he had written about the arrest of Leon LeBreton.

Barrie and Adam looked at each other, and Barrie joked, "Raj, we didn't know you kept a diary. I hope you didn't write down everything I did last Saturday night!"

Raj straightened his spine. "No, my booklet wouldn't have enough pages for you, and it'll always be the same—this girl, that girl... It's my work pad, and I've got to write down what happens each day."

"Really, and who can read your horrible writing?" asked Barrie.

"The sergeant has to sign it off. He manages..."

Adam interrupted, curious to find out why Raj looked unusually excited. "Having a good day then?"

"Kind of, not for someone, but a big day for me, my first..." Raj stopped in midsentence as if he didn't dare to carry on.

"Arrest?" asked Adam. "Come on, you can tell us, we saw it written and we know who it was. What happened then?"

"I shouldn't have, but I can trust you, right?"

"Of course you can! We're friends." Barrie gave Raj a friendly bear tap on the shoulder.

Adam first, then Barrie had taken a liking to Raj when he first arrived in the village. Adam had taken Raj under his protective wing, like an older brother. He was keen for him to settle in quickly and choose to stay. He was bright but modest, was very enthusiastic, and made him laugh with his expressions. The trio alternated weekly between a night at Heidi's and enjoying Raj's wife's delicious curry at his home.

"So?" asked Adam, coming closer to him with his stool so that he would not need to speak loud.

"You know, we didn't go there to arrest him at first. It's because he ran into my arms."

"You're good-looking, but there's a limit!" exclaimed Barrie.

Raj smiled, his eyes twinkling as Adam and Barrie laughed. "He jumped out of the window, but I was walking around the house because he hadn't answered the door, and we heard noise inside. He was running away! We just wanted to get confirmation that he and you-know-who were lovers."

"We could've told you that ages ago if you'd asked—the whole village knew!" said Barrie, looking surprised.

"Oh? Anyway, what I find weird is what was in his pocket." Raj was silent for a moment, as if he wanted to keep the suspense, until Adam nudged him.

"Yes, go on..."

"Aside from some hair gel and a comb, there was a blackmail note! That's got to be proof."

"Depends what's in it, no?" asked Adam.

"It says that he was seen. Anyway, the sergeant is happy now because he thinks we've got the man and the cases will soon be closed. He even told me to get some donuts for the office."

Adam didn't like casting a shadow on Raj's happy mood, but he felt compelled to ask, "So you're saying he's responsible in both cases?"

"Yes, the first because of the solar panel project, but we still need proof."

"And the second, why would he have killed his lover?"

"Simple, because she saw him cut the brakes and she wanted to push him to confess to her. Instead he killed her."

"I see, and did Leon confess that?" asked Adam, surprised by the logic. He had certainly not considered that option.

"Hmm, no, not really, not at all in fact. He confessed he went back to the crime scene to pick up her scarf the day after her murder, and he claims he had received the blackmail letter only that day." Raj's early look of contentment had vanished and was replaced with knotted dark eyebrows. Then, as if he wanted to hang on to his own truth, he exclaimed, with a head bobble, "Murderers lie, we know that! But whatever the speed of the lie, the truth will always overtake it. The sergeant will squeeze the truth out of him. He was already crying like a baby."

Adam carefully said, "So you don't really have anything against him then. You don't know who sent him that blackmail letter, do you?"

Raj deflated like a balloon, his shoulders dropping. He murmured with sadness in his voice, "No, we don't know who sent the letter. If we don't get more out of him soon, I fear it will be a grumpy afternoon at the office. Can you take my place?"

Raj wiped his brow with his tartan handkerchief, the subject of endless teases from Barrie when he first set eyes on it, until Adam got Raj to explain it was a present from a Scottish girl when he went there for his eighteenth birthday, and overnight it became a token of appreciation in Barrie's eyes.

Adam put his hand on Raj's shoulder. "Raj, I feel sorry for you, and no thank you, I'd really not want to be in your shoes... You'd better get him another dozen donuts. Humphries should have considered it without jumping to conclusions. Having said that, who knows, maybe Leon LeBreton is the mur—" Before he could finish, he heard a high-pitched voice behind him and turned around.

"So it's true then, they arrested Leon LeBreton? They think he did it...I'm not so sure..."

Tina Partridge stood there, her coat still on, looking at the trio arrogantly. Adam hadn't seen her creep up on them. He was usually aware of his surroundings. This meant the whole village would know about Leon. If Leon were innocent, it would be a blow to his reputation. But then he wondered what Tina knew. "You seem to have your own views on the case..."

"I do, like Maggie always seems present when a body is discovered...I saw her myself."

Adam couldn't believe his ears, and yet he had also been surprised about Maggie finding Fiona. Pursed lips accentuated the nasty look of jealousy in her eyes. He had no patience for that type of behaviour; he growled at her, "Miss Gossip, I'd be careful if I were you, spreading fake news..."

Raj stood up, capsizing his barstool in the process as he interrupted Adam, his finger raised under Tina's nose. "It's a crime spreading this type of gossip! Do I have to remind you that by law everyone is innocent until proven guilty! And don't even think of telling the sergeant this."

Tina's face turned purple. "If I want to speak with the sergeant, I will!" She spun around on her heels and marched out of the cafe.

Adam whispered in Raj's ear, "Better be at the office before she gets there... Go!"

Raj pulled out his wallet. "I still have to get those...donuts...and here for the..."

Adam stopped him short, putting his hand on Raj's arm. "It's on us, mate. Just go!"

Once Raj had left the cafe, Barrie sighed. "I know what we'll be reading in the *Daily Stumble*. I hope she'll have the decency not to name anyone."

Adam and Barrie watched Raj walk away from the donut shop, where he had gone in all the same, probably more afraid of Humphries even than Tina. After all, everyone knew Maggie found the bodies, so Tina couldn't do much harm by telling the sergeant what he already knew. Sipping their coffees, Adam and Barrie stood looking out the window of the cafe when the reflection of Raj's handcuffs in the sun reminded Adam of the reason he wanted to see Barrie.

"So how did it go with Maggie?"

"What do you mean? I'm not that fast!" laughed Barrie.

"Gee, is that all that's on your mind?"

"She hasn't changed much, although I've got to admit that my memory from that time is a little fuzzy. But she seems like a fun girl—woman...and single, am I right?" Barrie raised one eyebrow at Adam. "Don't see her liking my Molson Muscle somehow. But a weathered man like you..." Barrie stroked his beer belly, accentuating it by thrusting his hips forward.

"Barrie, come on..." Not wanting to carry on discussing Maggie from that perspective, perhaps because he had a growing soft side for her, Adam said, "What about the piece of metal, did you find anything?"

"It's aluminum. Could be a piece of a plane fuselage, but that doesn't make sense. Normally, planes don't lose pieces like that. Not your usual chrome bumper. I'll keep looking if I bump into a car missing a piece." He dug into his pockets to retrieve it and handed it over to Adam. "You can give it back to her. I know what it looks like. For the moment I think it's irrelevant to the snowmobile."

"If you hear anything else through the grapevine, let me know. And call Maggie if you get any bright ideas about that metal piece, that is, if your brain cells wake up!" Adam laughed.

"At least I've got one cell! It reminds me, I did see something weird this morning."

Walking back toward the garage on The Road, Barrie spoke softly, seeing a group of grannies in front of the garage pointing at the window of The Jolly Jumpers. "The mayor. I saw her speak with Fred Wigmott at the traffic light a week ago, I think. At first, I wasn't sure it was her; she was wearing a purple hat, not flattering to say the least. I couldn't hear what they were saying, but I'd say she was angry, while he had a smile on his face. Of course, it could have been a mere political discussion, but somehow I think it was more than that. With all your questions, I'm starting to think you've an eye for her. Funny, I wouldn't have guessed she could be your type, but we all have our secrets."

Adam laughed. "Thanks mate, thought she might be more your kind of babe. Seriously, I'm only interested in her in relation to this murder case. I found the body with Maggie, and Raj might need a hand with the sergeant. Perhaps we can help him figure out the truth."

"Watch out, though," said Barrie, waving his finger at Adam. "We might still have a murderer at large."

"No worries, I'm not into solar panels or politics and neither are you, so we should be fine. Cheers!" Adam slapped Barrie on the back and took his leave.

Soon after, Adam relayed his lunch conversations to Maggie, knowing she would eat out of his hand to hear it. He was curious to see how she would interpret the information; she always seemed to grasp the details and their context, thereby getting a good overview of the situation. He sensed she might be the one who would eventually find out what really happened and why. He had never met anyone like her who seemed so hooked on a case, like a terrier digging a rabbit hole without giving up. He smiled, thinking like master, like dog. Beans was a real match for her.

Chapter Twenty-Six

Constable Gupta, loaded down with a box of donuts, pushed open the glass door of the police station, quietly listening for the sergeant. The sergeant's voice emanated from the office at the end of the corridor. "Yes, sir, I understand, sir. I'll get a statement from Leon LeBreton about the letter. Yes, I should have asked, but everything still points to him. No, he doesn't have an alibi. No, he hasn't yet confessed. I understand, sir...yes, sir, but I'm sure he did it, and he did trespass. If we let him go...yes, sir. I will. Goodbye, sir."

Sergeant Humphries slammed the phone down. He stormed out of his office, through the corridor like a tornado, into the entrance of the police station, where Raj was standing, still holding the box of donuts.

Raj noted with regret that bad news had come from above, and nothing, not even donuts, could appease the sergeant now. Sergeant Humphries said, "We can't keep Leon LeBreton. Not enough evidence, they claim! Better safe behind bars, I say. What if something happens? I've warned them. I could've cracked the guy. Gupta, release the prisoner."

Raj kept a low profile and simply nodded and proceeded to release Leon LeBreton. Leon walked out of the cell looking haggard and surprised. "So I'm free to go?"

"Yes, you are," replied Raj.

"No longer a suspect then?"

"You're still the prime suspect, and if it were down to me, you'd still be in there." The sergeant pointed at the cell. Leon jumped because he hadn't seen the sergeant standing behind him. "And you'll still be on trial for trespassing and attempting to divert the course of justice. This means you can't leave town without my permission, understand?"

Leon looked down at his feet and nodded. He let the sergeant escort him by the arm to the front door. As soon as the glass door closed, Sergeant Humphries walked back in like a bear, his arms by his side. Slightly hunched and with a grunt he said, "Gupta, keep a close eye on him. I want to know where he is at all times."

This was the first time that Raj had to follow a suspect; he wasn't sure how to proceed. "I follow him with the car?"

"Why, yes, or do you want to run behind him! But he mustn't see you!"

Raj rushed out excitedly, grabbing his coat and cap.

Back at his desk, the sergeant slumped into his reclining chair with a sigh, his eyes moving in the direction of the appetizing scent. There on his desk Raj had placed the box of donuts, open to let out the aroma and ensure they would be found. He had managed to sneak in quickly when the sergeant was distracted by Leon's release.

Sergeant Humphries picked his favourite donut, the Boston cream, placed it on a napkin in front of him, and went out to get a refill of coffee in his large insulated mug. Back in his office, he decided to enjoy the moment, brushing aside his case and peering into his in tray to see if there was any interesting newspaper or magazine.

He picked up the green leaflet on top of the pile, wondering why the mayor's face was smiling up at him. The sergeant read the details; it was an invitation to the open discussion on the solar panel project and the increase of garbage disposal fees. Although he wasn't particularly interested in the topics, he always liked an excuse to get out of the office and enjoy a few nibbles and local gossip. He had taken particular notice of the little bit of text at the bottom indicating there would be free sandwiches. He picked up the next paper, the *Daily Stumble*. He thought it was his duty to check if he had missed any local news and settled back into his chair to enjoy a quiet moment reading it. He wondered why one of the pages was missing; he would have to ask his constable about it.

*

Leon LeBreton rushed back home, relieved. After a shower, he regained his normal high confidence level, now that they had released him and didn't seem to have any evidence against him. He decided to proceed with business as usual, brushing aside his sorrow.

Checking his diary, Leon realized the following day was the mayor's public meeting, and he had promised her he would give a presentation on the solar panel project, hoping to gain acceptance, and even better, support from the locals. If this didn't work out, he would go bankrupt, as he had invested all his savings into a number of solar panels and was locked into a deal for the remainder. Once Ms. Stilton had been elected mayor and Peter Wigmott could no longer interfere, he was convinced the project would get the funding from the township. Confident of the outcome, Leon had committed himself completely to the deal before the official approval had gone through.

*

On the way to her letterbox, Maggie heard her familiar frog call from her pocket. "Barrie, how's it going?"

"Good, good, I can't speak long, but you know the metal piece you asked me about?"

"Yes..."

"Well, I know where I've seen it. I polished the mayor's Airstream trailer."

Maggie smiled, thinking of her narrow escape from the Airstream. "So it's a piece of it?"

"Yes, I'm sure of it."

Maggie's mind raced. Suddenly the image of herself standing in front of the Airstream looking at her reflection came back, and the puzzle unravelled itself before her eyes. She muttered, "That's it, I've got it!"

"What? I can't hear you?" replied Barrie.

"Sorry, thanks, that's really helpful! I won't keep you..."

"Glad I could help, have yourself a great day."

"You too, bye."

Maggie walked across the road to reach her letterbox, wondering how on earth she could make the truth come out now that she had some proof.

The municipal leaflets had been distributed that morning to all the residents and were sitting in their letterboxes. After dislodging the green paper that had been crushed to the back of her box by her package delivery of a book on how to fly, she glanced down at the crumpled black and green photograph of the mayor's face...that was it, the solution. She only needed to gather a few items of evidence to allow her to expose the murderer.

This public gathering is the ideal setting. No one will suspect the agenda will be different from solar panels and rubbish. Now I just need to get them to go to the meeting.

Maggie listed in her mind the key players she wanted present. Leon LeBreton was the speaker; he would have to be there. If not, he would be making his case worse. Joe Johnson had to attend; he was, after all, Leon's right hand for his solar installations, and Heather, given the chance, would not leave Joe out of her sight. The Millers were very vocal about the solar panels. Likewise, Barrie would go; he had mentioned to her that he was upset with the proposed increase in dumping fees for oil.

There was still Patrick, Fiona McLenny's widower. He had no direct reason to go, unless she suggested to meet him there to hand him some photographs for her website. She could always add that his presence at the meeting would be a sign to the community of his innocence.

Maggie hadn't forgotten the slippery Fred Wigmott but felt he might be the hardest one to tackle. Perhaps the reverend could ask Fred to come? She changed her mind: no one must know her plan. Fred had openly shown his dislike for Leon LeBreton and the mayor, accusing them of being involved in the murder of his brother. What if she played on his pride and desire for recognition? She could highlight that it was a unique opportunity to avenge his brother in front of the villagers who liked Peter. She settled for initially using the excuse of discussing his quote to casually ask if he was planning on going to the meeting.

Having completed her calls, Maggie smiled at herself, thinking she was like a movie director setting the scene for the actors to play out. She would still need to intervene, an active role rather than cameo, for it to work out. For a moment she hesitated, nervous about what she was about to do. Was she right? She was choosing to influence the fate of another being for the sake of justice, her view of justice based on her observations. What would happen if she were wrong? She never ruled that option out and wanted to make sure she would not be manipulating people but rather coaxing them into telling the truth. Maggie concluded it was therefore ethically acceptable; this would be her angle, together with the evidence she had gathered.

She needed corroboration from sergeant Humphries on the DNA testing. She thought he would not tell her the results they found, but Raj might. Amy had at first been reluctant to help her, warning her of the dangers, but then Maggie managed to convince her it was a matter of helping her clear her name. Amy had even said she would try to get access to the investigation file to see if she could find anything mentioning Maggie.

Maggie had managed to gather many DNA samples: the mayor's top, Fred's cigarette that she had retrieved from the floor, pretending to drop a tissue when speaking with Barrie; Leon's from a cup she had kept when he visited her for the solar panels; Adam was easy, as she had picked up a tissue he had used when visiting him; and Patrick, again a cup she was careful not to wash when he visited her.

She still had a few to gather but had already sent the ones she had and was waiting for Amy to contact her with the results and hopefully other information. She might get enough evidence without it, though, she hoped, if she could get them to speak and if her hypothesis was correct. On the one hand, Maggie wanted to involve Adam in her plot, but on the other she was afraid he would talk her out of it, and if it didn't work out as planned, she would take all the blame.

Feeling excited with the prospects, her doubts pushed away, Maggie spent the rest of the afternoon and evening finishing off the details of her plan. The meeting was at ten o'clock the following morning. She would go for a long walk early morning with her dogs to thrash out any points she might have missed and to test her assumptions. Hopefully by then she would have the results from Amy.

That evening Maggie picked up the *Daily Stumble* she had received in the morning, intent on having a relaxed moment reading it with a cup of tea before she went to bed. She opened the second page and there on the third page was a large photograph of herself in her car, with the police and forensics team working on the scene of Fiona's death in the background. The headline was *"Death of a realtor in Foxton, likely foul play."*

She couldn't believe what she read as her eyes moved down the paper with fury. No names were mentioned, but the arrest of a man and his release were, and one sentence did it for Maggie. *"Everyone who has been seen at the crime scene and/or is related to the realtor remain suspects."*

If anyone read this, they would of course put two and two together. What was she doing there? Even if they would not suspect her, there was a form of subliminal message with her picture. She would have to corner Tina, even if it could hurt Denis, which she certainly didn't want to do. Tina should not get away with it. The mere thought of Tina's presence at the meeting the following day made her stamp her foot with rage.

Maggie feared Tina would be able to topple her plan just by opening her mouth. Her only hope was that she would not come, which was very unlikely, given she was the local journalist...

Chapter Twenty-Seven

Sandra, the plump blond clerk from the municipal office, was arranging rows of plastic chairs in the large room of the community hall. She seemed cheerful as always as she hummed tunes. She stopped midway as if she wanted to catch her breath and sat for a moment looking around when a loud noise of a crashing metal object broke the silence, followed by a loud swear in French.

She rushed toward the door and was confronted by a red-faced Leon LeBreton fighting with a presentation white board, papers scattered all around him on the floor. Sandra's first reaction was, "Let me help you." She knelt down, picking up some of the papers, then stopped short, looking up at him with a worried face. "Were you—I shouldn't ask, but were you the one arrested?"

"Wrongly so, yes. So all the village knows then," replied Leon angrily.

Sandra looked down at the papers, her hands shaking, and stood up as if she had been propelled by a spring when Ms. Stilton entered the room. She moved quickly toward her as if she wanted to hide behind her tall frame.

The mayor was a confident person and believed the law had to be respected; she would treat Leon as innocent until proven guilty. She would therefore act normal with him, and since she had supported his solar panel project, she couldn't pull out of it now. She played her motherly card as she spoke. "I think we've got all the good arguments. You'll see, they'll support us, and all this mess will soon be behind you." She smiled at him.

"I sure hope so…" Leon sighed, having gathered his papers and setting them on the pulpit.

For the occasion, Ms. Stilton had slipped into a moss-green dress, appropriate for her environmental mission, and a thin belt, attempting to break the silhouette but not enough to take away the focus from her bosom. Knowing she couldn't hide it, she had long ago decided to decorate it instead and always wore long necklaces. This time she had matched her dress with a beaded coral necklace, smaller beads at the back of her neck and the larger ones to the front.

She knew she would look even taller than usual standing on a pair of orange stilettos, but she loved high-heeled shoes, the higher the better. Ms. Stilton felt this meeting would be the turning point of her career in Foxton. She had to convince the audience, or else she would have to resign; there was too much resentment building up now that they thought Peter Wigmott had been murdered, resulting in her election. She made a final check of the room before reviewing her speech notes once more.

*

Maggie wanted to be among the first to arrive to watch the different attendees trickle in and check if they were all there, as she hoped. She was sitting in her Big Jay, waiting for the community centre front doors to be unlocked when she saw Raj on his knees just under a side window of the building. Thinking he had lost something and might need help, she walked up to him and stood just behind him.

Maggie bent down to his ear level to ask him if he needed help, and one of her curls touched his cheek. Raj sprang up. Maggie, startled, let out a shout as she was accidently pushed over by Raj's elbow. She fell noisily down against the window and onto the ground among the bushes. Raj was franticly rubbing his cheek while doing a sort of tap dance. She looked around her at the ground, worried that he had spotted something dangerous. "What is it?"

Maggie twisted her head to see what Raj saw through the window. Leon stood on the other side of the window, pale, moving his eyes from Raj to hers, holding papers in his hand. Reassured, Maggie stood up, brushing her trousers and said, "Phew, I didn't mean to scare you!" She smiled at Leon with a thumbs-up to show him she wasn't hurt, assuming he had heard her fall.

Leon shook his head and walked back to the pulpit. Raj straightened his jacket by tugging at it. "What were you thinking of! I could've hurt you!"

"I thought you'd lost something, I just wanted to help..."

"I thought it was a spider..." Raj rubbed his cheek once more. "And now you blew my cover!"

"Sorry," said Maggie, feeling awful, only now understanding what he had been doing.

Raj sighed, shaking his legs one after the other. "I guess now that Leon knows I'm here, I'd better go inside and stay next to him."

Relieved that he didn't seem too upset, she said, "I'm also going to the meeting. I'll join you." She hoped her plan would go well.

As they made their way to the door, Maggie felt comfort in seeing Adam arrive in his vintage Land Cruiser with Barrie, waving at them. The Millers, together with the reverend, were lined up at the coffee table, debating whether they would have a wet or dry summer after such a warm spring. The turnout appeared small so far. Richard Miller interrupted their discussion to greet Maggie. "Maggie! So are you for or against the solar farm project?"

"I don't know yet, I want to hear what everyone has to say. I like the concept of green energy, but it depends at what cost and if we really need it with all the hydroelectric energy around here. In any case, I've got lots of questions for Leon LeBreton." *And not just about solar panels...*

The reverend waved at Maggie from the other side of the room, clasping his hands together to shape little wings with his fingers. She replied with two thumbs up. The sergeant looked at John, surprised, then shrugged and made his way to the coffee table with the cookies.

Maggie stood a little away from the table, examining the crowd. As she looked on tiptoes for a sign of Patrick, Joe, and Fred, she felt a light poke in her back. She swirled around and couldn't believe her eyes. Amy stood in front of her clutching an envelope. Her joy at seeing her friend turned into fear, thinking she might have uncovered something ghastly.

Amy put her hands on her cheeks. "Don't look at me like that. You were right. Here, I've done the analysis, but I didn't want you to be on your own just in case, you know…"

Maggie felt a surge of warmth and hugged her friend. She whispered in her ear, "I'm so glad you're here. I feel a lot stronger, and now with the proof too. Not sure I'll use it, though."

She moved back, tapping her pocket, feeling the envelope Amy had just slipped into it, the DNA data. Maggie, still stunned at her presence asked, "But you must've taken a day off for me?"

"I had a bunch of days to take from my overtime. So are you going ahead with the plan then?" asked Amy with a wink.

"Yes, I found out a lot more too, you'll see. Adam and Barrie are here. You should meet them."

Amy tilted her head toward a tall man with a ponytail speaking with someone. "Is he Adam?"

Maggie nodded as she walked toward Adam, Amy in tow, when Denis stepped across their path.

"Maggie, you're here! Amy, that's a surprise. Are you moving up here too?"

Amy laughed. "No, no, just visiting."

As soon as Denis stepped slightly aside, Maggie caught a glimpse of Tina. In an instant she felt her energy drain away, but then she heard Amy.

"Maggie, there's someone here who wants a word with you."

Maggie turned toward Amy and saw Patrick and Damien looking at her, Damien waving his hand. Maggie had agreed to give the photos for her website to Patrick before the presentation. Happy to avoid a confrontation with Tina now, Maggie rushed toward Patrick, leaving Amy with Denis.

"Hi, you wanted to give me the pictures? I brought Damien with me because he has questions for you, but that can wait until after the presentation if you like," said Patrick, letting his son take over and stepping behind him.

Damien, with excitement in his eyes, said, "I've got lots of ideas for your website, but don't worry, it'll be two of us for the price of one."

"Really it doesn't have to, I know what it means, so—"

Patrick interrupted, his voice rising above the chatter of the crowd. "We insist. It's a good opportunity for us to test working together. But let's discuss it later; it's a bit too loud for me now."

After handing Patrick the photos, seeing that Amy was now talking with Adam, Maggie toured the place in search of Joe and Fred. Peering into the parking lot, Maggie saw Heather arguing with Joe with large gesticulations. She closed the glass door behind her, waving at them, thinking *Good, business as usual there...and now Fred Wigmott.*

She walked around the brick building and was puzzled to see the mayor standing in her dress in the cold air, talking to Fred Wigmott, holding his hand on top of hers in an affectionate way. They were too engrossed in their conversation to see Maggie as she slid back into the building, content that everyone she wanted present had shown up. She said softly, "Let the show begin."

She hadn't seen Adam standing behind her. He asked in his familiar deep voice, bending down to her ear level, "And what show is that?"

"This debate. I think it might turn out to be very interesting." She smiled at him. "I don't want to miss anything, and for that I need to sit in front. Shall we go there before the seats get taken? Get Amy and Barrie too."

Maggie searched her pocket for the paper with the DNA results and for the ring Patrick had left behind on her table; both were safely tucked in it. Adam sat next to Amy with two free seats next to them. She looked around to see where all her suspects were positioned.

The mayor made her entrance from the side door she had just gone through with a concerned look, swiftly replacing it with a broad smile directed toward the small audience. Fred Wigmott entered through the same door, and as soon as Maggie's eyes met his, she had the impression he deliberately made his way toward the free seat on her right side, the chair meant for Barrie.

Ms. Sue Miller's clear voice bounced off Joe's guttural voice as they feverishly discussed the recycling cost. She glanced over her shoulder and saw Barrie had found another seat. *I'm missing the three knocks before the curtains open. I mustn't think that way. This is serious.*

Ms. Stilton walked to the lectern looking like the school headmistress everyone feared. She was calm and composed as she addressed each and every person with her gaze, her hands resting on the pulpit, the coral nail polish shining in the light. She only needed to stand there for a minute, scanning the small audience, for the voices to die down and all eyes to focus on her coral beads...

"Thank you for coming. I see the most important decision-makers of the village are here, although I would have hoped more people would be interested in turning Foxton into the green example of the Highlands. You won't be disappointed. To start off, I'd like to discuss the wonderful solar farm project, about which I know some of you have questions. I am sure I can answer all of them and allay your fears. Afterward we will talk about recycling. I am eager to hear your suggestions for this topic."

Ms. Stilton turned to Leon LeBreton.

"Leon LeBreton, an expert in solar installations, will explain to you why the solar farm is ideal for Foxton and will benefit everyone. I am sure he will convince you as well as he has convinced me."

Leon stepped forward, grinning broadly, rubbing his hands

together, making him look nervous. Maggie understood why he might feel that way, with everyone staring at him in an accusatory way. He finally broke the heavy silence by clearing his throat, the sound reverberating through the room via the microphone. He launched into his presentation at full speed, as if he wanted to run away as soon as possible. As soon as he finished and asked if there were any questions, Fred Wigmott stood up, brandishing his fist at him.

"You shouldn't be here! In prison is where you belong! You killed my brother."

Maggie, who was sitting next to him, hadn't expected such a reaction. She stood up, put a calming hand on his shoulder, and with authority no one would have expected from her, announced, "Please, before everyone accuses Leon LeBreton, I'd like to share with you some facts, and then you may decide."

The attendees, who had nearly fallen asleep during the presentation, lulled by the voice and changing slides, sat up straight in their chairs, excited, as if they had all gathered to watch gladiators in an arena.

"So, Maggie, I wonder what you've got to say for yourself!" exclaimed Tina, only to be shushed by Denis, who squeezed her arm. Tina shook him off, yelling, "Ouch!"

A wave of whispers flowed along the rows as if carrying Maggie to the lectern, where Leon stood shrinking away. Maggie wiped Tina from her mind as she took her place next to Leon. The whispers died down as soon as she opened her mouth.

"Yes, it is understandable, Leon, that you are considered a prime suspect in the murders." Maggie was now facing him as she spoke. "You've been hiding your relationship with Fiona McLenny without even realizing everyone was aware of it. Did you meet her the day she died at Mr. Bern's house?" She waited for her words to take effect: all eyes were now on him. He seemed to break like shattered glass, his face contorting into a painful grimace.

"Yes, I met her there, but I didn't kill her. I loved her. That is why I went back to retrieve her scarf the following day. I had given it to her as a present. She loved tulips... I needed a memento from her, and I was drunk."

Maggie pursed her lips. "Only a murderer might be foolish enough to go back to a crime scene to remove evidence, don't you agree?" Before he could answer, she added, "And what about Peter Wigmott? The solar project you just presented to us would have never had a chance had he been elected mayor, is that true?"

Leon's head drooped as he nodded in response.

Maggie went on, "I also understand that it's thanks to the agreement you had with mayor Ms. Stilton here that should she be elected, your project would stand a chance. You both benefited from Peter Wigmott's death..."

Maggie turned toward the mayor, and all the eyes of the audience shifted to Ms. Stilton, who fiddled nervously with her coral necklace. Maggie went on, "I've something to show you, Ms. Stilton." She took the ring Patrick had left behind out of her pocket. "Do you recognize this ring?"

A loud ahhh came out of the members of the audience as they craned their necks to catch a look at the ring. Ms. Stilton shifted on her high heels, avoiding Maggie's eyes.

"As you don't seem to think it's yours," Maggie insisted, "please take a look at this photograph of you wearing it."

The mayor looked down at the blown-up picture of herself standing with the two Wigmott brothers. She took the unmistakable golden A letter-shaped ring and stared at the photograph, murmuring, "So that's what she had against me."

Maggie, hearing her words, inaudible to the audience, asked, "Someone tried to blackmail you? This photograph proves you knew Peter Wigmott a lot better than you led us to believe." She waited a little for a response and then asked, "Were you not his girlfriend at the time? Why did you lie and claim you didn't know him?"

Sergeant Humphries seemed too surprised by the turn of the

events to interfere. Everyone was hooked on Maggie's lips, as if they were wondering whether it would be their turn next.

Ms. Stilton slowly turned to face the villagers and in a clear voice said, "Yes, I guess I owe you the truth. Fiona McLenny. At first she used this same ring to threaten me to expose my relationship with Peter, and it was thanks to him I got my position here, not out of merit. I don't know how she got hold of it or why she would think it had any significance. It was only a ring. However, she came back to me later and claimed she had proof that I had been Peter Wigmott's girlfriend. She accused me of having killed Peter Wigmott, and if I didn't go to the police myself, she would go. I knew I had to explain myself but wanted the right timing for it. Here it is. I admit it."

She stopped for a moment, everyone sitting at the tip of the chair as if they expected her to be the murderer, when Ms. Stilton continued, "I loved Peter." Tears welled up in her eyes. "But I didn't kill him. I moved to Foxton a few years ago to be close to him after my divorce, having heard he was single. I had not realized Fiona was with him at the time. He rejected me as a lover and even as a friend. I offered him my help for his campaign. He also turned that down. I was hurt and wanted revenge. I decided to run for the position of mayor to compete with him on his grounds. I did want to hurt him, but I didn't kill him."

Maggie couldn't believe her luck at the mayor willingly sharing her story, aspects of which filled the gaps for her. She listened carefully, her arms folded against her woollen sweater, fiddling with her zebra-patterned scarf, glancing at Patrick and Fred Wigmott. She unwrapped her arms all of a sudden, placing her hands in tight fists on her hips. "You must've really disliked Fiona then. Her death would've been very convenient for you, no more evidence...until Patrick found the ring."

Maggie pointed toward the crowd to show that he was there. She took a step back to increase the distance between them and decrease the height advantage Ms. Stilton might use to dominate her.

As soon as she did this, Ms. Stilton automatically took two steps forward until she towered over Maggie and angrily replied, "I'm telling the truth! Why would I want to kill Peter's girlfriend? She dumped Peter for Leon over a year ago. I believe in Leon's project and thought he could talk her out of it. He was reasonable. Why not consider a more likely murderer—her husband, Patrick McLenny."

The mayor swerved on her heels away from Maggie to point straight at him. The small group shifted on their chairs, and some individuals stood up to take a better look at him. Damien gently squeezed his father's arm in a reassuring way. Maggie stared intensely at the mayor, attempting to read her.

"Yes, jealousy can be dangerous, but Patrick wasn't near the house at the time of her death. Were you?" Maggie looked at Patrick.

"No, I was at home," replied Patrick.

Hearing Leon shout, "That's not an alibi!" Maggie didn't need to intervene. Damien stood up for her and looked at the sea of heads turned toward him.

"I was on Skype with him, and I didn't lose sight of him. We were working together. Leave him alone!"

Patrick pulled on his son's jacket, forcing him to sit back down. Maggie felt the tension rise and sensed she needed to move quickly before a fistfight erupted.

She calmly said, "Patrick didn't kill his wife, and he didn't kill Peter Wigmott, although his jealousy was real. He disliked Peter for taking his wife away from him and Leon even more for bringing the final blow to the relationship, leading her to ask for a divorce. Am I right, Patrick?"

Patrick nodded. "She wanted a divorce to marry him..." He looked at Leon. "I now know, sadly, thanks to her death, that she was right. She wasn't happy with me. I did love her in my way and couldn't dream of killing her. I miss her." He rubbed his eyes with the back of his hand. "Today I would have wanted her happy and accepted the divorce." Without warning and seemingly out of character, Patrick stood up and shouted, "I want to know who killed her!"

Maggie scanned the room, worried he might have triggered a

mob reaction against Leon. Reassured, she slowly said, "No one did! Leon?"

Leon looked at her with astonishment in his eyes. The murmur that had started stopped short as Maggie continued. "It was an accident. You had an argument with her regarding her accusation of Ms. Stilton, and she tripped on the large solar panel cables that were lying outside the shed. Is that right?"

"Yes, but how?" replied Leon, stammering.

"Fiona electrocuted herself as she picked up the end of the cables to put them away before anyone else could trip on them. I nearly stumbled on them myself. And the electric shock made her fall backward, hitting her head on a stone."

"Yes, yes it was an accident!" replied Leon.

"You panicked and put the cables away to hide the evidence; the cables shouldn't have been connected to the solar panels until after the installation was completed."

Sergeant Humphries stood up to move toward Leon, pulling out his handcuffs. "So it was really electrocution? How did you find that out?"

"I noticed her hand was stiff. It had rigor mortis, while she had only been dead for a short period. And I asked my friend Amy here, who is a forensics expert, what could cause it, and she said electrocution," replied Maggie.

Sergeant Humphries reached Leon, who was standing next to Ms. Stilton. The sergeant sneezed, and in spite of the violence of the fit managed to ask him, "Leon LeBreton, did you leave the cables lying there, and did you argue with Ms. Fiona McLenny, as Ms. Flanagan suggests?"

Leon nodded. Sergeant Humphries triumphantly announced, tears rolling down his cheeks from his sneezing, "Leon LeBreton, I'm arresting you on suspicion of unintentional manslaughter of Ms. Fiona McLenny." As the sergeant was about to read the charter of rights to Leon from his memorandum book, he stopped short in his tracks and turned to Maggie, adding hesitantly, "And what about Peter Wigmott? You seem to know who did it. Was it Leon LeBreton?"

Maggie, her back turned to Ms. Stilton, whose rare perfume had enveloped the stage, pirouetted around to face her a little too fast, nearly losing her balance.

"Ms. Stilton, I've a few more questions. You knew Peter intimately. You must have been very jealous of his relationship with Fiona. You just told us you were so upset with him that you decided to compete with him for the position of mayor out of revenge. You knew he was a good snowmobiler. How can we be sure you didn't cut his brakes? You had the opportunity during the Christmas dinner. It would have been very quick for you to pop out from the party and come back in."

The mayor stamped her right foot like a child. "I want a lawyer. I will not speak anymore. I've played fair."

"This is not a game. Perhaps you can help me then. I don't think you killed him, but do you know what this is?" She pulled out the small piece of metal from her pocket and lifted it to the light. It glowed in the light.

"No, a piece of metal?"

"Yes, from your Airstream trailer. You own an Airstream."

Half of the group was now standing to see what was going on.

"Yes, and what about it?" asked the mayor defiantly.

"This piece of metal was found at the scene of the snowmobile accident, and it matches a piece that is missing from your trailer. Barrie, can you repeat what you told me?"

Barrie cleared his throat. "Sure. Ms. Stilton, you brought the Airstream to me for polishing in January, and I pointed out to you that aside from the piece that had been ripped off, there were also a few red marks on the side of it, and I asked you whether you wanted me to repair it."

Ms. Stilton seemed to hesitate to speak, wavering on her heels. "Yes, I remember. If you must know, I had lent it to Fred Wigmott for a number of months as a favour, and he returned it to me in January."

Maggie signalled to Adam to stand next to Fred Wigmott, who appeared ready to leave any moment as he eyed the emergency door to his left.

"I see, and why would you lend such a nice trailer to Fred Wigmott? Had he also been your boyfriend?" Maggie would normally never use such a sarcastic tone, but she felt the mayor was too political to tackle without it. For some reason, since their first encounter there was always electricity in the air between them.

Ms. Stilton seemed annoyed, but to Maggie's surprise she walked up to Fred Wigmott and said, "You killed him. You were always jealous of Peter. He succeeded where you didn't. You even tried to separate us when we were young and tried to seduce me."

Fred Wigmott looked coldly at her. "You've got nothing on me. You expect all men to want you. You're wrong. Look at you, why would I've wanted to be with you when my brother rejected you. You might be mayor now, but it won't protect you against the truth that you killed him out of jealousy, not me. You are the jealous one, wanting revenge!"

Maggie walked up to Fred Wigmott and looked up at him. "Wait a minute, you're a little fast at accusing everyone here. First, it was Leon, and now the mayor. If you don't want to explain what really happened, I will!"

"You've got no proof." Fred stood with his chin up, hands in his pockets.

"You disliked your brother for his looks, getting all the praise from your parents and attending university. He was better than you at snowmobile racing. He had moved to the little town where you'd chosen to set up your business decades ago and ran for the position of mayor. This was too much for you; you had to get rid of him."

Maggie stopped to look at his reaction. He remained stone-faced. She had to carry on with her theory.

"You know snowmobiles well and how to cut his brakes in such a way that he wouldn't notice. You also knew how good your brother was at riding his sled, and simply cutting the brakes wouldn't be enough. You had to provoke a fatal accident."

Maggie heard a loud ahh from the crowd. For a very brief moment she felt as if she were on stage in a play, but this was for real. She had to push him further.

"You asked him to meet you that evening and told him it was urgent. He left the party early to see you. He would have done that for you. He cared for you."

Maggie took in a breath, hoping her hunch was right. His face was still and grey and his eyes two blank black pools. She went on, "Thanks to seeing my reflection in the Airstream, I know you parked the airstream across the road next to the beaver dam. You made sure you parked it close to the dam, its full length blocking the road and your truck hidden on the right behind it. You knew he always drove fast."

Maggie saw a flicker in his eyes; she must be right.

"As he arrived at full speed, his headlight on, a bright light seemed to be coming straight toward him. The Airstream acted as a huge mirror. He swerved to avoid what appeared to be another snowmobiler coming head-on and managed to miss the trailer. He scratched the side of it, and still trying to brake, he went straight into the beaver dam, one of the skis hooking a branch, thus toppling the sled over, propelling him into the water. He died on impact, hitting a rock in the water."

Fred looked at her and at Raj, who was now framing him with Adam and maintained, "You've got no proof. This is utter speculation and ridiculous."

Maggie walked up to Sergeant Humphries and asked him to stand next to the mayor. As if under the spell of her story, the sergeant obeyed and brought Leon with him. The sergeant burst into another sneezing fit.

"Do you remember sneezing when I gave you the purple hat?" asked Maggie.

"Ahhtchooo, yes! And not just then, any time I looked at that effing hat."

Maggie then asked the mayor, "Have you lost a purple hat?"

Ms. Stilton, her chest turning red, replied, "Yes, I don't know where it went, only a few days ago and the last time I had it, I think, was when I saw Fred…"

Maggie coldly looked at Fred Wigmott, then took a piece of paper from her pocket. "I found the hat you lost at the crime scene, and the perfume in the hat was yours, as Sergeant Humphries can confirm with his allergy to it. No one can forget your perfume." Everyone nodded in response. She explained, "The hat was placed there to incriminate you, but that didn't work."

Maggie waited for a moment for Fred to react. The sergeant stepped away from the mayor, trying to control his tearing eyes and runny nose, and stood closer to Fred, while Raj moved next to Leon. Seeing Fred refused to budge, Maggie added, "How can you explain then that your DNA was all over the hat?"

"How can you prove it's my DNA? I didn't give any DNA sample to anyone. It could have been my brother's DNA or someone else's, maybe even yours!"

Sergeant Humphries interjected, "We took your DNA, remember, when we wanted to be sure it was your brother, as the body was hard to recognize after being in the water for so long."

"But how can my DNA be on the hat?" asked Fred angrily.

Maggie was quick to respond, seeing the sergeant look to her for the answer. "There were hairs from the mayor in the hat; no surprise there, given it was her hat. We also found one of your hairs. This was a real mistake on your part to have put on the hat. Perhaps you wanted to get a closer feel of Ms. Stilton, who had rejected you?"

Maggie's eyes moved from Fred to Ms. Stilton, who was staring at him in disgust. Maggie addressed the sergeant. "This DNA is a match for your DNA, Fred Wigmott, not your brother's, and certainly not mine. Sergeant?"

Sergeant Humphries seemed to seize his opportunity to be part of the revelation as he pulled up his trousers with his belt. "Yes, we have the results back from the lab. We were about to question you and arrest you."

Maggie looked briefly at Amy, who winked at her as the sergeant spoke. Fred folded his arms tightly against his chest, his chin pointing away. "You've got no proof," he said again.

Maggie walked to Adam and whispered something in his ear, then stormed toward Fred Wigmott like a little terrier chasing a rabbit brandishing a shiny object. "If it is not enough then, what about this?" While Adam was immobilizing Fred's arm, she had picked Peter Wigmott's ring from his pocket, betting on it still being there.

"How do you explain this in your pocket? It's not yours. I saw it didn't fit your finger when you wore it the other day. You've not changed weight since the photograph of the university party. You never graduated. Peter always wore his ring. I saw it on a recent picture of a township meeting. This means you removed it from his finger when he was dead!"

Fred had managed to free himself from Adam's grip but was stopped by a human barrier of Patrick, Damien, and Barrie. The audience had all been standing for a while and had formed a circle around the stage to get a better view and be part of the action. Sergeant Humphries made his way over, pushing the Millers and Tina away to arrest him and finally charged both Fred and Leon according to the rules.

Chapter Twenty-Eight

With a broad smile, the sergeant escorted Leon LeBreton and Fred Wigmott, together with Constable Gupta, stopping on his way for series of pictures from the little forest of cell phones that was now pointing toward him. Sergeant Humphries made sure only his face would be on the pictures, the convicted burying theirs in their jackets while the sergeant's head popped out left and right to catch the line of the cameras. The sergeant looked forward to writing his report and making it up to his superiors. He hadn't needed their help in solving the case, and that was what mattered most. It had all happened so quickly that they would most likely not believe it. Before reaching the car, he saw Tina Partridge, who had followed him out, and smiled.

"Come to my office tomorrow. I'd be happy to fill you in on the details for this case."

*

The group gathered around the sandwiches. Sandra, the clerk, commented on the mountain of food and the small group there to eat it. The mayor bent over her shoulder.

"You are right, I had hoped more people would come. I'm sure Heidi, who prepared this, will find mouths to feed for the leftovers, don't worry."

A brouhaha of voices rose above the heads, as everyone felt

compelled to state that it was obvious—it was exactly what they had thought but didn't dare say earlier. Adam and Barrie joked with Maggie that she had taken a big risk and they hoped there would be no more cases. They nearly had heart attacks listening to her unravel the case. Amy hugged her, saying, "I'm so glad it went well. Not really how you thought it would, though?"

"No, I was lucky, and I never would have found anything out had it not been for you." She looked at the three of them. "I didn't do much. They merely needed a little encouragement to talk. I can finally settle down here…"

The reverend joined the little group. "What a story. Who would have thought, Ms. Maggie Flanagan, the secret detective and future pilot. I do hope you will take less risk when flying with me and be gentle with me. I wouldn't want to be quizzed by you, that's for sure! This village was so quiet before you arrived…"

Maggie laughed. "Don't worry, statistically I think we're done. I really don't want any more murders. How about we all meet at Mutti's?" Seeing Amy's confused look, she added, "The Horizon Cafe, tonight?"

*

That evening the cafe was alive with excited voices debating the events of the day and recounting them to Heidi, who stood at the head of the table, her hands on her hips, eyes wide, looking at her expanded group of adopted children. At the round table next to the window overlooking the lake, Barrie, Adam, and Raj were joined by Raj's wife, Indira, Amy, and Maggie.

Having heard what happened, Heidi was about to give them the specials of the day when Amy asked, "But there's still a mystery for me. What about the blackmail letter Leon LeBreton received. Who sent it and why?"

Amy was looking at Maggie, and Maggie lifted her hands to the sky and replied, "Dunno…I'm still wondering what that was about.

It came from the..."

The group turned toward Raj, who wore a smug grin as he tapped the table with his index finger.

Excited, having already consumed a number of beers, Barrie nudged Raj with his elbow and started hitting the table with his hand in a rhythmic fashion.

"Tell us!"

The others joined in as Raj was clearly enjoying his moment of attention. He cleared his throat. "Yes, I know why..."

Everyone around him shouted, "Out with it!"

"Sorry, can't give out the information, police matter."

Outraged, Barrie exploded, "Raj, you... Don't give us this now. Okay, fine, we're not interested anyway." Turning away from Raj, he looked up toward Heidi, "So, Mutti, what can you recommend tonight, I'm starving!"

Instead of answering Barrie, she was smiling at Raj, who was sitting his arms crossed, looking down, lower lip drooping as if he were sulking.

Maggie's curiosity got the better of her. "Raj, come on, you can tell us, pleeeease..."

Raj, regaining the attention, settled back in his chair with a large grin. With a twinkle in his chocolate eyes and a little bob of the head, he said, "Okay, just because you ask so nicely..."

All heads at the table leaned in, including Heidi, bowing forward to catch every word as Raj whispered, "It was Fred Wigmott. He had seen Leon going back to the crime scene and wanted Leon to take all the blame. If he could make him confess to the murder of Fiona, since he believed it was a murder at the time, it would be so easy to cast the blame on him for his brother's murder too. He thought the fear that someone already knew would make Leon crack up."

Amy asked, surprised, "But how did you get that out of Fred Wigmott?"

"For some reason he still had something against Leon, and I just asked him if he had written the note, since I thought he could have done it. He confessed."

"Well done!" exclaimed Maggie. "Finally, the entire mystery is solved. Phew, I can now settle in and relax. I really never expected this to happen here. But one thing that I am grateful for is that out of this terrible story, here are my newfound friends!"

Maggie put her hands on the shoulders of Amy to her right and Adam to her left, looking at the pairs of eyes smiling at her from around the table. The moment was broken by a laugh and Barrie saying, "Now that's all well and good. What about some food!"

All eyes were now back on Heidi as she told them her specials...

AMBER BOFFIN loves stories and writing. She started writing to keep in touch with friends from different continents and then to document her travels around the world. British-born, she worked and lived in a number of countries together with her husband before settling in Canada. The warmth Amber experiences living in cottage country, together with her passion for nature, inspire her to write the cozy mysteries with a twist—a little less peaceful than reality.